HN

# Out of Danger

*Also by Suzanne Lipsett*

Coming Back Up     1985
The Silent Garden *(with Paul Ogden)*     1982

# Out of Danger

Suzanne Lipsett

Atheneum 1987
New York

Copyright © 1987 by Suzanne Lipsett

All rights reserved. No part of this book may be reproduced or transmitted in any form or by any means, electronic or mechanical, including photocopying, recording or by any information storage and retrieval system, without permission in writing from the Publisher.

Atheneum
Macmillan Publishing Company
866 Third Avenue, New York, N.Y. 10022
Collier Macmillan Canada, Inc.

Library of Congress Cataloging-in-Publication Data
Lipsett, Suzanne.
Out of danger.
I. Title.
PS3562.I59098   1987   813'.54   87-14409
ISBN 0-689-11825-2

This is a work of fiction. Names, characters, places, and incidents are either the product of the author's imagination or are used fictitiously. Any resemblance to actual events or persons, living or dead, is entirely coincidental.

10 9 8 7 6 5 4 3 2 1

Printed in the United States of America

*For my sons, Sam and Evan—
and for Tom*

Her hair became leaves;
her arms became branches;
her foot stuck fast in the ground,
   as a root.

—From the myth of Daphne and Apollo
   *Bullfinch's Mythology*

# PART ONE

# One

Telegraph Avenue shone and clattered like a street fair in the afternoon sun. It was partly her high spirits, partly the year's first spring warmth, that let Elinor Landau see the place that way. Somehow the dark exhaust of the crawling one-way traffic, the impatient press of students racing to and from the university, and the city detritus clogging the gutters had all receded from her view. Elinor strolled from table to table looking over the pottery, jewelry, and carved wooden boxes on display—even choosing not to see the sour boredom of the street vendors, there since dawn—as if the goods had been laid out exclusively for her pleasure.

Normally Elinor avoided this strip of the avenue. It had become crass and dirty in the years since she'd moved nearby. Those sellers who lifted their gazes from the tables peered at passersby through narrowed eyes, doorways sheltered crazy chattering wraiths, and there was likely to be vomit on the sidewalk. She hated bringing her daughter, Laurel, down here.

But Elinor was pleased by the success of her trip to the city, and for the moment the street reflected her satisfaction back to her. She had taken her portfolio of designs to a pricey store in San Francisco and had made an unexpectedly large sale. The two buyers had loved her woven jackets and dresses—her new work in ivory and white had won them right away.

The orders they had placed would carry her and Laurel for a couple of months at least, and there was a promise of more if her things did well. Now, with half an hour to kill before she was to meet her friend Goldy and Laurel for an early dinner, Elinor headed up the avenue slowly, swinging her portfolio.

She stopped in front of a rolling rack hung with handwoven garments. A wavy full-length mirror, which threw back a streaked, warped version of the sidewalk parade, was rigged up next to a card table. Behind the table on an aluminum folding chair sat a slender young woman, knees up, reading a paperback novel. She wore jeans and a long woven top of muted violets and blues. With a practiced eye, Elinor admired the dye work.

"Fantastic blend on your top there," she said to the girl.

"Oh," the girl said indifferently, looking off down the street. No sale. "Thanks."

"Did you do it yourself?"

"Nah, I'm just sitting here for a guy." She never looked up at Elinor; she wasn't there for the chat.

My things could have wound up on somebody's street rack, Elinor thought, turning to the clothes on their hangers. But for some intuitive resolve, Elinor's passion for weaving could have petered out at some depressing street stall like this one, her designs hanging in a slack bunch an inch off the sidewalk and absorbing the traffic's fumes. This stuff wasn't half bad, she observed, holding out a skirt and studying the weave. But it was lost out here on the street.

Six years ago, when she'd finally taken Laurel and walked out on her broken-down marriage, she had somehow known how to begin selling her work. As the wife of a frenetic, incurably frightened young lawyer, she'd had plenty of free time to learn her craft. And while Allen was building his addiction to baby-doll girls in slingback heels, Elinor was playing with fibers, textures, and colors. By the time she rented the apartment in Berkeley for herself and her daughter, she was just good enough to try selling the clothes and wall hangings she dyed and wove. She had started walking into stores and showing her samples, and she and Laurel had been living from sale to sale, order to order, ever since. It was a pieced-together life, but it was working.

Today's sale filled in a nice-sized space in the patchwork. Elinor swung up the street toward the restaurant—long, tall, pleased with herself, ready to take an evening off for a meal and a couple of movies.

* * *

"Mom! Mom, over here." Laurel's high young voice pierced the noise of the stuffy little Chinese restaurant.

Laurel and Goldy had managed to snag a window table. Strips of light shining through the venetian blinds fell across them and the shiny formica table.

"Hey, great. I'm starved," said Elinor, squeezing into the chair next to Laurel.

"Hi, Mom. How'd it go?" grinned Laurel, only twelve but long involved in her mother's precarious economic adventures.

"Oh, it went well, sugar," said Elinor. She turned to her daughter and kissed her cheek firmly. "How are you doing?"

"Good," said Laurel, slinging an arm around Elinor's neck.

"Thanks for keeping your eye on the punk here, Gold."

Goldy shrugged and smiled—no problem. The three studied menus they knew nearly by heart.

A waitress came to take their order. "Will anyone share that seafood soup with me?" asked Elly.

"Uh—I'm just going to have tea," said Goldy.

"What? Are you on a diet?" The waitress retreated.

"No, I—"

"I don't think you have much to worry about yet, right,

Laur?" She flung the compliment casually at her beautiful friend. In contrast to Elinor's long-boned look, Goldy—Goldene Jewell was the name her mother had burdened her with—was small and elegant. She seemed carefully, economically designed, the opposite of the sumptuous excesses her name implied. Thick, dark red hair framed her delicate features, but a small gap between perfect front teeth added a flash of sass.

Goldy ducked her head, avoiding the compliment. She never participated for long in the banter Elinor indulged in when she was feeling good. But Elly and Laurel were used to Goldy's quiet ways. During their six years in the same building, they had shared enough meals, watched enough movies together, and talked each other through enough crises to be a makeshift family. Goldy's husband, Paul, an associate professor at the university, had never quite made it into their tight inner circle.

"I've got to get back, Elly," Goldy said quietly. "I've got to work."

"Come on, take a break. Have dinner and let's go to the movies." She turned to her daughter. "Want to, Laur? We could look for a double bill."

"Sure, great," said Laurel. "I love Fridays." At twelve, she was a gamine, stretching out of childhood into adolescence with new length to her bones and her odd springy yellow hair growing a little wild. Tiny tendril-like curls that never grew longer frizzed the hairline at her forehead. The rest was pulled back in a loose ponytail, puffing out in a mass of tight curls.

"I can't, El," said Goldy. "I've got to type Paul's article before he gets back on Tuesday. And it's long, really long."

"I thought you did that already," said Elinor.

"He rewrote it."

"So you have to kill yourself typing the whole thing *again?*"

A pause, a coolness. "Yes. I do."

"Goldy, you've been working all day."

"It's really long. I've got to start."

"Hey, the guy's not even in town. It doesn't seem right to me."

"Luckily, Elinor, what feels right to you doesn't have the slightest bearing on what I promised Paul I would do," Goldy returned, showing the energy she kept in reserve.

"Mmm, married bliss," murmured Elinor, glancing around the restaurant.

"It beats single motherhood," retorted Goldy.

"Hey," said Elinor, smiling broadly. "I haven't typed a paper for Laurel since we Xeroxed her sixth-birthday invitations."

"Yeah," said Goldy with a faint smile. "And I've never bounced a rent check in my life." She moved her chair back. "Listen," said Goldy, "I've got to go."

"Mo-om," said Laurel, alarmed. Do something, said her tone.

Elinor caught Goldy's hand across the table. "Wait. I was kidding," she said quickly, annoyed with herself. "I barged in, I wasn't thinking. And you even picked up Laurel for me today. Come on. I'm sorry. I ran off at the mouth."

Goldy relaxed but she still stood up. "It's okay, El. But I've really got to get going. Have a good time, though. Come by and tell me what you see, Laurie," she said.

She smiled at Elinor to reassure her—no bones broken—and then turned and squeezed through the crowded tables to the door.

"Damn," breathed Elinor.

"Mom, she hates it when you joke around like that about Paul. Why'd you do that?"

"Oh, God, I'm just a bulldozer. I should have gone easier on her. I think there's something wrong."

"You should anyway. Goldy's sensitive. You have to treat her more gently."

Elinor turned to her daughter and smiled. "Oh, Goldy's

sensitive, is she?" said Elinor. "I guess I can depend on you to keep me in line. Right, sug?"

"But I can tell—"

"You're right, Laur. I was a dope. But come on, honey," she said, laying her arm around Laurel's shoulders, "let's us go to the show and have a good time. You want to?"

"Okay, sure," Laurel answered, restored. Wild-haired, she bent to her menu again while Elly took the *Chronicle* from her bag and, squinting through the bars of shadow and light, looked for a double bill.

\* \* \*

They were glutted with two movies, popcorn, and soda. Laurel was nearly asleep on her feet as they walked the eight blocks to their building through the warm dark night.

Supporting the girl's weight, Elinor mused on the pleasure she took in Laurel's company these days. After six years of raising Laurel on her own, she was starting to reap the rewards. Going to the movies with her—no more Disney, no more stultifying afternoon cartoons—had become one of Elinor's chief pleasures. And twelve seemed to Elly not the nightmare she had been led to expect, but a wonderful age full of promise. Laurel was still unmistakably a child, and often suddenly regressed into fits of stubborn complaining. But there were islands of time now on which they both relaxed—a thirty-six-year-old woman and her twelve-year-old daughter—and floated peaceably together.

"My wonderful, beautiful bed," mumbled Laurel, as Elinor guided her under the covers. The aerators from Laurel's aquaria bubbled softly, a comfortable sound.

"Night, baby. I had a great time," said Elinor.

Laurel pushed out her lips in a mime of a kiss, but she was already out for the night.

Elinor felt her way to the kitchen in the dark and, by the

light of the refrigerator, poured herself a glass of wine. She entered her own room, put on a long t-shirt, and slipped into bed, relishing the perfect ending to a single mother's night out: a glass of cold dry wine, a gripping novel, and the kind of sleep that gets you midsentence from behind. Hours later, almost at dawn, Elly stretched out her arm to turn off the light and push her book off the bed.

# Two

And then Laurel was gone—plucked from the street like a shining coin.

She never came home from school one day—that was it. It didn't take long for Elinor, though deeply engrossed in warping her loom, to start wondering, then worrying, then straining to hear the front door of the building open. Laurel always came home right after school, at about three-fifteen, because of the fish. She had four aquaria, two of exotic tropicals. The water temperature needed checking; it was the first thing she did when she came home every day. At four, Elinor knew something had happened. Laurel was always thinking about those fish. She should have been home.

At four-thirty Elinor phoned the school. No one had seen Laurel after class. She called around at Allen's. She called all Laurel's friends. She also called the fish store; the man who answered sounded offended, as if he had been accused of something. At five-fifteen, knowing that Goldy would be home from work, Elinor phoned her and Goldy came over, carrying the makings of salad in a brown paper bag.

A stifled wail broke from Elinor's throat when she saw Goldy at the door.

"What?" Goldy cried at the sight of her friend's anxious face.

Elly hestitated slightly, superstitious at locking the truth into words. And yet it was so simple to say. "I don't know where Laurel is. She's more than two hours late." Fear poured through the hole the words had bored in the familiar atmosphere of the room.

Goldy closed her eyes for a long moment and said nothing. In a deliberate gesture to force time along, Elinor grabbed the sack from her friend and strode to the kitchen. They began to wash lettuce and chop vegetables, and at six o'clock Elinor abruptly dropped the knife to call the police and the local hospitals. As she punched out numbers on the phone, she gazed at the nearly strung loom and spotted a flaw in one brown strand. She would remember that as her last impression before the ax fell, splitting her world in two. On one side lay the life Laurel and she led together—breakfast, work, and school; homework, dinner, maybe some friends in to visit, movies and trips on weekends. On the other side was silence, the unknown that can swallow one whole.

The police switchboard put her through to a gruff, impatient-sounding man, and so Detective Frank Metzger entered Elinor's life. He was a man she wished she had never met, and she knew that beneath Metzger's professional demeanor was a similar distaste for her. They scraped each other's nerves from that first phone call, and never found a comfortable way to exchange necessary information. On the phone, that first time, he said he would be by within the hour.

Goldy and Elinor kept making the salad—Elly cutting vegetables evenly, cleanly, regularly, marking off the seconds with the knife's hollow sound on the wooden cutting board; Goldy drying lettuce and pulling it to pieces. Laurel did not come home. The silence seemed to suck air from the room. Chopping and chopping, Elinor seemed barely anchored by the steady work as panic whipped through her. She saw every kind of possibility: Laurel run over and lying in a gutter like a struck cat. Laurel sick and unconscious somewhere strange, with no identification that would lead back to Elinor. She even saw Laurel lured into a car and abducted by a craven sex maniac. But in her wildest imaginings she never came close to the reality.

They never assembled the salad, though Metzger didn't arrive for nearly an hour. They just kept finding things to wash and cut. They didn't talk. Goldy, silent, self-contained, gnawed at her bottom lip. By contrast, Elinor's brown eyes, as she worked, were wide and erratic with fright.

"Stay, okay?" said Elinor when Metzger rang the bell. Her friend nodded curtly.

Metzger's looks didn't jibe perfectly with his tough-guy voice, not at first. There was a with-it quality he strove to achieve in his appearance: young, hip, a little of the jazz musician's cool, but what was memorable was how badly he failed while still managing to suggest the desired effect. His black hair was cut in a long boyish banged style, but under it his fiftyish face was haggard, the skin loose, a triangle of heavy moles on one cheek the harbinger of true old age. Under the expensive turtleneck sweater he affected with his suit swung a heavy gulletlike bulge, another testament to the age he apparently had yet to acknowledge. His appearance was decidedly unhealthy, yet the eyes were darting and hawklike, light in color and fine looking, designed to spot hidden prey from a distance of five hundred feet. They were a predator's eyes, suggesting a bullet-quick intelligence that cut through Elinor's own thorough consideration of things to strike and conclude and return to searching. His impatience with the time she took to answer a question or weigh a possibility was brutal, and from the outset she hated him for failing to conceal it.

When she let Metzger in the door she knew she was conceding that Laurel was missing. Up to that point her daughter might still have been simply late (she was never late), waylaid by a friend (she had few friends outside the neighborhood), gone to another fish store (there were no others). Or she could have been with her father, though Elly knew for a fact that he and his wife had left that morning for the Sierra. And since she could count on Allen to worm out of even his scheduled visits, she knew he'd hardly burden himself with Laurel voluntarily. With a detective sitting on the couch looking through her photo album at recent pictures of Laurel, Elinor could not deny the true situation: Laurel had been missing for almost four hours.

"I'll take this one," Metzger said, not asking, and he peeled back the plastic to take Laurel's fifth-grade class picture. In it her teeth were clamped together in a mischievous smile, as if she were mugging a grin and then really smiling at her joke. Thick, fuzzy braids hung down behind her ears, and the flyaway hair that always escaped framed her face, which was pale from the winter but still olive and smooth.

"Does your daughter have any rough friends? Has she shown any mood changes, any weight shifts?"

"What?" Elinor said, confused by the questions he hurled like darts.

"I'm trying to establish if she's been in any trouble or if she was headed toward trouble before this."

"But she's only twelve. She's a child."

"I've seen twelve-year-olds with a three-year habit. Twelve has nothing to do with it. She could take off at twelve, she could take off at eight, nine. You two have any trouble between you?"

Elinor controlled her urge to tell Metzger to slow down. She knew better than to let loose at this man, whose job bred cynicism like mold.

"No, look, Detective Metzger. She's a baby, she's not the kind of girl who would run away. We've been getting along fine, wonderfully." She felt another wail pushing up behind her speaking voice. She stood up from the couch suddenly and grasped her upper body tightly with both hands.

"Is this your husband?" Metzger asked, leaning back down

over the album, and she could see the bald spot at the back of his head mocking the style he affected.

"My ex-husband."

"Yeah, ex. This him? Allen Berlin?"

"That's right."

"This was taken when? This about what he looks like now?"

"That picture is, let's see—"

"This about what he looks like now, Mrs. Berlin?"

"He doesn't have a beard now. The picture is about three years old—Laurel is about nine in that. Uh, also, I go by my maiden name, Landau." She let herself spit out the last remark.

"All right. You see Mr. Berlin often? How would you describe your relationship?"

It wasn't that he was interrupting her consciously; he just couldn't wait while she stopped to consider.

"Would he have any reason to pick Laurel up without informing you?"

"Would Allen kidnap Laurel, is that what you mean?"

"Yes, if you want to put it that way, that's what I mean—"

"No. He sees Laurel whenever he wants to. In fact, he himself chose not to have her with him at all for the present. He doesn't want the responsibility—"

"Do you have Mr. Berlin's address?"

"Of course I do, but . . ."

Metzger glided along, scouting, homing in on what he wanted to know, writing down addresses and pocketing the picture he took from the album. With horrible longing, Elinor remembered the day she had put that picture into the album. Her ignorance of this event then—it was seven-twenty!—struck her as pathetic now.

"All right, Mrs. Berlin—"

"Landau." She took up her stance against him.

"Yes, all right, Mrs. Landau. You'll be staying here tonight.

I'll get back to you later on. You haven't received any peculiar phone calls?"

"No, no calls."

"All right, well, I want you to draw a map for me of the route or routes your daughter takes home from school with all possible places where she might stop marked out on it. I'll come by for that tomorrow, early. Also, I want you to keep a running list of all the phone calls you receive from now on."

As if answering a summons, the phone rang. Metzger walked over to it and stood by while Elinor answered.

It was Allen. He was calling from Truckee to say they'd forgotten to let out the cat—it roamed wild on the frequent weekends they went away. This was the second time in two months Allen had called to ask Elly to check on the cat.

"Allen, listen. Something's happened. Laurel's missing." It was truer by degrees. Saying it further advanced its reality.

Goldy sat still as a statue, staring at her hands. Her long reddish hair shielded her face from view. Metzger listened intently as Elinor informed her ex-husband that the young daughter who had represented a colossal inconvenience to him all her life had been unaccounted for for more than four hours.

Allen's tiny voice pierced the air. He didn't even have time to feel the dread and already he was hysterical, Elinor noted with sudden fury. She had long suspected him of enjoying his hysteria and jumping on any opportunity that arose.

"El, I'll come back. We'll drive home tonight."

"Come back but don't come over. The police want to talk to you. They want you to come back."

"Look, we'll start now. I'll see you in four or five hours. I'll call halfway to see if you've heard."

Could she shut Allen out of this? Laurel *was* his daughter, no matter how Elinor felt about him. Elly knew she would have to let him suffer with her while they waited, but did she have to let his wife, vain as a cat, sit with her too? What was the etiquette when your child disappeared and panic threatened your composure? Elly wanted Laurel back the way she had wanted her to be born during labor: please, God, make it soon or I'll die.

Metzger checked his pockets for his notebook and pen and the picture. Then he left, calling her Mrs. Berlin again. "Start that list now," he ordered over his shoulder as she closed the door. "And draw the map." He didn't expect to hear, she could tell. He was sure he'd be coming back in the morning.

Elinor sat back down on the couch, and Goldy looked up at her. She hadn't raised her eyes at all while Metzger was there. She hadn't moved even when Allen called. Now Goldy looked into Elinor's face with an awful confirming sorrow. Elly glanced at her watch and felt the truth of the terrible time she had entered. It was ten past eight, and outside the city was dark.

# *Three*

Vera, Elinor's mother, came up from her bungalow in Hollywood to sit out the nightmare with Elly. The two rattled around the apartment like a couple of apples in the back of a truck on a sickening ride to nowhere.

Vera's presence seemed to fine-tune Elinor's anguish. With time already halted, the sight of Vera's straight back and set jaw turned up the suspense for Elly one notch past bearable. With Elinor's breathing shallow and rapid, Vera's chain-smoking was nearly suffocating. With Elinor's eyes pushed tight from behind by anxiety, the sight of Vera silently drinking coffee, waiting, sent a jolt of fright through Elly's body. And with Elinor's hearing painfully acute, the sound of her mother repeatedly clearing her throat was an infuriating distraction.

While Elinor feared she would fly apart, Vera remained composed. During fifty years as a geriatric social worker, she had grown accustomed to remaining still in the eye of a family crisis. Her body seemed streamlined for the purpose—efficient, economical, with no more flesh than was necessary to carry out the work at hand. At seventy-six, she was pared back nearly to the bone. Behind dark-rimmed glasses, her eyes were vigilant, and fear for Laurel whitened her already pale, stern face.

It wasn't their way to reach out. There was no desperate

clutching of hands. There had been the usual awkward embrace at the airport, and then the magic circle that always surrounded Vera had firmly reasserted itself. You didn't touch Vera, you emulated her: so Elinor had come to view the strange cordiality, the short but uncrossable distance, that had existed between herself and her mother and had mystified her since childhood. Now they settled at the kitchen table and sat through the hours together, and Elinor felt herself assuming Vera's posture, mimicking her composure, setting her lips and lifting her chin, as Vera did, to bear the silence. It had always seemed Vera's purpose to show Elinor how to endure, and it had long been Elly's frustration that she never quite grasped the secret or found the posture that would set her free, as Vera seemed to be, of life's claims. That she still tried now, in the pit of her suffering, made her long to be free of Vera to buckle under her misery as she may.

"Cereal, Ma?"
"No, no, let me—"
"I'm making some."
"No, nothing."
"Coffee?"
"Here, I'll put on a pot."
"It's on, it's on. Don't bother."

On Vera's second day in the apartment, Elly risked an hour tying up the phone in a desperate search for a television set to borrow. She had to fill the hollow silence that swelled between them throughout each day. Finally Elinor rented a set, and a delivery man brought it to the apartment, confusing the women with his friendly talk about the weather. He left them feeling that a strange world of daily life was proceeding outside, somehow familiar but incomprehensible.

Evenings were the worst. Each day concluded with finality: no Laurel, no news. How Elinor hated to count the days. She hoped the television would somehow carry them through the dark hours, for by seven every night she was speechless with despair.

But the television assaulted them with cruel parodies of suffering. Into the room it brought bloodless murders and violent attacks that gave no pain. They changed channels at the slightest hint of violence, but they couldn't escape the slick-talking actors impersonating police and the scores of make-believe victims with flashing eyes. Even the newscasts scraped at them with their antiseptic capsules of cruelty and rape.

At the unexpected showing of a woman being wheeled from a building strapped to a rolling stretcher, Elinor leaned over and nearly retched. Vera slammed the set off, and in the sudden silence the two surrendered to the impotence they had been fighting off together.

Finally Elinor was able to speak. "Ma, I think you should go back home. This is terrible this way."

"Terrible, terrible," Vera agreed.

"Really. I think I could work if you weren't here."

"Truly? You think you would be better off on your own?" Vera was practiced at asking and reasking the difficult questions that had to be asked.

"I don't know why it is, but we can't seem to give each other any comfort."

"Because there is no comfort to give. Because there is none."

Despair threatened. They sat motionless under its shadow.

"But I'll go if you like. Just convince me you'll be all right here, waiting."

"How can I convince you? What could be worse than this?"

"No. You're right."

"At least I could work. I can't seem to work with you here."

"Yes, if you could work, I think that would be very good."

Getting ready for Vera's departure gave them something to do—each detail moved them forward in an imperfect imitation of time passing. A reservation was made, Vera's bag was packed. They sat over a final pot of coffee in a semblance of companionship.

In the morning, when the cab drove Vera away, Elinor sat down at her loom. She lay her hands briefly on the fabric she had woven days before. Then she began going through the motions that nothing could take from her.

# *Four*

Three months into the ordeal, braced for whatever was to come, Elinor met Jack Shapiro. But by then, another massive presence had established itself: The police had invaded Elinor's life. They had put a claim on her.

Elinor had always hated talking to the police. They all seemed to her like bland boys dressed up and waiting to be told what to do. Working to keep their eyes dull, their voices flat, they now seemed bent on convincing her that they would never find Laurel if they showed any spontaneous feeling. And all the officers she talked to seemed to have silently agreed among themselves never once to remember her unmarried name, Landau, or her expressed preference to be addressed by it. On this she finally gave up, but with a sense of a larger futility. The fact that her last name differed from that of her child seemed to defeat every officer on the Berkeley force, and whenever they made the mistake she doubted, with a strange mixture of exasperation and despair, that they were up to finding Laurel. I'll have to ask you again, Mrs. Berlin—but not sorry. You'll have to come with me, Mrs. Berlin—not caring. Just wait here, Mrs. Berlin—not fathoming, by half, the loss of a child.

Fear sometimes shot through Elinor so suddenly and with

such physical force she thought she would die. It was a primal fear, she knew, which she shared with animals, a fear that became a widening horror as, of all the scattered herd, your own young one is chosen and driven out of view. And there remained, after that first terrible day, the inadmissible thought, always hovering, that all during Elinor's hated dealings with the police Laurel might be long dead.

For Elinor, it was a time of unbearable feeling—of eyes dry and hot from lack of sleep, of nerves alive and moving, of grinding love residing in her belly and a continual writhing at the separation from her child. As the weeks went by, she yearned to escape the intensity of it. She was poised to die herself at the news of final loss, ready to quit at the one call out of the hundreds, thousands, they hounded her with in which they would say Laurel had been found, yes, dead. Elly came to feel that she herself was staying alive just in case, on the outside chance.

Endless chatter kept her anchored in the here and now. Some pictures, Mrs. Berlin, we have some pictures we need you to look at. Do you have a more recent snapshot of Laurel? Have you ever heard of—? Have you ever been to—? The terrible one-question phone calls set her mind darting out of sleep or shooting up out of the blessed distraction of work.

Metzger woke her one night with a call, and she came out of sleep with none of the scared restraint that kept her civil during the day.

"Goddammit, Metzger, give me a minute, will you, for God's sake?" she yelled. She sat up holding the phone away from her as if it were some strange, repugnant object she had just found in her bed. She rubbed her face hard, shoved her fingers through her short hair, pushed off the sleep that was fighting her, trying to pin her down.

She snapped on the bedside light. As she gradually came to her senses, a latent fury at Metzger gathered and sharpened.

"All right. What is it?"

"Oakland's got a girl missing over there. Same kind of sudden snatch. I need to know some things."

"What kind—?"

He cut her off. "Did your daughter ever know anybody on Oakland's west side? Ever have any friends near the lake down there?"

"Oh, I read about—"

"*Did* she?"

Elinor felt the tight rod of anger lock onto its target: Metzger's gravelly, impatient voice.

"Look. Don't cut me off again," she said, enunciating sharply, only just controlling herself.

"Hey, now, wait a minute—" he protested. She could imagine him in the classic posture of denial: head tipped to the side to avoid a direct hit, phone held by his spongy chin, both arms spread wide to reveal empty hands, and the quick scoot backwards, body language for "get me out of here."

"I'm telling you, Metzger, if you've got something to ask me, ask me and let me catch my breath, let me think. I'm not one of those knee-jerk rookies you've got down there who can only think in a straight line. If you've got something to ask me, then let me answer you, all right?"

"Yeah, okay, okay—" she'd heard *that* tone more than once. "So answer."

"So no."

"No friends, no family over there? No visits around the lake? No connection you can think of?"

"No, but something *does* occur to me. I read about this disappearance in the paper. What makes you suddenly so anxious to ask me about it at two A.M. three days later?"

"Look, I was off for two days. This is my first shift back on—"

She let him have it. "Did you have to wake me up?" she yelled. "I have a hard enough time getting any sleep with this nightmare going on. Did you have to wake me up with this?

Are you any kind of a decent human being or what?" She was a hair away from shrieking.
After a short silence, Metzger said, "Okay, look, Mrs. Landau. Uh, Elinor. I'm really s——"
Shrillness erupted. "Don't you call me Elinor. You just find my daughter, Metzger. Just get off the goddam phone and get out on the street and *find Laurel!*" Panting, she slammed down the phone.
She sat rigidly still in the bed for five minutes, letting the craziness seep away. Then she punched in the station number and muttered his name to the switchboard operator.
"Metzger," he snapped, unfazed.
"Look, excuse me," she said as directly as she could. "This whole thing is making me nuts. I just kind of dumped on you. I'm sorry."
"No problem. It happens all the time."
"You've got to understand—"
"You know," he answered, interrupting her in the usual way, "no one expects me to understand what they're going through when they've got grief. It might surprise you to know how much I do understand what it's like, Mrs. Landau."
Something in his voice convinced her.
"Okay. Look, I'm sorry."
"You might not know I've been holding the press off here, who are dying to get at this case. This is not easy for you to understand, but I'm working for you down here, and I know how it is to be nervous."
"Look, okay. I'm sorry. Hey, you can call me Elinor if you want. In fact, it might make things easier."
"Are you kidding? I'm not trying *that* again." It was the closest he ever came to making a joke. Then, his need to scan and rescan the territory unquenchable, the old predator asked her once more if Laurel ever went to Oakland near the lake. Not until he was sure she had given the question her full consideration did he let her go.
Nights were hardest. During the day she managed to duck

out of her fearsome anxiety by working at the loom or sewing, sewing. Hunched down low over her machine or her handwork, she poured her attention into making long lines of tiny, perfect stitches. She still needed money, no matter what undreamed-of horror shook the world, and working helped, more than drugs. Sedatives took the edge of panic off the horrible pictures and possibilities that ceaselessly floated through her mind. But the loom especially, and the laying down of colors strand by strand, obliterated not only the images but herself as well. When she was lucky she could become for two or three hours at a time a mere adjunct of the machine, a station through which the fibers passed to become part of a whole.

And when she wasn't working, Elinor was wrestling obsessively with Laurel's fish. There were awful days when she awoke, if she slept at all, to find that some of the fish had died.

She came to believe that something in her bearing repelled comfort from others. Perhaps she'd learned Vera's lesson better than she thought. To herself, her face in the mirror never showed her turmoil; it actually appeared calm and slightly inquisitive, as always. She was a strong-featured, dark-browed woman, her short hair scrupulously clean. The hair, in fact, took the punishment. Washing her hair had always been a ritual with her. Sometimes in this terrible time she did it up to four times a day.

Besides her weaving, the hair-washing was the one link she had with her old life. Every morning she stood under the shower letting the water pound her head until it was barely warm. When she didn't have the chance to shower—when the phone rammed her out of sleep and she had to drive down to the station in a hurry, not knowing what they would tell or show her—those were the worst days. Her skin and hair felt vaguely alien then, and she really did fear she was going insane.

Looking back long afterwards, it astounded her to think of

meeting Jack in that state. It was funny, she thought, if you went in for sick humor. She saw a *Mad* magazine cartoon in her mind whenever she thought of their first meeting. It showed the debonair, Gable-type male meeting the mad divorcée, her ankles tipping in her pigeon-toed high heels, her enormous teeth jammed together in a crazy frantic smile, her clothes awry, her cigarette burning her fingers.

Their meeting was a casual accident—for her, a lifeboat floating by. Goldy had finally convinced Elly to leave her apartment and telephone to have dinner with her and Paul one night. Elinor had called the police to leave word where she would be—and Jack had dropped by to visit after dinner, bringing a gallon of ice cream and settling in comfortably for a talk.

Goldy had often mentioned this old friend of Paul's. Elly knew he was some sort of ad man who'd had a beautiful, flamboyant wife. The marriage had ended some years ago, and Goldy had recounted the story to Elly in an episodic way. Had Elinor known he might drop in, she would never have consented to come down the hall. She was stretched too taut to make small talk. In perpetual suspense, she crackled like a power line knocked down by the wind.

Jack didn't mind talking, though, not a bit. He was a large, dark-haired man whose expansive presence made the room seem suddenly small. He greeted Elinor with an open, frank gaze, which lasted a second too long. Audacious, she thought. Only just short of arrogant. No doubt he had heard of her as well.

"Elinor," he said, acknowledging Paul's introduction with an easy handshake.

Big-city manners, thought Elinor. A nice contrast to the clipped, pseudomilitary style affected by the Berkeley police, her most regular male contacts now. And another species from Metzger, the aging hunter.

"How's business, Jack?" asked Goldy when he'd settled down and the ice cream he'd brought had been served.

"Can't complain, can't complain." Turning to Elinor, he explained, "I've been launching a second career for myself." He sat across from her in the middle of the short couch with his arms stretched out along the back and his long legs loosely crossed at the ankles. The guy's wide open to the world, she noted. She felt like a double knot by comparison.

"So what's the business?" she asked, taking her cue.

"Ah, a little of this, a little of that, a little promoting, a little of what's known as marketing."

"Don't worry, El," said Paul. "That's about all we've ever been able to get out of him."

"Hey, look," cried Jack smiling and holding up his hands, palms wide for all to see. "No secrets. Loosely, what I flog is public-interest advertising—"

"Public-interest advertising? Sounds like a contradiction in terms." Elly realized too late how rude the remark might sound. Anxiety and sleeplessness had made her curmudgeonly. Her instincts all along had been right—she tried to beam this silently to Goldy—she shouldn't be let out in public.

"Hah!" Jack laughed, catching her line and playing with it. "A direct hit," and he took the opportunity to change the subject.

Elinor found a way to imitate a normal person. She took her turn and told Jack about her work, liking while she distrusted slightly the interest in his gaze. She didn't realize until the phone rang and her stomach clenched against the possibilities that she hadn't thought about Laurel in a full twenty minutes. This was her first twenty minutes of distraction without the loom since she had slowly understood, three months before, that Laurel was gone. Weeks later, Jack told her that despite her relief at having forgotten, her eyes had been stretched wide, like those of a scared horse, and she had talked in a breathy staccato rush.

Casually he told her he was interested in her work, asked if he could call on her to see it. Sure, she tossed back, hoping to match the smooth way he had. She went home soon afterwards, feeling guilty somehow for being so long away from the empty apartment and from Laurel's fish.

Jack called two days later, but not about seeing her work. "No, no, it's not the work," he said with a dismaying frankness. "I want to take you out."

No, she said, she couldn't. No, not now. But she would find that she had little resistance to his utterly direct approach. Now she felt warmth flood her face as he said, "Goldy told me about your trouble, of course. It's really because of that I'd like to take you out for a nice dinner."

She felt close to downright frightened while at same time she leaned toward his candor as to a cool stream. No one except those who had to—Vera, Allen, and the police—had ever made direct reference to Laurel's disappearance. And yet from the beginning, when she did speak she herself talked of almost nothing else. His grainy male voice spoke directly to a profound loneliness that she had not even noticed before.

To Elinor's silence, Jack said, "No, no, I don't mean out of sympathy. Elinor, I would have wanted to see you again no matter what, but God knows you must need relief from those four walls, from the waiting." Was he some sort of voyeur? Did this kind of thing excite him?

"Listen—," she said, trying to think of a way to repel his frontal approach. But her need to talk nearly melted her.

She had been going it completely alone. Allen had been worse than useless during the whole ordeal. Like a ten-year-old boy, he believed Laurel's disappearance was a punishment for his rampant infidelities during his marriage to Elinor. Inevitably, on his visits, he would cry and light a joint. Elinor would reassure him perfunctorily as his eyes glazed over. The marijuana seemed to absorb what little volition he had, and he would sink by degrees into the couch and his own self-pity. As for Goldy, she hated to talk about Laurel's disappearance. She looked aside quickly at the slightest mention, warding the subject off. And Vera brought more distress, not less. So Elinor had been on her own with the thing for three months, on a leash to the police station via the girl at the switchboard.

Voyeur or not, who cared? At the sound of Jack's invitation she pressed the phone to her ear with both hands, wanting to hear him say again how she must need relief, God knows. A rough, tired underside to the voice convinced her to trust him despite the alarming self-confidence his phone call seemed to suggest.

He told her later that indeed he had been fascinated with the situation. There *was* an element of voyeurism in the attraction he felt, but it was an attraction to the heightened reality, the intensity of it all, not to sex and violence. He himself was just emerging from a life-transforming two years that had put him outside the flow of ordinary life. He had a new knowledge of how deep life could cut, and into the wound flowed a loneliness astonishing in its profundity.

About the intensity he was dead right: she felt strapped to the wheel of life, simply whirling. As for the loneliness, it had affected her at the sound of his voice and set her leaning toward him despite all her reticence and natural good sense.

Their love affair took hold on the first night. They achieved a level of easy intimacy then that Elinor knew to be a rare accident, a genuine balance of temperaments. From the start she had the awareness, and a deep satisfaction from it, that they were two adults talking, two fully realized human beings partaking of each other with pleasure. It was a feeling she determined to keep and protect.

The police hadn't called all day, and late in the afternoon of the day she and Jack had agreed on, he phoned to say he would bring food to make dinner, apparently divining her habitual reluctance to leave the apartment and the phone, even for a few hours. Now, that took thought, she realized appreciatively. Any apprehension she felt faded with his call.

He came loaded down with food and wine and with a little

bag of marijuana in his jacket pocket. They made dinner together—linguini with clam sauce and exotic vegetables for a recipe he knew. They drank while they cooked and moved past each other, doing their separate chores, with a casual touch of a hand to an arm here, a guiding of the hips there: they got drunk and hungry and warm from cooking while Jack elaborated on himself. By the time the sauce was simmering he was touching, but lightly, on his ex-wife, Lee, who had remarried quickly after their divorce and moved to Mexico with their two-and-a-half-year-old son Mike. Yes, in a way he had lost a child too, though not so horribly, not with such cruel suspense. More than once he stood still over the skillet, wooden spoon poised, as he described to her a person central to his narrative or demonstrated a reaction on his expressive face.

"She simply said 'fuck you,' there would *be* no arrangement. She was marrying, going to Mexico—but *tomorrow!* I had my choice of going to court and having her move blocked until we got a judgment or kissing Mike good-bye at the airport. Kids teach you patience, as I suppose you know. So I sent my boy off docilely as a lamb—here, I bet you're a chocolate lover," and he tossed her a bar of Italian chocolate from one of the bags he'd brought.

Thoughtfully, he stirred the sauce. "I'd been partners in the agency for years, and my partner hated it that Lee left. That only puzzled me for a minute. I took the opportunity to do what I'd been thinking for a long time—go off on my own, see what I could do, pick and choose accounts so I would never have to advertise another household product in my life. It was beautiful. 'Okay,' I said to my partner, 'so you're going to miss Lee? Well, my considered reaction to your hypocritical sympathy, my son, is that you can take your vaunted partnership and shove it squarely up your ass. And here's some advice—the next time you make a business deal with somebody, try not to fuck his wife.'

"So within a very short time I was out one marriage, one

son, at least on a daily basis, and one business. Instant nothing." He stirred the sauce. "Instant nothing," he said again.

Elly felt deliciously drunk, momentarily suspended above her own life. A pressure was gone from her head that she hadn't even known was there.

Over dinner he talked of his plans—camping trips with Mike, a drive down the Baja Peninsula, a series of spot ads he was working up to show prospective clients. He had a knack for the business angle, he said. He was going to let the new agency grow slowly while he plotted its course deliberately. He had money now, he had time. . . .

There was a vagueness about his plans and an optimism for the future that Elly noticed immediately. In his leisurely sense of experiment, his high tolerance for seeing how things went, she recognized money in the bank, and registered a pang of envy. She would never have that kind of edge. Even in the midst of personal disaster, she was living on the brink, swinging like a trapeze artist from one sale to another, once or twice accepting, but with the greatest reluctance, Vera's standing offer to help. Still, she enjoyed seeing him relishing his freedom and, over their meal, imagining himself living out a hundred different possibilities.

By dessert—pastries, his passion—they were finished with Jack and, truly drunk now, ready to start on her.

She hadn't laughed at all in three months, but their dinner had been punctuated by his jokes, and she had even made some of her own.

"You feel good, Elinor, I can tell," he said, when they took their coffee to the overstuffed couch. "You look like you just lost about twelve pounds . . . right here." He touched her forehead with his finger.

"Oh, shit. I never cry," she said, as tears slid down her cheeks.

"Your daughter's been missing for three months, and you never cry? Are you kidding?"

"It's true, I rarely do. It's not my style. And anyway, the

whole thing's been beyond crying." The tears coursed down her face in flat streams. "You don't cry in hell. You ache. You throb. I even shake a lot, though you can't see it."

"Yeah, I think that's right."

The promise of release was like the growing certainty of orgasm. The effortless tears were a bath of flowing juices, the murmuring exchange of words the intentional winding down of conversation. With one convulsive breath, she let her head drop to his chest, and then she cried out her suffering for five minutes or more. It didn't escape her that at one point he kissed her on the neck, and she felt glad, as the paroxysm subsided, that she had washed her hair twice that day, once on sudden impulse just before he arrived.

\* \* \*

That was a Friday, and he didn't go home until Monday morning. They barely got out of bed the whole weekend. For Elly it was a glory of tearing down walls. She talked and talked in a torrent, and Jack listened intently and asked direct questions that she had barely had the courage to pose herself. Was there anyone at all—anyone at Laurel's school—who might have been sick enough to take the girl? Anyone who hated Elly herself? Or Allen? Would Laurel have run away? Could she find her way back home if she were dumped somewhere and abandoned? Did Elinor have confidence in the police? Feel they were doing all they could? Might it inspire more confidence to seek out a private detective or publicly offer a reward? Was there *anyone*, anyone at all, Elinor suspected in her deepest inner soul? Someone she had never dared to implicate but still distrusted?

It was a feast of words. Elly alternately talked and cried and blew her nose. She sat on the bed and rocked, gripping her chest with crossed arms as she had many times in the middle of the night during the time Laurel had been gone.

The difference was that Jack rocked with her, holding her shoulders from behind.

Long afterwards she could feel the flush rising when she thought of burrowing her face into Jack's skin for the first time to breathe in his smells. He was a big, solid man, and Elinor was tall herself. Stretched out on the bed, they seemed to go on forever.

Elinor knew Jack's coming had saved her life. She took sustenance from him in every way, from the food he brought to the rich banquet she made of his body (and he of hers, oh yes) to the delicious sympathy he offered to her cramped and frightened soul. Often, at her weaving, Elinor would think of that first evening, of her discovery and relief, and a sound of satisfaction would escape her throat at the foretaste of safety that Jack brought into her torn-up world.

*  *  *

The love affair quickly became a settled thing with its own routine. They were too old, they agreed, to sneak up on it gradually. Either it was going to work or it wasn't; at forty, or nearly forty, and with Elly stretched to the breaking point on the rack of Laurel's disappearance, neither had the inclination to play games. Jack kept his apartment in the city, a rattlingly empty penthouse. He had lived there with Lee and Mike, but now it was a working bachelor's dream whose style harked back to his old agency days. He hated it, and actually seemed embarrassed the first time Elinor saw it, an unlikely reaction for him that helped her forgive his owning the place. She, in turn, felt downright irritated by its fashionable elegance and wide view of the bay. The place struck her as vacuous and cold.

The situation held them tight, like a fist, but Elinor soon gave up feeling she had to pretend it was otherwise. Jack gave her the power to cry, to shake with fear, and to show the whites of her eyes at the sudden scream of the phone. He stayed over weekends, and they never did much. He read, she sketched out new designs, they cooked a lot together, and finally he managed to urge her out on walks and even to the movies. She never left the apartment without calling the station to leave a number or say when she would be back.

They made dinners for Paul and Goldy sometimes, but there was a sense of vigil about those evenings that made them all give up the effort with relief. Seeing how terrible it was for those two to enter into the suspense made Elinor know how fully, mysteriously, Jack had accepted the situation. She understood him to find in her—frantic, frightened as she was—something that matched his new knowledge of life with the scrim ripped off. The dissolution of his own family and the virtual loss of his son had apparently spoiled his taste for the sporting life. With Elinor in her trouble he never had to pretend he was the golden boy he apparently had once appeared to be.

Come Mondays, though, Elinor needed to crawl back down into the tight, safe den that her work provided. The loom filled half the living room. When she sat down to it with the light just right—it was for the rich light that she had rented the place years ago—and the movement of her hands, feet, and back found the rhythm, at some early point the motion would take hold and she would become part of the machine. Sometimes—from long habit she knew when to try—she put on jazz to direct the rhythm, and if she was deeply enough engrossed, and only for the length of that session, the panel of new cloth emerging before her would seem a physical manifestation of the music.

There was no place for Jack in the apartment when she worked. In the old days, during her marriage, it had annoyed her that Allen took no interest in her weaving. He had considered it a form of busywork. To her gradual mastery and her excited experiments with color and form he remained utterly oblivious. Now she discovered it had been a blessing to be left alone at her loom. With Jack in the apartment, even when he was unseen in the bedroom, a crucial shred of her awareness stayed hooked to his presence and kept her from merging with the mechanism.

"Go," she would tell him on late Monday mornings. Gradually, as their habits of being together took hold, he grew more reluctant to leave.

"God almighty, just a minute. Give me a chance to get dressed." He hated going back to his apartment across the bay, though he ran his business from it. In fact, it was more suited for business than living, but he loathed the evenings and nights there. It didn't take him long to suggest that he stick around, doing business on the bedroom phone.

"You know I can't tie up the phone, Jack."

"So we'll get another phone."

"No. And the place is too small. I need you to go."

"You need the company, El. You're going weird here alone, waiting and working fourteen hours a day."

"Don't tell me what I need, Jack. I'm telling you, I need you to get out of here now."

"Okay. You're the boss," he would shoot back. He had a way of forcing air out between clenched teeth that pumped up the tension between them.

But she toughed her way through these exchanges. Let her get back her daughter, she thought, and she'd see about the weekdays. For now, just let her dive down into the weaving of cloth, dulling the hot-eyed tensions of the week while she sat at the loom and created and re-created her fierce, defiant hope.

# *Five*

The memory of that last drive to the station never lost its potency for Elly. She had had to leave the car windows open, gulping air to keep from bolting through the red lights in impatience. But she wouldn't let Jack drive that night. Nobody would take that drive from her. She had earned every second of the jubilation pushing up through her belly and sending long delicious tremors through her body. It was her hands clamped to the wheel like mechanical grips that kept her upright and driving.

They had been to the movies, and the phone was ringing as they walked in the door. At the sound of it, images of the movie congealed for Elinor into vapid stupidity. Whenever the phone rang, she always knew suddenly that they had found Laurel, long dead—like a cat or raccoon on the side of the road. Each time she reached for the phone a picture crossed her mind of headlights picking up something barely visible, unidentifiable, in the dark.

"We've got her," shouted Metzger. "We've got your girl down here!"

She might have fainted for a moment then, though she remained standing. Speechless, she just stared at Jack, who had stopped in midstep, and held the receiver high, high, high in the air—like a prize she'd nearly died to win.

\*   \*   \*

Metzger tried to stop her that night as he always did, old predator that he was. And now a new face rose up as Elinor ran ahead of Jack into the station house. A large unfamiliar female shadow threw itself over her headlong path across the shiny black institutional linoleum. This was Janet Lovejoy, forensic psychologist. Elinor had time later on to contemplate the rich pun in the name of one who spent her life studying the hatejoy, or was it lovesorrow, or fuckhate—whatever it was that kept the city's outcasts craving and searching out the healthy.

Lovejoy was a well-groomed woman of forty, beautifully cold, composed, and towering over the men there. She was probably six-foot-two in her heels, which were moderate but conceded nothing to her height. She didn't give in, as even Metzger had, to Elinor's wild progress across the room toward the closed door she barred. She filled it nearly to the top of the frame and showed no intention of moving.

"Mrs. Landau," she said softly, with authority. Even in her agonized impatience, Elinor noticed she had gotten the name right. Lovejoy would prove always careful and perfectly composed as she studied the discarded victims of the damned.

"Mrs. Landau, you must be told what to expect. Please let me talk with you for a moment before you go in."

A suspended orgasm, drawn out into a band of irritation—so went the last moment of Elinor's five-month stretch of hell. She could almost taste the end of the ordeal, but Lovejoy held her off.

"Laurel is very different now from when you last saw her," said Lovejoy, still barring the way and talking quickly to secure her advantage. Jack watched from the hall. They both knew he ought to stay out of Laurel's sight at first. He was a stranger to the girl, would have to be broken to her gradually. They had agreed in the car that he would remain in the background but close by. Now, with Lovejoy stopping her at the door, Elinor wheeled and stared back at Jack in exasperation, and he caught it and pressed his lips together, shaking his head slowly with the delicious empathy that Elinor drank from him.

"She's in pretty bad shape, Mrs. Landau. You need to take a minute to prepare yourself. She looks bad and she is bad. She's been through a very tough experience. You're going to have to prepare yourself for some rough changes."

Elinor suddenly heard what Lovejoy was saying and looked straight up into her eyes.

"I'm telling you that you're not going to like what you see when you look at your daughter, Mrs. Landau. You're going to have to take a minute here and compose yourself to expect the worst so you don't scare her with your shock when you see her."

It was the start of Elinor's grudging and then growing respect for Lovejoy. From that first hour, the psychologist was looking out for Laurel. Whatever she did in connection with the case, Lovejoy was always looking out for Laurel.

"Okay," Elinor conceded in a whisper. "I'll tell you though," she went on with more certainty, "with Laurel alive, just alive, I can handle anything." She became aware of tears streaming down her face and swiped them off impatiently.

"All right. Are you ready?"

"Let me by, for God's sake. I'm her mother."

Lovejoy opened the door, and Elinor flew through at a run. It was crossing a bridge.

She stopped cold at the sight of Laurel, wrapped in silence and utterly still.

She could smell her from across the room. The exotic hair of memory was slack and stringy, oily and dank, clotted together at the bottom and long, hanging down her back and sticking to her neck. She wore men's jeans much too big for her and a filthy t-shirt that might have been picked up from the floor of a garage. No shoes. The feet were horny and caked with dirt.

She sat at the corner of a table in one of those big wooden chairs like the ones in the principal's office at school, somehow wrapped around herself. Her thin arms made a protective cage around her upper body; her legs, noticeably longer than when Elinor had last seen them, were crossed tightly; and one bare foot was hooked behind a bony ankle. She watched her mother from the side, her face nearly turned away.

After a single frozen minute, Elinor reached her and caged her own arms around the girl, feeling with alarm the sharp wedged shoulder blades as she encased Laurel and nearly lifted her from the chair. Later, Elinor wondered at how light and unresisting Laurel had been. But surely she must have stood up on her own, Elly would think without conviction. Surely she rose to meet me, her mother, after all those months.

They stood together, and Elinor whispered Laurel's name, like the name of a lover, into the girl's filthy hair. Laurel was taller now and so thin that Elinor's hands retreated from the bones, seeking a softer place, less angry, to caress. Standing quietly now, she felt the girl's trembling, a steady quaking like her own in the car, and heard her sharp breathing. The child was petrified! Safe at last in her mother's arms and she was rigid with fright!

They stood together in the otherwise empty room—a table, a chair, someone's raincoat and umbrella, and on the windowsill an overfull ashtray. Elinor held onto Laurel until the girl struggled to get away, making her first vocal sounds down in her throat. She struggled more and Elinor held her more until she pushed out of the embrace and ran to the corner, first breathing loudly, then gasping once, then throwing up on the floor.

\* \* \*

The highway patrol had picked her up at dusk somewhere on Highway 5, a desolate high-speed road that cuts vertically through California and proceeds on up to Oregon. Elinor and Laurel had driven it back and forth many times to visit Vera in Los Angeles. The highway dissects scrub desert marked at infrequent intervals by ugly clumps of gas stations and restaurants, astroturfed and floodlit. Laurel had been standing on a long, empty stretch between two of these fluorescent oases about two hundred miles south of the bay area—just standing there, apparently not even hitchhiking. The officers who picked her up guessed she had only just been dropped. Why else hadn't she been trying to stop a car to escape that terrible emptiness before nightfall? Why, indeed? Elinor passed up the chance to ponder the image of Laurel in the desert at night.

She was barefoot, filthy, and totally silent. The patrolmen reported that they weren't even sure she was registering them; they were certain she was on drugs. They drove her to a hospital in Fresno and radioed around on the sixty-mile ride to determine her identity, managing to extract from her a small confirming nod when the correct information came back through the receiver. In Fresno they got in touch with Metzger, who told them to put her on a plane—forget the hot bath and cocoa, make sure that every hair, every thread, every smudge she was picked up with remained intact. Elinor could imagine the hawk rising to the surface as Metzger talked: spoor is what he wanted, evidence. So two female officers had accompanied Laurel up to Oakland, and Metzger met the flight. He got seven words out of her, that was all. "They got drunk. I just walked away."

Elinor sent Jack home for some clothes and rode with Laurel to the hospital. All during the physical and the detailed collection of evidence, Laurel stared blankly into the middle distance, her gaze never wavering regardless of what passed through it. For Elly, this look on the face of her daughter was much worse than the dirt and greasy hair. It was an expression, she knew, that should never be seen on a child. She imagined it to be the look of war babies. The expression marked the end of resistance: whatever came in through the ears and eyes, whatever pain forced its way into the body, whatever knowledge drove into the mind so easily folded, this child would receive it unprotesting. Perhaps it masked the hope that, in a like manner, the sights and sounds, the pain, and the knowledge would all pass out again.

After the exams, Elinor dressed Laurel as she had when her daughter was too young to dress herself, feeling near bliss at lifting the bony ankles to slip her feet into soft pants, and stroking the warm vulnerable neck under the tangled hair as she pulled it free of the sweatshirt collar.

Later, she bathed her. She had to see her daughter's naked body, reclaim her right to look at it. She could see all the girl's bones, all her bones. And the hot bathroom was filled to the stifling limit with a clear cold message: Don't touch.

# PART TWO

# Six

Nothing fit—all the delicate cogs and wheels that formed the connections between mother and daughter were jammed. From the first night, Elinor wanted to bring Laurel into her own bed but Laurel ignored the suggestion, apparently preferring to sleep in her own room. She left the aquarium lights on and retreated, door closed, into the green glow, while Elinor chided herself for standing in the hall feeling like a spurned lover.

Yet there was something to the feeling. Laurel suffered Elinor's embraces, her strokes of Laurel's cheeks and wild hair, but Elinor sensed an instant recoil from the touch of fingers to skin. The easy physicality they had shared—the arm flung around small shoulders, the held hands—was gone. In the days that followed her return, Laurel could take nothing from Elinor but the safety of her presence. Elinor's passionate relief, her tender urges to ease the girl's obvious distress, were met with sullenness and quick exits. Sensing that Laurel's spirit, so lately free and expanding, was cramped and pinched nearly paralyzed Elinor. How was she to proceed?

The telephone continued to drive Elinor crazy. But now, in addition to Metzger, it was the various pieces of her life on the line clamoring to be fitted back into place. Jack, banished for the time being, called throughout the day; when he didn't, she called him. And Allen called often, always in agitation. Soon she would have to let Allen see Laurel face to face, but he seemed terrified to come on his own. He insisted on bringing his wife. Instinctively Elinor balked.

"I'm trying to keep things simple, Allen. Let's not make an onslaught on her this first week, okay?"

"What onslaught?" Allen whined at her over the phone. "You're calling it an onslaught to bring Debby over to see Laurel? It's not like she's a stranger, Elinor."

"Have a heart, Allen," said Elinor, thinking about the stranger she herself had in store for Laurel. "I'm trying to feel my way here. I don't think she's ready to see a lot of people at the moment."

"Look, Debby's my wife. She's concerned. She wants to see Laurel for herself." Elinor thought she could hear Allen's breathing speed up. Toward the end of their marriage, she had started thinking of Allen as the Victorian Lady. Strong emotion simply sent him to bed, rendering him useless in a crisis. But at least in those days it had kept him out of the way. She wished he would retire now.

"I'm going to ask you again to come on your own, Allen," she said in the controlled voice she always used when she heard his voice rising. "You think about when you want to come and get back to me. There's plenty of time now. Laurel's not going anywhere again."

"You betcha, Elinor," he breathed. Then he made a sound of disgust with his tongue and hung up. Amazing how Allen could be counted on to make things worse, she thought as she hung up the phone.

\* \* \*

It took Allen days to make up his mind, and when he finally showed up and knocked on the door, Debby stood a little behind him in the hall, as if she might try to sneak into the apartment by means of a modified Marx Brothers routine. However, one arm encircled Allen's narrow frame, and the row of polished nails rested on his windbreaker like five shining, bloodred medals. Debby never talked much, Elinor had often noted, but she never failed to find a way to assert her link with Allen. The two were always just short of entwined with each other. With Goldy, Elinor referred to them as the Siamese twins, joined by the hand to the hip.

"Where is she?" Allen asked in a nervous wet whisper at the door. Elinor knew that at least part of his urgency lay in pushing past the issue of Debby. It was his frequent strategy to avoid confrontations by creating a diversionary flutter.

"She's in her room. Hey, I see you worked it out to come by yourself—" I must quit, she told herself, or this meeting will be a disaster.

Allen and Debby settled on the couch in their typical formation, each with a hand on the other's knee. As if, she told Goldy later, they were preventing each other from rising up and floating away.

"I'll get her."

Laurel was on her bed going through magazines on tropicals.

"Laur, your dad's here to see you."

Obediently but silently, the girl followed her out of the room.

Allen and Debby looked as if they were paying a condolence call. They emanated a morbid sympathy, mixed with a palpable self-consciousness. Allen jumped up and wrapped Laurel in his arms. Elinor had the feeling he was embracing the girl so he could avoid looking at her for as long as possible.

"You okay, Laurel? You okay?" he called to the ceiling.

"Yeah, Daddy. I'm okay," whispered Laurel. Her hands lay lightly on Allen's back while he pounded and squeezed her.

Elinor sat down and concentrated on keeping her mouth shut, for years her main preoccupation whenever Allen was around. After all, he is the girl's father, was the repetitive phrase she used to control herself on these occasions.

Debby reached over and squeezed Laurel's arm.

"Oh, Laurel, Laurel," moaned Allen. He released the girl and sat down, shaking his head like an old man. "Tch, Laurel." Elinor was fascinated to watch the whites of his eyes turn suddenly red. Though his facial expression remained unchanged, his eyes brimmed with tears. It might have moved her to sympathy for him, but she knew he was stoned to the gills.

"No, Daddy. I'm really okay. Don't worry, please." She really meant it. She didn't like him crying over her. Her whole body twisted with discomfort as she stood before them.

When Allen cast his eyes down, searching for something to say, Elinor perceived another emotion on his face. Not only was Allen concerned and relieved to see Laurel, he was embarrassed. Awareness of the muck she had been dragged through was keeping him from looking directly into his young daughter's face. For Allen, Laurel had stature now. Like the teetotaler to the seasoned alcoholic, the pot-smoking college kid to a swooning junkie, Allen showed his deference to Laurel's new street knowledge by the hanging of his head.

Elinor released Laurel. "That's okay, Laur. Your dad just wanted to see you for a minute. You can go back."

When she was gone, Allen whispered, "Jesus, El, she looks awful."

"Yes. She's very thin."

"I don't know what to do for her. Look, do you need some extra money? Let me give you something extra so you can get her something."

"When she settles in why don't you ask her how you can help her with the fish? She'll always need more for her fish."

Automatically he patted the pockets of his shirt, looking for a joint. He thought better of it and sat back.

"God, I can't get over it. She looks like death warmed over."

"I know. She's not eating properly. She's probably barely eaten for months. I'm going to have to work with her gradually on that."

"Elinor, you've got to be careful. You can't let anything happen to that girl again—"

"What?" she snapped. Her body readied itself to do battle even before the meaning of his remark sank in.

"I mean this isn't the best area, and with a young girl like that you have to be extra careful. Here you are in a front apartment right on the street. I just mean—"

"Allen," she said steadily, "shut up."

"What do you mean, shut up?" His voice took on an injured tone. "I'm just saying you've got to make sure you know where she is, what she's—"

"Shut up," she growled.

"Come on, Elinor," said Debby, half whining, half placating. "Things are hard enough."

Quite right, thought Elinor. A good point. Without another word, she rose and strode down the hall to Laurel's room. "Honey, I'm going outside in the back for a minute," she said. "Your dad's still here." She crossed back in front of the two on the couch as if they had left while she was out, grabbed her keys from her purse, and let herself out the door.

The building's yard was tiny and confined by walls, but it contained three giant elm trees—ancient, judging from their size. She and Goldy had bought cheap lounges and often sat out here in summer reading in the filtered moving light, waiting for the sun to appear between the tops of the trees. Now, in the cool darkness, the trees absorbed the city sounds she knew to be all around the building, and she sat on one of the plastic lounges within the triangle they made. Elinor let Allen's words blow away in the dark as she listened to the light wind in the trees. Hundreds of thousands of invisible leaves tapped rhythmically against each other. Quieting, reminding herself that Laurel was home and life was moving again, Elinor sat still despite the chill, waiting until she was sure her visitors were gone.

\* \* \*

Vera received the news of Laurel's return with a short, soft "Hallelujah." It was typical of Vera to say no more than there was to say. She was a highly practical woman whose directness and economy of speech had been her stock in trade.

After a silence on the phone she asked, "Do you want me up there?" Elinor could tell from her voice that Vera wasn't up to coming.

"I don't think so, Mom, not yet."

"Let me know when I can be of some use, and I'll come," she said. It was Vera's genius to anchor a calamity in practicality. Yet whenever Elinor contemplated Vera's calm reliability in the midst of high feeling, the unanswered question arose: how deeply could Vera be touched?

"How is she, El?" asked Vera.

"Oh, god, Mama, she's scaring me to death. She's like a zombie, she's not eating. I don't even know what happened to her. She won't talk."

"Mmm," murmured Vera in acknowledgment through the line.

"I don't know what to do for her. And the police are already beating down the door. They want her to talk—"

"Has she told you anything at all?"

"Two men took her to a house somewhere—some horrid hot place. There were other children—"

"Good god—"

Yes, thought Elinor. This was beyond even Vera's realm of experience.

"The cops show her pictures—of men, of children. She just

looks and turns away. She's sleepwalking. I'm scared for her, I really am. She's like another child."

"It's early yet."

"Yes, but the police—they're like mad dogs for leads. They're calling night and day. It's worse than before. I'm afraid they'll eat her up. She can't take the attention."

"Can you hold them off?"

"Not forever, I can't. She has to tell them what she can if they ask her. I can only insist they go easy, stand between them and her. And they are trying, in their way. They're keeping the press out of it completely. They've got it straight about keeping her anonymous, I'll grant them that."

"Good. That's good."

"But what do I do for *her*?"

"You have to follow her lead, Elinor. That's all you can do. You can't push her, El."

"Yes." Vera's words echoed Lovejoy's level warning on the night of Laurel's return. "Don't push her in anything, Mrs. Landau," the staid, serious woman had said in a quick aside at the station door. "Laurel's been forced enough."

"Yes," Elinor said to her mother, abstractly wishing for more, for practical guidance, for simple how-to instructions. How do you shove back time? How do you turn a scared stranger back into a guileless child?

"All right, you'll call if you need me," said Vera. "Or when you want me to come up."

Elinor hung up feeling cheated. Surely her mother could have given her more direction, some downright reassurance. After all, family trouble was Vera's daily bread. She knew how to maneuver through it, had steered Elinor herself—sternly, competently—through her father's long illness and death, always seeming certain of how to proceed. But Vera was tired now, there was a new drag to her voice, as if she might be assessing this pack of trouble as too great for her to take on.

With Laurel home and everyone informed, with Jack suddenly banned as too new and exotic—too potent—to expose to Laurel too soon, Elinor felt as lonesome as she had ever felt during her daughter's absence. And a new fear dogged her that she hadn't often felt: it was the fear, where the consequences might be lifelong, of doing the wrong thing.

* * *

Lovejoy agreed to see Laurel on a private basis in her basement office at the police station. At first, even those rides to the station were a teeth-gritting battle of wills. Laurel had to be home all the time. On the street, even going in the car to the market, she broke into a sweat and visible trembling. Sometimes, when it was unavoidable, Elinor urged her out, gently cajoling, cooing, stroking the air around her. In a month, Laurel went back to school, carefully shepherded to and fro. But she went with such awful, silent resignation that Elinor felt cruel making her do it. Still, they had to have a life: Laurel had to be in life.

The style of their existence now was so stiflingly claustrophobic that after the first few weeks, Elinor could barely tolerate it. She would work every day after taking Laurel to school, then go out at three to pick her up and try to sneak in a trip to the market. There Elinor would soak up the people in the aisles for as long as she could, but soon Laurel would start to breathe audibly and pluck at Elly's clothes, trying not to clutch her arm in panic. She would have seen something, or bumped against someone, or seen somebody bump against Elly. A friendly word from the checker at the register could send her into a frenzy of belt-pulling or pocket-tugging on Elly's clothes, though all the while her expression would be blank, and she would gaze down the aisle in a flat bored teenage way.

At home she stayed in her room, caring for her fish. And

Elinor would face the walls, nearly mad with boredom. She would call Jack just to talk, working hard to keep a new concern out of her voice—that their fledgling relationship wouldn't survive the separation she felt she had to impose. And she would listen for Goldy coming in the front door from work. On the many evenings when Paul was out, Goldy came down for dinner, and the two women talked around Laurel's silence, pretending with brittle cheerfulness that nothing about their familiar threesome had really changed at all.

# *Seven*

Dr. Lovejoy adjusts the blinds, and the light in the room is cut by half. Such ugly blinds, thinks Laurel, dropping her gaze.

She senses the psychologist composing herself in the wooden chair across from her. She can see her feet: shiny brown high-heeled pumps, long tendons smoothed by a film of hose, the cuffs of sharply creased pants cutting firmly across the ankles. Her view of the feet planted and waiting causes Laurel to draw up her knees and push back more deeply into her chair. It is not a comfortable chair. Her back sticks to the imitation leather through the thin cotton of her blouse.

Silence settles and the expectancy grows. Laurel's breathing speeds up, though she tries to bring it under control. She is afraid the woman can hear it.

Outside, from behind the blinds, a man shouts. "You go on ahead. I'll catch up with you." The voice comes from above them. The surface of the police department parking lot lies just level with the bottom of the office window. A car starts. A car door slams. An engine grinds into reverse and then forward, and a shadow across the window momentarily darkens the room even more. Quick footsteps on concrete stairs fill the void.

Laurel suppresses an urge to move her head. She is practiced at remaining motionless in order not to draw attention to herself. But the woman is looking at her now, she can feel it. She will not be able to keep still much longer.

Dr. Lovejoy breaks the tension. "Laurel, do you know why you're here?"

"Uh, not really," the girl mutters into her shoulder. After a pause, she adds, as an awkward courtesy, "I don't know what to say."

"I'll help you," says the woman. She lets a long time go by in silence. She seems to consider it natural for two people to sit face to face in a basement room without speaking.

Then she makes a speech similar to the one Laurel has been expecting, and dreading. "I know that terrible things have happened to you. I know that you have been frightened very badly and for a long, long time. You have been in danger, you have been kept away from your mother. Perhaps you have been hurt—I don't know. You can tell me about that if you want to—"

Tears threaten. Laurel swallows them back with a fierce determination not to cry. To cry at all, or to take up the invitation to talk, would only prolong what is finally finished, past. All that is over now. That door has been slammed for good.

She looks up at Dr. Lovejoy's face. Her firm resolution not to speak of that time ends her self-consciousness at remaining silent. She lets her legs drop down over the edge of the chair; her feet, in socks and sandals, dangle high above the floor.

But the woman's steady gaze shatters her momentary confidence, sending her glance skittering around the room.

"And, Laurel, I want you to understand that everything you say in this room is confidential, between you and me alone. I won't tell anyone what you say here, not even your mother. She understands that. Do you? Do you understand that this is a place where you can talk about anything, say anything, without worrying about who might find out or whose feelings you might hurt?"

"Yes," says Laurel, looking up quickly. "But I still don't know what to say."

"Then say nothing. I'm used to that."

"So am I," she says, and drops her gaze. She is unaware that these three words touch back on the time gone by and drive a small wedge into the slammed, locked door.

Laurel, her eyes downcast, can still see the woman's feet. One leg crosses the other at the knee now, but there is no motion, no ticking off of time. The dangling foot shows patience, a willingness to wait. A restlessness grips Laurel and, though she manages to remain still, she wrestles boredom and embarrassment for the rest of the wordless hour.

# *Eight*

It shouldn't have surprised Elinor that she and Jack would argue at the first possible opportunity. The fashionable penthouse mocked them with cool indifference as their first evening together after three weeks of phone calls turned sour and went bad over dinner.

"She needs deep therapy, *real* therapy," said Jack, sipping wine.

With a desire like hunger to talk of anything else, Elinor fielded the remark. It was headed directly at the source of her seemingly ever-renewing uncertainty.

"No. She's staying with Lovejoy."

"But Lovejoy's a cop," he said, his voice rising. He stood up from the table and carried his wine to the serpentine couch in the adjoining living area.

Elinor had to pivot in her chair. "She's *not* a cop. She's a psychologist. She just does her practice there—"

"But that's what I mean," Jack returned, leaning forward on the couch for emphasis. "You'll have Laurel drowning in law enforcement, El. And she needs a psychiatrist, from what you tell me, for what's at stake for her. She needs a *doctor*, somebody who can medicate her if she needs it, somebody with all the tools of the trade—" He punctuated his separate points with his wine glass and then sipped from it. "Besides, Lovejoy *looks* like a cop."

That pricked Elinor's uneasy composure. "Goddammit, she's *not* one of them. She's smart, she's direct. And she's *experienced* in this kind of—" No words came. They never, in all their talk since Laurel's return, ever got close to naming it.

"Yes, but in a kind of first-aid way," said Jack, "Laurel needs some intensive work—"

"That's just it, don't you see? I don't want anybody pounding at her. Intensity is exactly what I don't want for her. And I'm scared to death of those things they could do to her—those medicines, those treatments. Don't you hear what I'm saying? I don't want anybody doing anything to her at all. And I think Lovejoy feels that way too—that she's just got to be made to feel safe. That way, she can tell us—"

"*Tell* you? She's been home nearly a month, and you said yourself she barely speaks, she barely eats—"

Elinor flew off her chair and planted herself in front of him.

"You let me do it. Shut up," she hissed. She had seen suddenly that it was impatience driving him to insist. How long would Jack wait for Elinor's undistracted attention? She fended off the pleasure she took even now in his presence by clenching her fists and teeth. Very quietly she said, "This is the way I'm doing it, Jack. You'll just have to sit back and watch. Quit trying to do your persuasion-for-the-public-good on me."

After a moment he raised his eyebrows and tipped his glass in mock concession. He leaned back and crossed his legs at the ankles on the low glass table between them. "You really like to be right, don't you, Elinor? You sure do have a line on the one and only way to do a thing." His voice was maddeningly calm.

She made a tentative move toward him to cut the tension and barked her shin sharply on the table. Her fury redoubled.

"Oh, *how* did you ever raise a child in this frigging place anyway? It's like a goddam showroom, for god's sake."

Their wills met like crossed swords, hers shaking with fury, his resting implacably, she thought, complacently with that infuriating certainty he never seemed to lose. Their words and breath, the heat of their exchange, collected around them and drained them of their energy. Elinor had been looking forward to this evening for days and had all but bribed Laurel to spend the night with Goldy. Dinner had been eaten, wine had been drunk, all was in readiness for a grand bout of celebratory lovemaking—and misery pressed the spirit from the room.

"Look, Jack—"

"Hey, let's give it a rest, okay? Since you can't seem to manage to talk about the subject without laying down the law?"

He would always win, she could see that. She was never completely sure of her position, there was always an element of bluff to her defense. The same certainty that fueled his candor defeated her now and repelled her.

She returned to the table to pick at her cake. Her anger warred with the knowledge that she could lose him now, tonight.

And even if they made it through the evening, how long could they go on seeing each other only when she could cajole Laurel into spending the evening with Goldy? Jack hated this place too, was ready to leave it for good. He wasn't joking any more when he talked about moving in with Elly. And she didn't even dare to have him over for an evening. She couldn't dislodge the feeling that it was still too soon.

What a balancing act, she thought, exhausted. The firm path she had been treading with Laurel before the abduction had become a tangle of taut wires. Every step Elinor took in any direction had her rocking on her feet and waving her outstretched arms.

"Let's go to bed," she said suddenly, her back still turned to him. She wanted to strip away his arrogance before she began to hate him for good.

She heard no movement. It took him a full minute to come around.

Finally, she heard him get up. He was milking the silence for all the suspense he could get out of it, she knew. "Might as well," he drawled finally. "Conversation's getting a little bit touchy around here."

It was a new kind of lovemaking for them, who had found a common language so easily before. Now their fluency had left them. But the unwillingness and withholding on both sides traced back to a heartiness of spirit, a clarity of personality that, in the end, when the last resistance gave way, took them farther and deeper together than they ever had gone before.

# *Nine*

Elinor held Metzger off Laurel for as long as she could. He'd had to be satisfied with the monosyllabic descriptions he had squeezed out of the girl by the hypnotic repetition of his clipped questions during several grueling sessions of interrogation. What he got was whispered references to two greasy-haired men, a green van, a house in a hot place. There were other children there. Dry-eyed and white-faced, Laurel had recognized two from their pictures.

Metzger clearly hated these sessions as much as Laurel and Elinor did. He had to inhibit his search-and-destroy method or he would have mowed down the thin young girl on the first sweep. But trying to temper his style made Metzger even more irritable than usual, and the interminable pauses that always preceded Laurel's sullen, one-word answers drove him wild with impatience. Each of the sessions had ended with Metzger pacing the small interrogation room, which jacked up the tension to a nearly unbearable pitch.

One morning Metzger called with his version of a bright idea. He had some men for Laurel to look at—"they won't *see* her, no. Come *on*, Mrs. Landau, let's get these scum where they belong." But he would put what he called a lady officer on the assignment to relieve Laurel of his own presence.

"Oh, hell, Metzger. It doesn't even matter. It's still terrible for her."

"Tell her to think about the ones who are still there. Tell her to think about their parents."

"All right, I'm not arguing with you. Just tell us when." Brusquely she cut off Metzger's graphic mode of persuasion. It wouldn't take him long to start recounting gory details.

"One-thirty," Metzger answered.

Less than an hour, she noted, annoyed.

It was a half day at the university. Goldy would probably be home. She dialed Goldy's number. Both she and Laurel could stand more company. And Laurel seemed to be feeling more at ease with Goldy these days than with Elinor herself. Maybe Goldy's quiet presence would make it easier for Laurel to sit down in front of a row of people Metzger and his boys had just scraped off the street.

But Laurel was nearly sleepwalking between Elinor and Goldy as they climbed the station stairs. Elinor remembered Laurel as an energetic eight or nine, when moving her out of the apartment for anything was like catching and wrestling a muscular, untrained puppy. The girl had teased and bolted, playing with Elinor's plans for the day as if they had been the morning paper. But since her return, Laurel seemed stunned, all the playfulness whipped out of her.

They entered the corridor and stood for a moment to adjust to the dimmer light. With a clatter of echoing footsteps, a figure approached at a near gallop.

"Mrs. Landau, Mrs. Landau—" It was a young woman, panting from her run down the hall, even giggling slightly. "Oh. Which of you—?" Elly made a sign. "Oh, good, good. Mrs. Landau, I'm Officer Fenton—I guess I should say Loretta Fenton? Inspector Metzger assigned me to take you to the observation room? And this must be—?"

"Laurel," Elinor responded instantly, well used to the infuriatingly poor memory for names that seemed to be a departmental affliction.

"Yes, Laurel. Laurel, I'm Loretta. And this is—?"

"This is our friend, Goldy Ives," said Elinor.

"Goldy, good, good. Fine. All ready?" she asked, beaming at the three of them as if she were leading the way to the event of the year. Her round, good-girl face shone like a pumpkin over her starched tan uniform collar and brown tie. When she turned down the hall, wide round hips bulged irrepressibly beneath the black regulation belt, and the narrowness of her back and shoulders was emphasized by the starched-in creases of her shirt.

She rushed ahead of them at just less than a dead run and gave a breathless commentary on what to expect, like a sportscaster hurrying to the main event and yelling back to the camera.

"Nothing to worry about here, nothing at all. Inspector Metzger told me to put your mind at rest right away. That's why he put me here—thought you might be more comfortable with a woman to show you the ropes, although I always thought he couldn't scare a flea. Don't you think he's a great big bear, not scary at all? So here—" She held a door open and urged them in with wild swings of her arm. "Here we are. Just file in and find a seat, make yourselves comfortable."

They entered a small empty gallery. Three rows of folding chairs faced a black picture window. When they were seated, Loretta let the door swing closed and in the pitch darkness resumed her pregame chatter. "Now, this is only routine, nothing at all to worry about—you're not worried, are you, Laurel? In a minute or so the lights will go on behind that window, and you'll see six or seven people. But they won't be able to see you. They'll be looking out this way, but they won't be able to see through the glass. That's one-way glass, just looks black to—."

Elinor felt a hand—Goldy's—reach across Laurel's lap to seek her own and squeeze it hard. And now Elinor could hear, above Loretta's din, Goldy's suppressed shouts of laughter. She could even feel the back of her connected chair shake with Goldy's hilarity. Instantly she was infected, squeezed the hand back, and sought Laurel's with her other one. If Metzger imagined that this hyperactive ball of crazy energy could ever put anyone at ease in any situation. . . . She nearly gave vent to a hoot and swallowed until her throat ached. Laurel's hand covered her own and squeezed too. If the girl wasn't hysterical, she certainly had caught on to the joke. The three of them sat rigid and shaking and squeezing each other's hands, choking down the laughter that threatened to break out.

"And you can feel completely free to say anything at all about anyone. You can just talk freely, nothing will happen, they won't be able to hear you, so we want you to feel completely comfortable to say anything that crosses your mind, even mention the slightest resemblance, the slightest gesture or piece of clothing that might remind you of something about—" She dodged the subject and barreled off along another path. "I always feel better when I hear people talking, then I know their minds are working, that they're at least trying to answer the question, or, you know, make sure they're right—."

Goldy coughed, choked, and Elly took the opportunity to lean across Laurel and concern herself with Goldy. "Are you all right?" she hissed through clenched teeth. Goldy kept coughing to hide the laughter bursting free, until the light went on behind the window.

Six men climbed the stairs to the platform, and all the mirth drained from the gallery room. Laurel was completely still between Goldy and Elly, and despite her absolute assurances that they couldn't be heard in the next room, Loretta's monologue trailed off into a whisper and mercifully ended.

The men squinted into harsh lights, which heightened the pale, sick look of most of them. These men would look commonplace enough on the street, especially on Telegraph Avenue, but in this institutional setting they seemed to make up a museum diorama of humans at the end of the line.

"See anything?" asked Loretta.

"No," whispered Laurel.

"Nothing at all? Nothing that even reminds you of anything you forgot to tell us?"

Laurel didn't bother to answer.

They sat in silence for a minute or so before Loretta slapped her knees and cried, "Well!" jumped up, and held open the door. The light from the corridor reflected off the window and blocked the figures from further view. All the way out to the front door, Loretta raced ahead of them and threw back over her shoulder detailed recollections of her own first lineup and assurances that talking about what you saw, saying just anything, always seemed to help.

Outside, after an ordeal of good-byes that Loretta couldn't seem to end, the sunshine and relative silence seemed blessed. Then Elinor, Goldy, and Laurel, still glancing at each other in wide-eyed amazement, took themselves out to lunch.

# Ten

Slowly, carefully, Elinor began to introduce Laurel to Jack. She was a chemist, mad with suspense, mixing a new element into a potentially explosive substance.

The first meeting, nervously anticipated, occurred without incident. "Hi," Laurel managed, and then turned her chin to her shoulder, looking off into a place far beyond the living-room wall. Within a minute, she was back in her room. At dinner, while Jack and Elly exchanged hearty non sequiturs, wildly careful to include the girl in the conversation, Laurel made a pale pantomime of eating and disappeared again after fifteen minutes, this time for the evening.

One night, after the three of them had eaten a dinner during which a pleasantry or two had been exchanged, a joke had been successful, Elly dared to let Jack stay the night. For her, the evening was more exciting and fraught with adventure than the first time he had stayed with her. Laurel, on the other hand, appeared not to notice or care that Jack wasn't going home; eventually she went to bed. Next morning, Jack bought pastries and left some out on the table for Laurel in a new variation on his old ritual. It was like leaving an offering to an angry goddess. As she ate practically nothing now, they viewed her taking of one of the gooey things as a wordless acceptance of Jack's presence. Nothing was said, but this sort of ritual food talk appeared to be as conclusive as anything.

\* \* \*

There came a point when Elinor knew a threshold had been reached: this much Jack and no more. I'll grant you Jack for this many hours, Laurel conveyed to Elly without seeming even to see her. Okay, fair enough, agreed Elly every week. No Jack until Friday. They reached these contracts wordlessly, silently passing in the hall. But when the tension finally snapped, they were hit by a blast of talk that took them all by surprise.

They drove up to Point Reyes one day, to the ocean, leaving the brilliant winter sunshine in the countryside for the gray, foggy coast. Laurel brought her backpack to collect shells for her aquaria, but she sat on a cliff overlooking the ocean all day, not searching, not moving, just huddling up there in the cold wind watching the gulls. Jack and Elly poked around in the tidepools, waving her down to see this or that, but she just sat up there keeping them in sight.

The cool wind whipped the two on the beach into exhilaration. Having grown used to Laurel's silence, they didn't worry about it much. Elly was able to have a good time without feeling guilty or anxious about her not joining in. She and Jack let the day flow by, feeling lashed together by the wind.

They stopped at a café on the way home, a place where Elinor and Laurel always used to stop as a ritual for drawing out the day.

The three burst into the small warm room, its decor countrified and a little coy, and settled down at a corner table still wearing their puffy down jackets. Their faces burned in the heat of the room, and their bodies were exhausted from walking against the wind.

Laurel took her jacket off last, and as the waiter set steaming crocks of soup before them, she glared across the table in anger.

"He looked at me," she mumbled as the waiter retreated.

"What? The waiter looked at you?" Elly asked.

"No. *Him. He* looked at me," she said, practically hissing.

"I don't get you," Elly answered absently, dipping into her soup.

"Yeah, well, I'm not surprised, because you never see what's going on. But your *boy*friend here was looking at my boobs when I took off my jacket. *Weren't* you, Jack?" she added, spitting out the question like a streetwalker baiting a cop.

The restaurant, which was half full and very small, froze. In the silence, Laurel's words rang in a dozen pairs of ears.

Then the other diners pulled themselves together. They rustled, and fell on their meals again, everyone suddenly thinking of something to say.

The three sat together around their cute little table as if carved in stone. Elly would remember the image as if recalling a photograph—a memento of the day on which they started to understand what it was they had been living with.

Never had Laurel struck that tone before. She had barely even spoken above a whisper since she'd come home. But as Elly had told Jack many times, before Laurel was taken she had sounded like any other twelve-year-old kid—sometimes whiney, sometimes shouting with joy or verve. Now the meanness, the certainty, the audacious edge to her voice—it was as if a stranger were talking through her mouth.

"You've got to be joking," said Elly, sitting straight up, alert. "Are you kidding? Do you really think Jack was looking at you funny?"

Jack sat stark still, hands flat on the table on either side of his soup. He looked as if he had just seen a wild animal across from him and was trying to decide if he could safely back away.

"I can't believe what I'm hearing," Elly continued. "Are you saying that Jack looked at you funny and that I'm taking sides against you with him?"

"He didn't look at me funny, Mom. He looked at me very serious. He didn't think I would catch it, but I did."

"Honey, I don't know what you're talking about," said Elly, but of course she did. She was buying time to get over her dismay at the whole day's cracking apart, at the whole delicate illusion that was their lives together cracking apart to reveal the danger they were in.

"No, Laurel. Honey, you're wrong. Isn't she wrong, Jack? Jack wouldn't, Laur. Baby, come on, you're wrong." She was begging. The Laurel behind the silence and the fish tanks and the surreptitious clutches to her mother's belt had been sitting on her hatred and her rancor, but it was leaking out now. Elly was begging her to keep it in, begging her daughter to let her have Jack and her life as a woman.

"Jack, tell her."

He did not speak or move. He made no attempt to reassure her. He knew somehow that the only thing to do was to sit motionless with his hands on the table, shaking his head back and forth slowly with his eyes slightly lowered, not looking at her directly. It was how he would behave with a frightened animal about to spring or tear off into the bush. He saw that she was that.

Laurel still had her hackles up, like a wolf meeting a man in the wilds. It was all the wilds to her, Elinor thought, out here with all us innocents. We have no idea what she has been through, we forget that she is different from us now. Finally, Elly realized, after more than three months, the shock of coming home had worn off and the defenses that had failed to protect her when she was out there by herself had come into play.

They finished their soup and continued the long drive home in silence, all three wondering what would happen next and dreading to find out.

# *Eleven*

Laurel cannot lose Lovejoy's eyes, which are clean and clear as water. She twists and turns in the chair, feeling danger under the cool gaze. Eyes are her enemies. Elinor's brown eyes narrow when they find Laurel—scouring her minutely. Jack's eyes avoid her now. They slide away to protect them both whenever she is near. Her father's eyes shift too, but in embarrassment, which is far worse. And Lovejoy has a dangerous magic in her eyes. Spreading out from them and filling the room is an imperative: Laurel must speak. To its top corners, the room is a box of expectancy, pressing Laurel to talk, while Laurel resists, curling up in her chair, wishing she could sleep to speed up the hour.

Sometimes, not often, Lovejoy lays down a quiet question across the space between them. "Do you think about the men who took you?" These words swell too, like her gaze, to fill the room. They touch upon the walls, ceiling, and floor, bringing up cold sweat where they press on Laurel's skin.

She is not able to hold out against the pressure.

"No, no, not often," she whispers, tucking her chin into her shoulder, wrapping her arm around her chest.

"As quiet as you are, what *do* you think about often?"

"I just do my fish now. Nothing."

"Only the fish?"

There is something she sometimes wishes she could say. The silence rolls on, a ponderous stone wheel.

In a burst of courage she says it. "I hear them sometimes."

Lovejoy must ask, "Them? You hear the men?"

"I think it must be them. I hear rumbling voices anyway, maybe angry. Always men."

"You hear the men who took you?"

"I think it must be them."

"What do they say?"

"I can never tell. I don't know." Laurel is sitting upright now. Her voice is gaining range, timbre. Her bewilderment at the voices is coming through. "I just hear men in the background, no words."

"When do you hear these voices?"

"A lot," says the girl. "I hear them a lot."

"When you're in your room working with your fish, do you hear the voices?"

"No." She thought about it. "I hear them with my mother. When my mother looks at me."

"Only when she looks at you?"

"No. I hear them whenever anyone looks at me. My mother, my father, Jack."

"Do you hear the voices when your friend Goldy looks at you?"

"Goldy doesn't look at me. Goldy is as quiet as I am."

"Do you mean Goldy doesn't talk to you?"

"Goldy is like me. She doesn't talk much. I never hear the men when I'm with Goldy."

"Does that mean you feel safe with Goldy?"

"Safe? She's so quiet. I guess so."

"Mmm," says Lovejoy. "Do you hear the voices in here with me?"

Laurel realizes the answer with surprise.

"No, not with you. I've never heard them here."

"I see," says Lovejoy.

Silence absorbs what has been their longest exchange. Faint echoes of their words resound within it. As they wait out the hour, pale spectres of the men, now cast into words, make themselves felt in the room.

› PART THREE ‹

# Twelve

Berkeley, 6:00 A.M.

Gray light from a low sky pervaded the bedroom. Elinor stared vaguely at the ceiling, stealing a few more moments of warmth from Jack and planning her day. It was a late morning at school, so Laurel could sleep until nine. If Jack slept for another two and a half hours, Elly would be able to get in some time at the loom. There was no time to get dressed, though. She'd have to get up and work straight through until Goldy came by.

She pushed herself up and out in a single motion. In her long jersey and socks she looked like a girl in the dark bedroom, but she was now thirty-eight, and in the bathroom light, her face, though unwrinkled, showed marks of time and change. She peered closely at her face in the mirror. Age seemed to be bringing out the structure more sharply. A flash of Vera came and went in the course of a single movement. She noticed changes almost daily now. The eyes, of course, had altered; there was definitely more of Vera there now in their dedicated watchfulness. No question, they had lost their decorative quality over the last two years. Eyes to see, not to speak. She shut them against the sudden image of Vera standing here at her own bathroom sink, brushing her teeth, washing her old white face, becoming enmeshed in the dailiness of Elinor's grown-up life.

Brusquely, Elinor ran a comb through her short hair, pulled on the soft pants that had been hanging on a hook on the door, and turned off the light. Once more, walking quietly down the dark hallway, she looked like a tall young girl.

Making coffee in the kitchen, Elinor heard the newspapers slap the building's stoop. She poured herself a cup of coffee and took it to the corner of the living room where the loom waited, as it waited patiently in her mind every night, every meal time, every moment she wasn't there.

"Okay," said Elly aloud to the empty room. "All right." She flicked on the desk lamp, and the light pulled the disparate elements of the corner together. The colors of the design emerging on the loom blended easily with the living room's tones of brown and rose, coming up now in the growing window light. "Okay," she breathed again. Now for April, she was thinking. She needed to get some work out and make some substantial sales to cover the rent for April. With an hour and a half now, plus a full day after Jack left, she might be able to finish this panel today.

Outside, as the morning brightened and the gray gave way to blue, the birds reached their highest pitch and the first real traffic started rolling, bringing the day into motion.

\* \* \*

Laurel slept on in the weird green glow of the five aquaria lining her bedroom walls. The sound of the aereators bubbling seemed to intensify the soft color that bathed the room, the steady bubbling noise somehow green itself. The fish hung within their tanks like streaks of paint on watery pages. Some moved, silently gliding or shooting through the water.

The girl, now fourteen, slept comfortably inside the green room, for it was an environment she had created for herself to meet her needs exactly. It was long ago that she had changed, nearly two years now—though to her the time was measureless since every creak of the floor in a rundown dirty tract house, uncarpeted and balled with dust, had signaled certain degradation. Sometimes humiliation was followed by damp food in paper bags. Now, to place eons between herself and that house and to absorb all memory of it, she slept here among her fish, which if they moved at all, had no effect, barely seeming to exert pressure on the warm water that held them.

She had begun keeping fish at ten. First a bowl, soon a small tank her father had bought and assembled for her. Within a year she had progressed from familiar tropicals to the rarer breeds, astonishing dabs of color requiring much special attention. Over that year she read and read about tropical fish, pored through books in the library, special-ordered others through a collector's journal, and came to know and consult extensively with a pet-store owner—the fish man—who shared her growing passion.

Very soon her interest in the fish gained the stature of an adult occupation, an artistry really, for she created tiny worlds for them. She made each tank into a living picture of a place totally different in feeling and detail from the ones she had made before it. The very sand was distinct, and she laid down objects that she selected from the beach on serious collecting trips with Elinor or sometimes with Allen, under duress, for he was too impatient to move at a beachcomber's pace. She kept a supply of these objects and was always prowling for new ones whenever she could get someone to take her away from the city's barren concrete. She even saw things at other people's houses that she craved and sometimes asked for. All these she washed, often boiled, to remove all traces of their former environments, and kept in her desk drawers for use as she needed them.

Into the tanks Laurel worked the fish—wild, iridescent blue, yellow purer than that of flowers, fantastic patterns of oranges and black—the way a painter wields color. Each tank gradually took on its own look, with its own distinctive kind of plant life—filamentary or broad-leaved or treelike—and its own kind of fish—combinations of silvers and wisplike transparents coupled with dramatic black velvets and a few darting reds. In abundance, too, were the clownlike fish looking whimsical and sometimes foolish, but whose colors seemed mysteriously pure and excessive, the result of a special urge within creation to make living beauty.

These tanks were Laurel's canvases. She had always done well at school, and now she did her schoolwork as if filling out forms, quickly, with dispatch. It was easy to stay beyond the edges of the raucous life at school. She made her eyes blank to discourage anyone who approached her, and many did, both students and teachers, fascinated by her disregard and her angular, slightly wild looks. Onto her fish she lavished the energy that she withheld from daily life, where she remained watchful and silent, guarding against the eruptions of raw feeling that could take her by surprise. She knew and feared the power she had to shatter the tentatively forming household. Each day she came back to her room with relief, returning to the fish for safety.

In the early days she had turned off the tank lights at night. Now she slept lightly, wrapped in and held by the green.

\* \* \*

Goldy Ives, dressed for work, balanced her coffee cup in one hand and pulled her apartment door closed with the other. Waking up to an empty apartment had gotten to her again. She had been relieved at the note from Elly she'd found stuck under the door last night. "Stop by for coffee in the morning if you have time. E." She would take a few minutes with Elly in one of their ritual early-morning talks to clear her head of the loneliness that had hounded her all night. Outside Elly's apartment door, Goldy could hear the muffled slam of the loom.

She used the key Elly had given her long ago and let herself in. "I'm here, El," she said softly as she entered. At the dining-room table she set down her coffee and settled herself, swinging her legs, muscular and efficient-looking in dark sheer hose, across the seat of the adjacent chair. She was just coming around to seeing her own legs without remembering how Paul had always loved them. Just legs in hose, she thought now, irritated at having him enter her mind already.

She watched Elly, sitting arrow-straight and wholly focused on her work, her back to the room.

"I need to talk," said Elly into her work. The shuttle whooshed.

"What's up?" asked Goldy, blowing across the top of her cup.

Elly studied the end of the panel, combing down the fiber with care. Finally she turned around and faced her friend. "I talked with my mother last night. Something awful happened."

Elinor grabbed an afghan off the couch and wrapped herself in it, then went to the kitchen to pour herself more coffee. She arced the overfull coffee mug onto the table across from Goldy, sweeping away a spilled drop with a brisk swipe of her hand.

"I called her before I went to bed last night." Elinor raised her brows as she lifted the mug to her lips. "For maybe a full two minutes she had no idea who I was."

Goldy inhaled sharply. "Oh, no," she finally said.

"She didn't exactly come out and say who is this—you know how you keep talking to somebody while you're trying wildly to remember who the hell they are? She sounded so preoccupied and embarrassed I just kept talking. When she finally got it straight, I could tell she was absolutely mortified."

Goldy grimaced in sympathy. "Oh, Elly, how awful. And she isn't really even old."

"Seventy-eight? To me that sounds old. For my mother,

that's old." After a pause she added, "It's true. I usually think of her as she was at about forty-five, wearing a black dress and looking sharp, ready to go downtown. I can't believe she's coming apart like this. She's always been so absolutely put together."

The two women sipped their coffee in unison.

"Sooooo," Elly went on, picking up a theme they'd covered often. "I've got to get her up here. I just don't see how I can let it go any longer. I can't leave her there by herself. It's too risky."

"But she's still managing her job at the clinic, isn't she?"

"She says she is, but who knows? The thing is, she can't really get down there without driving, and how safe is it for her to drive around in the L.A. city traffic?"

Goldy received this in silence.

"Hell, it could be great. Who knows?" Elly continued, her voice pitched high with bravado. "I'm dying here under the expenses, and I can't exactly let Jack help me on a regular basis without letting him move in. Vera could help with the rent, and she'd be here where I could watch her. I can't take the thought of her just sitting in that poky little house by herself." She pulled the afghan up around her shoulders and shifted in her chair. "Goddammit, Goldy, the idea of living with Vera again—trying to work with her around, trying to keep things going with Jack . . . Jesus Christ."

Goldy made a sympathetic noise.

"And then there's Laurel. I worry about throwing things off with Laurel." The girl seemed so precariously balanced; after nearly two years she still tipped easily into fear or sullen withdrawal.

"Maybe it would be good for Laurel to have Vera around," Goldy ventured.

"Yeah, maybe," said Elinor absently. "And what's *Jack* going to make of Vera, I wonder. Oh, lord," she sighed, "life just keeps coming at you, it really does."

"That's the truth," Goldy answered, shifting her legs on the chair. Then she asked, "What about some kind of home? Or having somebody come in?"

"Oh, sure," said Elly, with a wry smile. "Fifteen hundred a month either way, and all the soaps you can watch. Vera? Can you picture it?"

They grinned at the thought of fierce, impatient Vera sitting still for daytime TV and then looked past each other across the dining-room table. They sipped their coffee in silence.

"So," said Elinor after a long moment.

"So," echoed Goldy, pushing back from the table.

"So, how's the hot single life? Wild nights and dreamy days?"

"Insomnia. Don't ask." Stopping at the door, Goldy called, "Hey, it'll work out, El. From what little I know of her, Vera seems great."

"Sure, Pollyanna. For somebody's mother." She picked a balled piece of fiber off the floor and threw it at her friend. "But hey," she said, her expression turning sly, "maybe I could send her down to you. I have the feeling you could use the company."

Not quite up to a joke about her solitude, which was still new and full of demons, Goldy tossed the ball back at Elinor and slipped out the door.

# *Thirteen*

Vera recognized the expression. The old man was in pain. He smiled at her across the table, making an effort, but deep creases at the edges of his eyes meant distress somewhere in his body. She was so practiced at reading the signs that without conscious effort she could distinguish between the lines of old age and the newer ones laid down by pain and many sleepless nights.

She had long ago discovered that reading faces was a secret skill of the elderly. They needed to be able to recognize friends in the same way the sick and the very young did. But for Vera it was a practiced art. She had been doing it at the clinic, or at places like it, for more than fifty years. How on earth would she give it up?

The sudden question caused her to reach for her cigarettes. She lit one, drew deeply, and set the ashtray carefully as far from the front of the desk as she could.

"Now. Can you read and write easily, Mr. Lepski? The pencil is no problem for you?" she asked the old man sitting on a folding chair before her.

"Nah, nah, no problem," he said, waving his hand vigorously to show the flexibility. It was a small point of pride with him, she could see, that he could still wield the pencil, for he was very old. It meant the difference between coming into the clinic on his own and having someone come in with him to fill out the papers.

"Good," she answered. "You need to fill out these forms—they are nothing, you'll see. Come ask me if you have any questions. Fill them out front and back, and then bring them back to me."

As she spoke she watched the old man's shoulders drop in relief. He could use the clinic, yes. Yes, a doctor could see him today. He let his head fall backwards, lifting his chin and stretching his flesh-folded neck. A Scottish rag-weave cap, a present from a grown child or a grandchild oblivious to the state he was in, sat snugly on his head. The cap was a rich touch that contrasted sharply with the thin white hair showing beneath it. When eventually he took off his hat, no one he had spoken to in the clinic would recognize him except Vera. She would read his face again. And though it was March and warm even for Los Angeles, she would note at his collar line three shirts under his windbreaker, which itself was zipped up to the top. He took the forms she gave him and smiled, the web of wrinkles on his face deepening all at once, and then began the slow work of raising his old body from the chair.

Vera saw it as her chief business to give relief by speaking. Her tone was not soft or crooning, but somewhat brusque, even businesslike. It conveyed competence and the ordinariness of things. Signs of sleepless nights and months of worry inscribed on the faces of those who came to her intake desk often receded slightly at the first sound of it. It was the timbre of her voice, above all, that made her good at her work.

There was as little embellishment to her appearance as to her voice. She had no cushiony bosom, no somber traces of empathy around the eyes. Behind her glasses, the alert brown eyes were set within bony frames and half-covered, it seemed, by heavy lids. Though finely creased by age at seventy-eight, her skin was taut across the cheekbones, and her well-shaped nose showed white from the pull across the bone beneath. The short cut of the snow-white hair, which she had tried years ago at her daughter Elinor's urging, lightened her air of efficiency and lent a hint of youth when she smiled. But Vera smiled rarely; she showed little in her face of what she thought or felt. Most often she expressed a calm attentiveness in her work as listener—fifty years of direct, clear-eyed, undistracted listening.

In her day she had run clinics like this practically without having to think about it. She had been the nerve center of three or four such operations, where she would neutralize and handle the frenetic, often bitter complaints of her staff members, the frightened protests and confusion of the patients, and the endless details of keeping a place of business intact and doing its work—all with the clear focus of one who had no inner disturbances to break the concentration. She did it while she raised a daughter, while she watched her husband grow indifferent to her, falter in his work, take to other women, and then begin to die. Throughout his long, hopeless illness, she went to work each day ready to take what came and do what had to be done. With relief at the escape it provided, she took the opportunity daily to sharpen her expertise.

Now she worked as an unpaid volunteer at the intake desk of an inner-city public health clinic. She did what she had always done, to the amazement of the younger, dissatisfied staff, because there was little else she was inclined to do and hardly anything else she was suited to. And she saw herself now as an advocate for the elderly patients, whose embarrassment at being old in the presence of youth, beauty, and energy often, she knew, flustered and even paralyzed them.

Vera herself had never experienced any such embarrassment. Impatience with the younger staff members, some pity for their arrogance and limitless inexperience, occasional pleasure at the beauty of a young face, and very occasionally anger at the insane preoccupations with the superficial that the young perpetually indulged—these were the private reactions she allowed herself.

The clinic needed her, she knew, whether the staff realized it or not. They would miss her soon enough when she was— What? she thought, feeling a current of despair. Sitting through the days in a bedroom in Elinor's apartment, trying to keep out of the way? Trying to hang onto her mental wholeness as if it were a cracking bowl? She fought these threatening images of herself with a fierce draw on her cigarette and a practiced assessment of the rows of people in folding chairs before her.

As usual, several of them were asleep in the waiting area. Many slept their deep first sleep there, kept awake at night by anxiety or the lack of a place to settle. Vera remained undaunted at the steady flow. While the staff rolled their eyes and worried over the clinic's resources, she saw those who filed in each morning as simply more—more of the sick, more of the old, more defeated, more damaged, pregnant, diseased, drunk, exhausted, incurably mentally ill. More of the thousands upon thousands of people she had met with her direct gaze and calm, clipped voice over the years.

Today Vera was shaken. The night before she had spoken to Elly for minutes on end while thinking her daughter was Polly, a nurse at the clinic who had been off work for several weeks. Coming out of it and recognizing her mistake, she knew she had reached a crisis in the bizarre piecemeal disintegration she was experiencing, and she knew from the strain in Elly's voice that her daughter knew it too. Drenched in embarrassment, Vera had had to struggle to keep from hanging up.

It wasn't the first episode of forgetfulness by any means. She was starting to worry that she might burn down the bungalow some night. More than once lately she had found a cigarette she had just lit burned suddenly down to the end—

but instantaneously. And where had she been if she'd really been gone while it burned? Had she sat stock still? spoken? shouted out? danced a jig? Once she'd looked up to find she'd removed a picture from the wall. And once, a mere second after entering her kitchen, she found all her dishes taken down from the cupboard and stacked neatly on the table. They were arranged with some care, a fifteen-minute job, and she still held a cup in her hands. Between these episodes her perception and thinking remained as sharp as ever. But where—*what*—was she during these lapses? The mystery had forced her to the conclusion that she must move up north with Elinor. Still, the decision brought neither relief nor a sense of safety, but rather the intense anxiety that Elly might see her in one of her states, exposed, or find some mundane but puzzling evidence to show that Vera was coming apart.

At the moment, however, her distress was taking the form of intense irritation at a problem that had remained unsolved for two years. It was actually a table she sat at facing the waiting area, not a desk, a large wooden teacher's table topped with in and out baskets, plants, and her inevitable accoutrements: a pack of Lucky Strikes, a lighter, and an ashtray. Despite the tailored pantsuit she wore, Vera felt herself too exposed to view below the table. The shame at being old that many clinic patients exhibited was not a part of Vera's repertoire of feelings, but being visible below the table to the incoming clients felt to her unseemly for a woman of her age. For the two years since she had come to work at the clinic, she had been writing courteous notes to the director requesting a real desk. Finally, his assurances and hearty promises had yielded a scratched-up desk of the same vintage as the table. But for months now the desk had remained down the hall in an empty office.

To relieve her irritation—and further force her mind from its real cause, for she had blacked out after the phone call the night before, and for a very long time—she inhaled purposefully on her cigarette, put it out in the ashtray, and stood up, leaving the first row of clients to stare abstractly at her empty chair. She would get that desk moved out front today, she resolved, even if she had to cajole the two clinic nurses into shoving it down the hall under her firm direction.

\* \* \*

Four hundred miles to the north, Elinor sat at her loom. She sought the perfect motion that would connect her to the delicate fabric—beige and ivory shot with an occasional strand of near gold—that was growing out before her. Jack, Laurel, Goldy left her easily. The books and bills, a growing trepidation about approaching a certain exclusive city shop—all dissolved as the motion involving feet, hands, arms, back, and a certain lift of the head took over. But she was left with pictures of Vera. This worry was stubborn and rooted in the years of vague dissonance between them.

To live with Vera again! And with the eternal tension tuned higher by Vera's weakening health, Laurel's new peculiarities, and Elinor's fierce protectiveness of her love affair with Jack.

Oh, the gluttony of family life. Families ate up love and art. Elinor resigned herself to her failure to find the ancient weaving rhythm and gave in to her vision of Vera's face. She sat in silence, looking for a way to end her resistance to the inevitable and so get on with her work.

## *Fourteen*

It was a Monday and Jack woke late, at least for a working man. The clock showed nine-thirty. He stretched, groaned robustly, showered long until the water ran cold, and threw on his clothes, still gleeful after two years of self-employment at the lack of tie, collar, and jacket. He made a point of moving quietly through the living room so as not to disturb Elinor at her loom.

"Morning," she said, still working and not looking up.

"Morning, old lady," he said.

Her mouth twisted sideways in a wry half-smile.

"Don't call me old lady," she said to her loom.

"So don't wear your blanket to work," he responded, for she was still wrapped in the afghan she had pulled around herself during Goldy's visit. "Want some coffee?"

"Get a new woman if you don't like the look," she remarked.

"Got some, thanks. Where're you going?"

"To the office. Where else?"

"By which you mean out for breakfast."

"Exactly. Then back to the city."

"Okay. See you Friday."

"Bye," he said, kissing the back of her neck.

"Quit," she said absently, going on with her work.

\* \* \*

He strolled down the street as if he owned it, breathing in the March air with an awareness of approaching spring. Working people passed him as he walked down the slight hill to Telegraph Avenue—busy, neat, tailored people tapping the sidewalk audibly with their shoes. The nine-to-five shuffle, he called it, and he slowed his pace even more.

Jack had a knack for making money. He saw doing business as a source of excitement and a chance to sharpen his wits. But he liked it only on his own time, mixed with a reliable dose of freedom. He had great confidence that he was doing the right thing. He had a good reputation in the city; people knew what he was up to. And strolling down the street in the sunshine, totally dissociated from that nine-to-five world, was definitely part of the plan.

As he turned onto the avenue, a familiar-looking car inched by him, locked into the early morning crawl. Jack stepped off the curb and rapped on the window.

"Paul. Hey!"

His old friend Paul Ives leaned over and unlocked the passenger-side door, and Jack swung into the car. They hadn't seen each other for several months, not since Paul had moved out on Goldy.

"Where you headed?" Jack asked.

Traffic surged forward suddenly, and Paul concentrated on his driving. Jack studied his friend's profile—intense, serious, appropriately professorial. His horn-rimmed glasses rested midway down his nose, adding a rakish air. Paul's usually sardonic aloofness was marred now by a look of consternation.

"Thought I'd go by the place and pick up some of my stuff," he said finally. There was embarrassment in his voice.

"Join me for breakfast?" asked Jack. "That's where I was

headed. Hey, let's check out that new diner down on the pier. I can pick up BART down there to the city."

Paul hesitated slightly.

"Come on," Jack urged. "A person's got to eat."

"Sounds good," said Paul, following the flow of traffic west toward the bay. "I could use a cup of coffee."

They found a booth on the water side of the small noisy diner, and the whole bay spread out before them. The water itself was almost too brilliant to look at in the morning sunlight, but the city, bunched up at the end of the bridge, drew the eye. It was perfect and tiny, its edges sharp as paper against the clean sky.

"Some view," Jack remarked. "It was luck running into you. My car's back over in the city."

"Yes," said Paul, unable to generate much enthusiasm.

"So how's it going, Paul? I haven't seen you since you took a powder."

Paul smiled weakly down at the table. "That's a quaint way of putting it."

Three months earlier Paul had left Goldy to move in with a young man, a graduate student of his.

A harried waiter came to take their order, staring out impatiently over the bay while they read the blackboard menu over the counter. Paul ordered coffee to Jack's three-egg omelet and potatoes.

Jack caught Paul's evident discomfort during the interruption, and when the waiter left it was bumpy going.

"How're Elly and—"

"So what's—ha! No, go ahead."

"I was just going to ask how everybody's doing," said Paul. He sat up straight and threw his arm over the back of the booth. He seemed to be forcing himself to shape up.

"Doing fine, doing fine," said Jack.

The waiter brought coffee.

"Yes? Laurel's all right?" Paul asked, with the academic's

knack of suggesting, by the tone, that there were volumes left to say.

"Oh, yes. Things have been going pretty smoothly for quite a patch of time now. No panics, no frights."

"You think she's calmed down for good?"

"To my mind she's been *too* calm since I've known her. She's not a real forthcoming kid, you know what I mean? And that about kills Elinor, who wants her to pick up the pace a little. Have friends, do things—"

"Laurel did change. I can see Elly's point."

"Yes. El tells me she changed. And she wants her back the other way. I don't think it's going to happen. I'd say she's always going to be cautious, quiet, looking things over real carefully. Who wouldn't?"

"That's a point."

They had never discussed the situation when Paul had lived down the hall. Now they settled on it as a subject they could expand on while their mutual self-consciousness subsided.

"I'm just glad she can relax at all with me around. That's been a prime concern."

"She just gradually got used to the idea that you weren't going to go away?"

"Hell, no. It wasn't that easy or that cheap. I had to bribe her."

"You bribed her?"

"Sure. She couldn't stand the sight of me for months. But I started telling her about this aquarium store near my place in the city. It's a wild place—maybe fifty tanks in a dead black room. And all filled with these amazing fish from all over the world. The first time I took her there she thought she'd died and gone to heaven."

"Police still coming around and bothering them a lot?"

"No, that's petered out. They haven't been around since before you left, at least. They're never going to find those guys if they're counting on Laurel to help. She never had the slightest idea where she was."

"How does Elly feel about that?"

"Oh, she's relieved to have the cops out of her life. Those sessions were always hell on Laurel. I don't know. For myself, I don't like knowing those scumbags are out loose in the world with the rest of us. Makes me uncomfortable. I'd like to get completely out of the city, *both* cities, and away from the city weirdness."

It was an ongoing issue between Elly and himself, a source of constant frustration. Jack found it hard to understand how Elinor could apparently ignore the undiminished dangers of the city streets. He himself was often struck by the look of some crazed or alien creature hovering nearby. Most of these shells in the next moment inspired pity, but there was the odd man or pair of men who, by the obvious anger lacing their derangement, evoked the urge to run. Those two child stealers were out there with everyone else on the street, but Elinor kept her attention pinned on Laurel. She never seemed afraid, nor did she seem vengeful, as he often did when he thought back on the ordeal, a mental rat cage he tried to avoid. When the investigation was finally closed without anyone's having been turned up, Elinor's unmixed relief was apparent.

"Thinking seriously about moving?" Paul asked.

"Hell, I've been pushing for it for over a year. I'm getting tired of this commute I do across the bay three or four times a week—but Elly's so goddammed set in her ways. My god, she's stubborn. Doesn't want to upset Laurel with any big changes, not yet."

"Sounds reasonable."

"It might sound reasonable as hell, but meanwhile I'm thinking about how Laurel might get a lot out of leaving the city. And we could find someplace where we each had somewhere to work, get the loom out of the middle of the living room.

It's like sitting down to relax with your favorite cottage industry. But Elinor's so goddam independent. The money aspect drives her crazy—down payments and so on. . . ."

"Sounds like you two ought to get married. Wouldn't that ease the money thing?"

"Elinor's absolutely dead set against getting married." The waiter set down an enormous platter of food in front of him. "She has her own ideas about things," he said, "and that's a fact."

Paul looked prim sipping his coffee as Jack set to his breakfast.

"Have some toast," said Jack.

"No, thanks. Listen," Paul said. He pushed his fingers through his hair and dropped all pretense of trying to seem at ease. "How's Goldy doing? I mean, day to day?"

Jack looked up and stopped eating. He could see that Paul only half wanted to know.

"Goldy doesn't talk much to me," he said. "She looks real good. Elly gives me to believe that she's had her moments."

Paul began to chew at his lip.

"Well, you have to admit, it had to have been a pretty good shock after—how long were you guys married?"

"Fourteen years. But she shouldn't have been surprised. That's what I can't get over. I thought we'd been talking about it for months. But apparently she—misunderstood."

"Didn't want to know, maybe."

"And now I can't believe how much she hates me. I never would have believed she could hate me so much."

He turned to gaze distractedly out the window, and Jack felt as if he'd been visiting a sick friend whose mind had suddenly reverted to his illness. He finished his breakfast quickly, impatient now to get on with the day. Paul looked incapable of more talk as he continued to stare out the window, cupping his coffee mug in both hands close to his lips.

"It fades, you know," said Jack. He recognized Paul's incredulity at the storm of feeling unleashed by the seemingly clean resolve to end his marriage. He thought of his own blind rages, and the memory of his own unrestrained voice, accusing Lee, pulled vaguely at his throat.

"In a year, you two might even be able to have a conversation."

"A year of this," Paul mumbled at the window.

Breakfast was over. Wild to get out now, Jack grabbed the bill and swung out of the booth.

"Paul, stay in touch. I mean it. Let us know where you are, when you're coming over."

"Let me get that coffee," said Paul, making a move to reach for his change.

Jack threw up both hands—"Please!"—and turned to the register to pay the bill.

Outside in the sun, a red-skinned, frazzle-haired old man in a tattered army jacket lay sleeping against a doorway fronted by a locked wrought-iron gate. A grimy bedroll and a large paper bag of groceries stood next to him on the low stoop.

"Oh, boy," Jack muttered. "Another casualty." He wanted to stop thinking about where and how and with whom to live, or he'd soon be brooding about his son Mike. And it was too early in the morning to get started on Mike.

One thing about concrete, Jack thought as he lengthened his stride, it speeds you up. Once you get going on a concrete sidewalk you can really cover some ground. With determination, he turned his attention to his work, and soon he was weighing with pleasure the ways in which the day might sort itself out.

# *Fifteen*

"So many dishes," said Vera, thrusting her hands into the suds.

"Oh, Ma, don't. I'll do it. Not on your first night." Elinor was holding onto the back of the chair for balance, overfull from dinner and heavy with too much champagne.

"You have a nice man there, Elly," said Vera to the wall above the sink. "I like Jack."

"I'll take that as a professional opinion," Elinor said, trying for lightness. But she was as pleased by her mother's approval as if she had surprised Vera with all As on her report card. She had been besieged by worries since the decision had been made for Vera to move in. Not the least of these anxieties was that Vera would dislike Jack and thus add more weight to a love affair already heavily burdened with domestic concerns. Suspense on that score had added an unbearable edge to the preparations Elinor had been making to receive her mother into her life.

"I think if you had asked me I would have been very negative about your becoming involved at this stage," Vera mused over the dishes. "Speaking generally, I believe most people are better off without."

Elinor swung from relief to an old agitation, exaggerated by the wine. Into her gullet pushed the stony feelings she knew to be a rough physiologic translation of her childhood love for her father. Somewhere in the pause at the end of Vera's remark, Elinor's long-ago passion for her father, Sandor, met Vera's implacable coolness, the motionlessness that struck the old woman even at the mention of his name. Slowly the feeling sank from Elinor's gullet to her stomach. Would she vomit? With her mother in the house? The possibility struck her as inadmissibly horrible. Drunkenly, she strained for control.

"Where's Laurel?" asked Vera, turning to wipe off the counter.
"In her room. With her fish."
"That girl loves those fish."
"Mm."
"Almost as much as she loves you."
"She loves her fish, Ma. She only *needs* me."
"Same thing, darling, between mother and child. No difference whatsoever."

With a turn of her head, Elinor closed the subject.

"And that Goldy's a fine thing," Vera went on. "She's a smart girl. I've always liked her."
"Sure. Smart, beautiful—lonely as a rock."
"There's no reason for her to be lonely, with that job she's got. She has good work, lots of energy—"
"Her marriage is wrecked, Mama. She's suffering."
"So there are other men. There's plenty in life besides that, at any rate. There's no call for her to pine away her life with that work she does at the college. She'll get over it, whatever he did."

Elinor swore off champagne. Now, grown woman though she was, tears threatened, and she was struck with envy at Vera's approbation of Goldy. Drunken baby, she scoffed at herself. Begging your mama to say something nice.

At the start of dinner the wine had seemed the perfect antidote to Elinor's shattered nerves. After two feverish weeks of getting the back room ready, dragging Laurel around against her will to buy a bedspread, new curtains, and an extravagantly expensive rug—and all the while working past midnight at the loom—Elinor had finally picked Vera up at the airport that morning. They'd stopped at Greyhound to collect Vera's three cartons of belongings, and then rushed home so Elinor could create a welcoming dinner at which she would introduce Vera to Jack. She had made Goldy agree to come—hissed at her when she hesitated—and to provide the gaiety that Elinor was failing to feel.

Over the meal, Elinor seized on the champagne Jack had brought, and soon she was looking around the table with a contented expression like a beneficent matriarch. Her daughter safe by her side; her mother under her watchful eye; her kind, handsome man; her smart, pretty friend—it was all she could do, pressed on by the wine, to keep from raising a lugubrious toast to the cozy intergenerational picture they made around the roast and potatoes.

No one seemed to notice she was leaning on her splayed elbow. Laurel, keeping her eyes focused intently on her place, cut and recut her meat into tens of neat tiny cubes, organizing her plate in a tedious pantomime of eating. This was her regular mealtime behavior, but she seemed concerned with making her performance particularly convincing in the presence of her grandmother.

Jack carved and served with some grace and seemed to defer to the family atmosphere, restraining his usual mealtime enthusiasm for raucous conversation.

When Goldy asked Vera about her work at the clinic, Vera responded calmly, showing none of the nostalgia or longing that Elinor had feared hearing in her voice.

And Elly continued to drink, dispelling the cloud of worries that had grown and redoubled over the last two weeks, plaguing her mind like gnats.

Now, the dishes washed, Vera wiped the counter, sat down at the kitchen table, and turned her calm attention to her daughter.

"So, you. Working hard?"

Elinor managed to shrug, the champagne somehow solidifying her joints now, not melting them, and dulling her brain practically to sleep.

"You seem tired, El. You've been knocking yourself out with me coming, haven't you?"

Too tired to resist, Elly mumbled the truth. "I'm worried, Vera. I'm worried about you."

"Oh, me—" Vera answered, waving a hand, diminishing.

"Ma—"

Elly stopped short. Vera's short blackouts, their meaning, and her formidable seventy-eight years formed an invisible barrier between them. Neither mentioned them. Neither dared reach out to determine how real, how substantial, the barrier actually was. "Well, daughter," said Vera, lightly slapping the table and standing up, "life goes on."

In her near stupor of exhaustion, Elinor received this comment in silence. But not without registering how directly it contradicted the true insight that, at the very moment of Vera's speaking, she shared with her aged mother.

The dishes done, the wet towel hung flat on the edge of the sink, the pans put away, the lights turned off, Elinor and Vera left the kitchen. They walked the width of the empty living room side by side. Together they turned to check the room once before putting out the light, and then they walked slowly, single-file, down the hall and into their separate rooms. Elinor woke in the night to the realization that she would now have two sets of night sounds—rustles, turnings, stray vocal scraps—to interpret before she returned to sleep.

# Sixteen

"Look what I found," said Vera to the girl, who lay across the foot of her grandmother's neatly made bed. "Look. Do you know who this is?"

Laurel took the small, brown-toned snapshot. She looked at it for a long time without speaking.

"Who is that?" urged Vera.

"It looks like me, sort of. Is it my mom?"

"It's me. At the beach at sixteen." Vera didn't press the matter of resemblance, but it had moved her to the core once she noticed it. The girl in the picture, wearing a black wool tank suit with a long, modest skirt, knelt in the sand and stared into the camera with the same unswerving directness that Vera had always shown. The straight-ahead gaze, the face and slender body, the wild hair bunched on top of her head could have been Laurel's. Behind her in the photograph people sat and stood on the sand—young women in heavy bathing suits similar to Vera's, old women in dark dresses with braids wrapped across their heads—all with their backs to the camera, facing the unseen surf. Vera was galled, for she clearly remembered the moment at which that photograph had been taken more than sixty years ago, while in her mind yesterday—lord, this morning!—was a matrix of comings and goings riddled with empty spaces.

She was finding that Laurel triggered memories of herself as Elinor had never done. When she looked at the girl, she was apt to see some long-forgotten episode unroll across her mind. It bothered her to have old images and memories jarred free in this way. She really must, she resolved again, go down to the volunteer bureau and find a job. It had been the condition under which she had agreed to rent out her bungalow and come. Now, not without humor, she imagined her resolution to find a job bubbling up in her brain, holding itself together for a long brave moment like a stubborn bit of foam, and then drifting off to be lost in the deep reaches of memory and mind.

Laurel had taken to her grandmother's presence with a blessed lack of ambivalence. Every day for the three weeks since Vera had moved in, Laurel sought her grandmother the minute she got home from school, and for the first time Elly was free to leave and go about the city after Laurel came home.

For her part, Vera made sure to be home when Laurel arrived, fixed her a bite to eat, invited her to her room. Today she had gone out while Laurel was in school to buy a large leather photo album (she stood exasperated for a long moment in the stationery store, trying to ferret out the reason she had come). When Laurel got home, Vera beckoned her back to her room and slid a large paper carton of photographs out from under the bed. Now Laurel lay on the white chenille spread slowly going through and making piles of pictures. They were progressing through the top layers, mostly images of Laurel herself as a child and as a baby, and records of the marriage of Elly and Allen. Then came Elinor as a strong-willed, strong-boned young woman, a moody teenager, a shy pubescent girl; then layers of Vera and her three sisters, tall fashionable women of humor and obvious affection for one another.

Once a long time ago, Vera had gone through this box and taken out all the pictures of Sandor, even of Sandor's car.

Carefully she had stacked them, then slid them into a manila envelope, sealing it with deliberation before placing it in the wastebasket in her bedroom. The image remained in her mind of the fat yellow envelope leaning against the side of the wastebasket by her bed. She must have had to make the decision all over again to carry the basket downstairs and throw away the pictures for good.

And yet Sandor was everywhere in the pictures without his image actually being present. The middle layer showed Elinor's childhood and Vera and her sisters as adult family women, the moving forces behind the birthday parties, send-offs, Thanksgivings, and family gatherings recorded here. Looking at them now, she could remember how Sandor had taken his leave—whether clandestinely, angrily, or lying glibly—on nearly every occasion. Whatever it was went on without him.

There was something in Laurel herself that opened the old wound in Vera. It was a wound buried under layers and layers of protective scar tissue. She hadn't felt anything at the thought of Sandor in thirty years or more. It had been that long since she had nursed and then buried him, buying a perpetual-care contract in the end and never returning to the cemetery after the funeral. And no tremor, no dream of him had disturbed her sleep since then. Now often, with the image of Laurel's face fresh in her mind, she lay awake in her new room—her last, no doubt, unless she couldn't manage to die before she had to be turned over for custodial care—and the figure of Sandor rose up before her as she stared at the ceiling. Rakish in his hat, as handsome as a thirties gambler in the movies, and exotic with the Polish accent touched with a South Brooklyn edge, he split her in half with his words, cut her to the spine with his insolent comings and goings. "I need women around me, Vera. Always have. You'll just have to live with it, that's all." Cruel memory, to let those words ring on through the years while whole recent days disappeared.

Vera was proud, and she had managed to meet with utter

silence his mean dares to raise a ruckus. She remained silent about it all through his illness, when his efforts to dress and leave the house grew increasingly pathetic and desperate.

Occasionally she would see past the wreckage even more deeply into the past, and there would be Sandor's hands on the steering wheel of his dashing Oldsmobile, thrilling her with his mastery of the car and his casual, mannish ways. He sang when he drove; he threw his arm around her across the seat; and he seemed to barrel noisily across the barriers that held her, as a serious working woman in the 1930s, in check. But in the end such memories struck her as ridiculous, with no real connection to the old woman she had become. Of Sandor there was nothing left at all. There was none of him in Elinor that she could ever see, and in Laurel there was only this memory-stirring reflection of herself.

\* \* \*

Laurel watched Vera light a cigarette and skim off six inches of pictures, digging down deep for more snapshots of herself as a girl. She sifted through the photos, casually wielding her cigarette, and to Laurel Vera looked like a woman who had never been hurt by anything. Straight, tall, and alert, the old woman spread safety around her as she laid down the pictures as if playing a dignified game of solitaire. There was no excess of feeling. Only light amusement played around her thin lips as she looked closely at first one image, then another.

Laurel picked up the photos, cracked and discolored and soft with age, that Vera laid down. It was true that the girl in the pictures bore a striking resemblance to herself, but in a certain bearing of the shoulders, a lift to the head and chin, Laurel saw a surety, a poise, that she had started to crave. Laurel resolved to watch her grandmother closely. There was something important that Vera had to teach her.

# *Seventeen*

Laurel likes the sense of Lovejoy towering over her as they walk down the hall to their room. It is really just Janet's cheerless office, but over the two years Laurel has come to think of it as their shared warren where no one else ever comes. Stupid, it's a police station, Laurel chides herself. The place is crawling with people. But it makes her sick to think of a stranger sitting in her chair, using up the air into which she spills her dreams. She has to think of that door as locked all through the week.

Janet is tall, looming, and you can feel strength coming off her. Laurel often imagines seeing through the thick cloth of her skirt: long muscular legs, firm thighs, and a flat protected midsection, like a man's.

Janet always meets her at the front desk and walks with her downstairs and through the corridors to the office. Inside—how many times by now?—they sit down across from each other, and Janet inevitably reaches behind herself to adjust the venetian blinds. It is part of the ritual that makes it all safe: it gives Laurel the power to speak.

Then Janet turns onto Laurel her fantastic, awful eyes—barely blue, barely even colored, the irises transparent and clean. After the blinds, Janet begins the session, as always, by looking at Laurel as if there were nothing else in the world to see.

In the early days, Laurel saw that gaze as a weapon. Janet's eyes pierced her. Into the wound they opened flowed self-consciousness and a feverish desire to get away. But now it is different: Laurel takes the gaze the way a hot, dusty hiker drinks water, feeling it enter and slide coolly down, bringing alive her insides, which all week have lain desiccating, nearly dead.

"How'd it go this week?"

Laurel always meets the first questions with a long stretch of silence before she begins. It takes her that long to drink from Janet's awful, magical eyes.

Then: "Sometimes the way my mother looks at me, you know, Janet, she starts it all going. Just one look and the voices start up again. Just like always. The angry men."

Janet nods in recognition. She has heard about the voices many times before.

"I want to scream at her sometimes. Oh, please, *please* stop looking at me, *you're starting them up*, look *away*. But I'd just screech it out once I started, I know I would."

"You never do."

"No, of course I never do. I wouldn't. She's my mother. And I know how much she's been through because of me."

"Like what?"

"Like trying to be with Jack, for one thing. I know I ruin it for them."

"How 'ruin it'?"

"Oh, you know. How would you feel about having some weird kid hanging around all the time—not eating, never going out, just poking around with her smelly old fish—when *your* boyfriend came over?"

The idea of a boyfriend for Janet strikes Laurel as funny, and she ends with a transforming grin.

"Mmm." Janet lets Laurel settle down. "But she loves you."

"Oh, yes, love," impatient, looking around the room. The rush of words is over. Janet shifts slightly. It is an invitation, an encouragement to continue. But their little globe of time revolves on toward the end. Seconds tick into minutes while Laurel draws herself together for another splurge of words.

"I get to school and back, I go to Goldy's a lot, I can go with my mom to the store or even to the movies, but—I don't know why—I can't go out. I just can't go out yet. I get the shakes about it. It's the same when I have to eat. I get the shakes, my stomach clenches up, my teeth smash together. I can't do it yet."

"You're just not ready," says Janet. "You're still coming out of it, Laurel."

The girl waits a beat. "But that was such a long time ago."

Silence wells up again. It is their medium. Without self-consciousness, they drift, they float in silence like two of Laurel's fish.

"Oh, I'm a funny bird. Can't go out, can't eat, can't leave my mommy.

"You should see me at school. You wouldn't, though. Nobody does. I keep out of the way. I hide out. Nobody sees me. My main job is keeping anybody from finding out just how funny I am."

"How are you funny?" Janet asks softly.

Laurel looks up, then away, then down. The unanswered question stretches over the silence all the way to the end of the hour.

Janet performs the final ritual. Lightly she touches her hands to the wooden arms of her chair in a stylized suggestion of departure. "It's time," she says, and Laurel withdraws the new green buds of her freedom, at risk for another week.

# *Eighteen*

"What is it, El?" Jack asked into the warm dark of the bedroom.
Silence.
"What?"
She gave up staring, looked back over at him unseeing.
"My mother in the house, what else?"
"I thought you felt better with her here."
"On a practical level, yes."
"So?"
"I feel better and worse. I love her and I hate her. I'm a saint for taking her in and a total idiot for wrecking my life. Things aren't so simple, Jack, you know?"
"Who said things were simple?"
"Nobody. Nobody."
"Hey, good, Elly. Get irritated with me now."
"No. Come on, I'm sorry," she said, backpedaling. She rolled onto her side and faced him, deciding to talk. "But I'm a wreck. I can't do anything right, haven't you noticed?"
"Somehow Vera doesn't strike me as passing judgment all the time," Jack offered very cautiously.
"No, but she's here," said Elly. "She makes an impact, you know?" She sat up in the darkness and faced him, cross-legged, pulling the quilt up to her neck.
"There are just so many things—I can't get it straight. She's

not judging me or running a finger along the mantel to check for dust. It's just that I can't get *to* her. Having her here day in, day out, I feel I ought to get closer to her somehow. It never mattered to me very much when she was down in L.A., but now I just can't get to her, and she's here living in my own house. Do you know what I'm trying to say?"

Jack grunted.

"Plus seeing how she is now, honestly I can't believe it. I cannot believe these confusions, these endless pauses in the conversation while she looks for a word. Vera *never* pauses. I'd always marvel at the way she talked on the phone or the way she was at work—listening, nodding, staying right with what the other person was saying. Then she'd just wrap up the conversation. Like a tennis pro serving for the set. She'd just say what had to be said, and that would be that. It was fantastic. But she's losing her touch. And when I hear those pauses, my mind starts in with 'She's going to die. Vera's going to die' until she finds the word she's been searching for. It's excruciating."

"Maybe she could still do it, maybe she's just bored. She wants to get a job. She must *think* she can do it."

"Oh, maybe she can. But—oh, god, even *mentioning* this seems dangerous to me—I catch her staring. Do you? You're talking and she's staring, and you know suddenly she's not there with you. Have you noticed?"

"Yes, I know what you're talking about."

"It happened today at dinner, but it just slid by. I thought about it later. She was gone for a minute. Did you see?"

"Yeah, maybe."

"She's just so old now," she said, grabbing his t-shirt and twisting it. "And I feel like I ought to be able to get closer to her somehow."

After a time she lay back down and took hold of the hand he lay on her.

"And there's Laurel," she said to the ceiling.

"Ah," he answered. "I wondered."

"Oh, you wondered, did you, know-it-all?" with half-hearted brassiness. "What exactly did you wonder?"

"I wondered if you were jealous of Laurel's obvious affection for Vera."

The direct hit made her breathe in sharply and feel a passing anger at his marksmanship. After a long pause, she gave her self-mocking half-smile into the dark room.

"Well, I am." She turned away from him.

"I am," she said again in a flat voice. "Laurel went straight to her, didn't she, Jack?"

"Yep."

"I should be happy that she feels that safe with Vera. But I'm hurt. It's absurd."

A pause. "I know why she goes to her. Vera's not anxious about her like I am. Laurel says I bug her, that I stare at her. God, I'm only looking."

"You're looking with worry, with concern. You're listening to her breathe. You're searching her face for clues. You're always wondering about how things are going to work out for her, and it shows."

"So what do I do? It's just loving her."

"It's only natural, El. I don't see how you're ever going to change that. You're her mother. A mother worries, and you have what to worry about with Laurel, let's face it."

"So why doesn't Vera worry? You know, when Laurel went to bed one night, Vera turned to me and said, cool as could be, 'That child is ready to explode.' It was a completely quiet night—no fears, no ripples—and still she saw that, she said that. I don't know. Is it true? And if Vera thinks that, why isn't she worried?"

"She's not the mother, El. Her worry goes for you. And Vera's a professional, after all."

"You're right there," said Elly, rolling onto her back. "Vera is a professional in the business of people flying apart. Fifty years she's been watching and listening to people in anguish. I've got to learn to use her. She could be so much help now if she could just keep her head screwed on straight. I've got to get myself to listen to her and let her help instead of always feeling that *I* have to be the one."

"That would be good."

Long after the conversation ended, Elly spoke again.

"I've got an odd idea."

He was almost asleep. "What?"

"I want to go to Jade Mountain tomorrow to hear the teacher there speak."

"What? To that Buddhist center up the coast?"

"Yeah. They open to the public on Sundays so anyone can go hear the teacher. He's supposed to be an amazing person, calm and smart. I have this tremendous need to hear a wise person talking, Jack. Would you feel like going along if I can get Laurel and Mom to go?"

"Are you joking, Elinor? I've never heard you even remotely interested in religion before."

"Wisdom. I want to hear wisdom, not religion. I need a new point of view. I don't want psychology. I don't want social work. I don't want religion. I want wisdom."

"What makes you think you're going to get wisdom by dropping in at this place on a Sunday morning?"

"Goldy's been going. It's helped her with Paul's leaving. And it's beautiful out there. The farm's set right above the ocean. I want to, Jack. Will you go with me?"

"Oh, man, Elly, a Jew in church? It makes me start itching just to think about it."

"Just for the ride, Jack? I'm not that wild about the idea of driving out there with the two of them by myself. In case it doesn't work out, you know?"

He answered after a pause. "Oh, Christ, can't you think of another way to do this?"

"I've been racking my brain."

"Well . . . it's a beautiful drive, at any event. I wouldn't mind some ocean air."
"Great. Thanks."
"Look, I've got to get to sleep."
"Okay. Good night, Jack."
"Sure. Good night, good night. Look, El—"
"What?"
"Relax, will you? You're wound up to the hilt."
"Cripes, Jack. Thanks a lot."
"Go to sleep."
"Sure. Good night."

\* \* \*

Laurel slept dreamlessly in the pale green light, the filters gently bubbling all around her.

\* \* \*

A hint of death visited Vera's room as soon as she closed her eyes. It seemed ironic to be awakened by the feel of death, but Vera had long ago begun to fear that death had no relation to sleep at all. The suspicion petrified her. She fought for control of her breathing, which had accelerated into a panic rhythm. How often had she brought back a fear-crazed patient with the clean regularity of numbers? Inhale one. Two. Three. Four. Exhale one. Two. Three. Four. Five. Six. Seven. Eight. Steady gaze, steady breathing. Inhale one. Two. Three. Four. Exhale. The numbers formed a seamless wall between Vera and death, which entered through cracks, she knew. Finally in firm control of her breathing, Vera too sank into sleep.

\* \* \*

In the back apartment, down the carpeted hall from Elly's, Goldy sat up in bed, reading. She held off loneliness with her book in the creamy white light of the bedside lamp. She had turned her clock to the wall. Its red digital numbers reflected back a pale pink glow. Thoughts of Paul, their good times and recent battles, flew at her like moths. She forced her eyes across the lines of print, blocking her memories' entry into the circle of light. She would force herself to read on, and at some point soon the book would take hold and swallow her. She had only to hang on, pushing her gaze across the page. She would read all night if she had to. With sleep she risked dreams.

In the darkness, outside Goldy's apartment, the city stretched to the wild mile-wide border of hills, where creatures and birds lay motionless in burrows and trees. Beyond that slept neat suburban towns. Neighborhoods, houses, and lawns. Everyone still, everyone sleeping. There, deep in one of those houses, behind its tidy fringe of shrubs and blooming oleander, behind artificial shutters painted just last year, in a back bedroom dimly lighted by the television's flicker, Paul and his lover, a man of twenty-four, did dangerous, unimaginable things.

# *Nineteen*

The Jade Mountain outing was not a success. Both Elinor and Laurel rode home red-eyed. Vera sat up straight in the back, forcing herself to study the glorious Marin County landscape, the crisp, clear view of the bay. Goldy sat still, somehow managing in the close confines of the car to remain outside the general distress. And Jack drove and drove, gamely trying to buck off the sullenness that filled the car and pressed against the back of his neck.

\* \* \*

At the center, Laurel had panicked, and now Elinor rode unseeing along the twisting, redwood-lined road. She couldn't believe her stupidity. How could she have failed to see it coming? The crowd had been too strange, the atmosphere oppressive. Of course Laurel would panic. She had nearly fainted with fright.

Elinor and Jack had known what crowds could do to Laurel. They were both used to protecting her through the first few minutes of a movie, while the theater was filling up and before the house lights dimmed. Elly would squeeze her hand, and Jack would refrain from speaking. Once the lights went down and the audience became invisible, the girl was somehow, inexplicably, all right.

This morning, though, Elly hadn't thought about the crowd. She was hoping for insight, a new way of seeing. Taking the usual precautions hadn't occurred to her.

In fact, as they parked in the dusty lot, Elly felt relief at finally taking an active step toward roping in the chaos of her feelings. In their own little knot, they followed Goldy into the quiet stream of people, moving down a path to the prayer hall, passing a pond charmingly complete with lily pads and ducks, and breathing in the complex smell of eucalyptus and bay. Even the air there felt healing to Elinor. For a moment she slipped her arms around Vera and Laurel as she walked.

The prayer hall was in a gray barnlike building. Around it stood other rough, unpainted structures, including a small glass and stone one, its large interior room visible and looking invitingly cool and quiet. A plaque labeled this the library. Behind it ran a small creek. And behind the prayer hall stretched orderly planted fields.

Several hundred people were clumped at the two large doors of the hall, a mingling of healthy, well-dressed suburbanites, young students singly and in pairs, and the center's acolytes, monks and nuns and scholars. Some of the latter wore black robes. Many, both men and women, had shaved heads. Some, the children of the confirmed, were very young.

Goldy fits in here but Vera looks strange, thought Elly. She sticks out. It wasn't her age but her direct searching gaze. There was no softness to her mouth or eyes, no anticipation, as on the faces of the others, of something good and important about to happen; rather, she remained alert. She's probably dying for a cigarette already, Elly thought. With the press of people behind them, she felt the familiar tug of Laurel's hand grabbing lightly at the back of her skirt.

Slowly, the silent crowd inched into a crude, clean anteroom where people bent down to take off their shoes and line them up neatly in rows against the wall. Everyone seemed to know exactly what to do. Elinor glanced at Jack. He rolled his eyes at the ceiling, then looked sideways at his feet. She knew he was making a silent joke about his socks—they were mismatched or had holes. She grinned.

Vera and Elly followed Goldy slowly through the inner doors, with Laurel close behind clutching Elly's shirt in a fist. Elinor flinched slightly as she noticed that each of those entering the huge hall bowed their heads and lifted their hands, palms together, up close to their faces, as they passed a large golden Buddha set on a table and breaking the flow of the crowd into two streams. "Oh, lord," she thought, "I *have* dragged them to church." She imagined Jack barely suppressing a sigh of resignation as he inched into the room behind her.

The crowd filed into folding chairs, gradually filling the hall from the front row back. Around the sides of the room stretched long, wide platforms where students in black robes sat motionless, hands lightly touching, on round black pillows. Sitting down between Laurel and Jack, with Vera and Goldy on the far side of Laurel, Elinor realized suddenly that everyone who was seated was motionless and completely, inhumanly silent. Eyes throughout the hall were lowered or focused on the middle distance.

Slowly all were seated. No one moved. There were creaks. Suppressed coughs. The sounds of fabric rubbing against fabric. Sighs penetrated the air. Vera dared to clear her throat; Jack stared through his knees at the floor. Elinor could hear Laurel breathe. "What on earth have I done?" she asked herself in sudden realization. "I've trapped her. How in hell am I going to get her out of here?"

The huge block of humans sank one more degree into silence, and Laurel's childish fingers grabbed and twisted Elly's belt.

\* \* \*

Clamped together in their metal chairs, Elinor sat with Laurel through many circuits of panic and temporary relief. After what seemed hours, eons of stillness, a gong sounded, sending Laurel onto a new plane of fear. The sound entered from the corner of the silent room and moved across the crowd. Slowly, ever more slowly, it pulsed, dragging hundreds of people into tighter bondage with each other. By the time the gong had gradually, painfully, played itself out, they were a solid cake, a boulder of humanity encased within the walls of the prayer hall. And in the silence that rolled in behind the gong like an ocean wave, a new, dreadful, truly sinister sound followed. It was a hum, shaking the air, as from a tree filled invisibly with bees, and it grew rapidly into a word, a chant of rumbling power, driving the air out of the room. Under it, barely penetrating, was a piercing sound escaping Laurel, an emanation of pure animal fright. Elly could hardly breathe, so tightly was Laurel gripping and turning the waistband of her pants.

Jack nudged at Elinor sharply, caught her eye, and gestured toward freedom with his head. He had heard. He promised escape. No, Elly signaled with her eyes. They couldn't leave. No one left. They were nearly in the direct center of the hall, hemmed in on all sides by the huge vibrating sound.

Laurel was now plastered up against her mother, nearly shrieking in her ear. Vera looked across at Elinor, commanding *go!* with her eyes. With sudden determination, Jack reached around, circled Laurel and Elly with his arm, and literally dragged them to their feet and down the row, herding them against the solid line of knees. He pulled them out, up the aisle, past the beautiful, stern golden Buddha, and through the sound as if through a vibrating web, a screen of thin singing wires. He pushed them, pulled them, out the swinging door, and in a controlled dancer's gesture, quickly dropped his arms and wheeled to keep the doors from flapping back inward.

In the outer hall, the homely rows of shoes brought them back to the everyday world. It was then, witnessed by the worn sandals, the sturdy boots, the slip-on fashion skimmers, the multitude of health clogs, that Laurel nearly fainted from the fear of contact that had been building inside her for more than an hour.

Elly saw her swoon and kicked out a place for her among the shoes. She sat the girl down against the wall and gently forced her head between her knees. The innocent pink fabric pulled tightly over those knobby teenage knees brought tears to Elinor's eyes while Laurel gulped air. "Oh, baby, I'm so sorry," Elly crooned. After a moment, hearing a shift from within the hall, she pulled Laurel to her feet, and the three left as one. The two adults' arms wrapped around each other's shoulders with Laurel sheltered within, and neither Jack nor Elly missed the significance of their grouping, for it was the first time ever that Laurel had taken refuge between them. Behind the prayer hall, they slowly walked down a path among the planted rows that stretched before them for a quarter of a mile, fanning out toward a rugged hillside that dropped down to the ocean. They studied the blossoms, corn, melons, lettuce, potatoes. And they slowly gained the distance, gradually leaving the mass of humming, and then the droning of a single voice, that sought them from the hall.

# Twenty

Vera sat on the stone bench smoking into the fog. Amazingly unsatisfying, she mused, watching the smoke blend into the thick white air almost as soon as it left her mouth. It struck her as ridiculous that she should still, after all these decades, be attached to the sight of smoke leaving her mouth in a well-defined stream. But then, she had always used it literally to draw the line. An angry nurse, a suffering patient, a sharp or jaunty or impatient word from Sandor set Vera to pause, to take a cigarette from the pack, to light and drag and emit a perfect line of clean white smoke. Ridiculous, she concluded again, with a quick deprecation of self that was a habit almost as old as the smoking. What with the smoke, and the years, and now this aimless wandering in the middle of the night, she noted with sardonic self-regard, surely, at seventy-eight, it was time she was dead.

The fog had whitened another degree while she smoked, yet it remained as opaque as it had been when she'd left the house in the dark. Vera hoped Elinor wouldn't wake early and find her gone. Elly would certainly conclude that Vera was wandering in the head, not merely taking to the streets.

Vera had awakened to a savage restlessness at whose heart burned an image of Laurel. After long hours of alternately sweating and shivering in her bed, with the image of Laurel's closed face keeping her from sleep, she got up suddenly in exasperation, dressed hastily, drew on Elinor's big padded coat, and let herself out of the apartment like a thief. It was five-fifteen on a cold dark morning. Fog from the bay covered the city down to the surface of the streets.

She had walked the two blocks to the university campus barely conscious of the muffling darkness or the wan power of the streetlights to make a glow in the swirling white air. She felt only the relief of escape and of finally turning her full attention to a knotty problem. As in her clinic days, she needed to break from the familiar when a problem began to nag at her. Finally, she would simply walk out, tramping the downtown streets with her face blank and lowered, her eyes nearly unseeing as she worked out what to do.

How to release her granddaughter from her pain: here was an urgent problem of daunting proportions. She felt certain that Laurel's life was literally at stake. Perhaps Laurel wouldn't die of misery, but she would inhabit it forever if no one helped her to break free.

Two things impeded Vera. One was her own confusion. This she saw with fury as the beginnings of senility, the dissolution of her clarity. Whose image was it, really, that kept Vera awake? In the darkened room, Laurel's face became Vera's own as a newly married woman. And the booming voice she sometimes thought she heard was Sandor's, droning on as she used to hear it through the wall thirty-five years ago.

The second impediment was Elinor. Could she tolerate Vera's interference? Elinor was feeling her way with Laurel and above all was reluctant to give more pain. It was a mistake familiar to Vera, a novice's mistake. She had seen families and clinicians mired in it all through her career. Vera knew it was her special genius to be unafraid of giving necessary pain and acknowledging the suffering at hand. Thus she could go straight to an illness, a loss, a patient's fear and let it out into the air.

One could see the patient start to breathe when Vera let the secret out, and then they would all move on, as if in a movie a freeze-frame had been set to life. Vera saw Laurel frozen by the savagery she had experienced two years before, and she saw Elinor inching around the girl, fearful of reminding her of what it was impossible to forget.

Vera would need all her confidence, even some audaciousness, to press through Elinor's caution and her possessive mother love.

It was Vera's intolerable new uncertainty of her abilities that had sent her out into the fog. She had always been competent; now suddenly she was frail. She considered her predawn confusions and her increasingly frequent blackouts to be the first stages of nothing less than the disappearance of herself. The old smooth-mindedness, on which she had always relied not only to solve problems but also, ironically, to seal away her own secrets, was leaving her. This was why she took flight. She would do anything, things far more radical than taking a walk in the dark, to escape the helpless knowledge that she was coming apart.

It was nearing six, she imagined, and the fog was white now with the light of the hidden sun. Vera's concern for Laurel receded, her alarm at herself dissolved, and suddenly a huge tree was revealed across the path from where she sat. Farther off a ragged skyline became discernible, and she saw that she was on a knoll. Now she felt a sense of the limitless space that started just above the clouds. Yes, the fog was lifting, or rather simply disappearing. Green showed through at her feet; the white above showed blue.

She saw that she was sitting near the campanile, the needle-sharp clock tower that marked the campus from a distance, even from across the bay. As she watched, a small dark man appeared from behind the tower and began to unlock the door. Vera had often walked on campus since she had come to Berkeley, but she had never been drawn to the campanile.

Now she stood, stubbed out her cigarette, and drew Elly's coat tightly around her.

"Not until eight, not until eight," the man called to her in staccato East Indian rhythms.

"But, come. I will take you if you like," he smiled, holding both his arms wide and fluttering his fingers in an outsized gesture of welcome. She hesitated and then crossed the small plaza at his invitation.

"It is one dollar to go," he said.

"I have no money with me."

He assessed her frankly, and smiling broadly with eyes downcast, held the door wide. She entered a dark foyer and then an old-fashioned wood-paneled elevator.

"To the top," he announced, clanging the grating closed, and up they creaked, gaining speed as they went, while rooms filled with cartons and old-looking machinery glided past at an ever-increasing rate.

On the balcony at the top, with the huge bells silent and ponderous above her, Vera beheld the city, the bay, and the newly lit ocean beyond. The air was cold and clear now, the fog a vanished dream. Confusion, memory, the pain and love humans give to each other lay far below, invisible. Up here, she herself was part of the clarity.

"Ah, yes," she was moved to breathe out, though in affirmation of what she could not have said. Suddenly elated, Vera gripped the stone balcony and took in the view, letting her gratitude for the final disappearance of another sleepless night flow in all directions. She would bring Laurel some solution, she would strain for as long as she could to keep herself together. And she knew what would save Laurel: it was just this power to stand high and clear of the world, to step free of the press of people, and to understand the utter indifference and limitless beauty of things simply as they are.

# Twenty-one

"Oh, Vera. Oh, my god," hissed Elinor to no one. She pounded the steering wheel in frustration and squinted down the row of chrome bumpers for a parking place. She had already circled the block three times.

"Vera. Vera. Oh, Ma," she muttered, her fist beating time on the wheel.

The theater disgorged its crowd, and she finally double-parked across the street and scoured the mass of people for Vera and Laurel. Hunched over, intent, she moved her head with the rapid, sharp movements of an alarmed bird. Maybe they couldn't come out. Or perhaps Vera had come to her senses and taken Laurel out early.

It was Saturday. Elly had been to the city to take some work to a shop, leaving Vera and Laurel to spend the day at home. When she returned she had found a note on the table in Vera's spiked script: "Gone to movies. Can you pick us up at the Cinema Theater at 4:30?"

As she turned into the block where the theater was, the words on the marquee assaulted her: TAXI DRIVER with Robert DeNiro RETURNS!

"My god," she whispered, nearly gunning the motor. Laurel at *that* movie—she'd never be able to walk out! Was it just a horrible accident that they had gone there? Or was Vera up to something? Several years ago, Elinor herself had been sickened by the vicious climax of this same disturbing, nerve-scraping movie.

Thinking now of the weird loneliness and obsessive, dark illness of Travis Bickle, the movie's horrifying central character, seemed dangerous to Elinor herself. She felt her mind repel the memory of the actor's face. Bickle lived in a terrible dirty room; she remembered that. And when he went outside, the sunlight was always a shock. He nurtured, cultivated, his violent impulses as if they were plants thriving in the dark. He loved no one, only weapons and himself. Hadn't he loved himself and the raw evil that showed in his mirror? It was a decadent, pain-obsessed story masterfully portrayed. Many people near her in the audience had applauded, whistled, and stamped their feet when, after two hours of relentless tension, Bickle finally opened fire on a roomful of people. When he blew apart a pimp, two or three viewers positively screamed with delight.

What on earth would the sight of that close-up on insanity—and the bloodbath finally, the flying limbs—do to Laurel? "Vera," Elinor breathed again, squinting into the crowd in the low, brilliant afternoon light. "Oh, Vera. Goddammit, Vera, please."

\* \* \*

She saw them. Vera waved, guiding Laurel by the elbow. Elinor pounded her fist in rhythmic little punches against the outside of the car, wild with impatience to pull Laurel in close to her and drive her away and back home. But they progressed across the sidewalk and street with maddening slowness.

She thought she would grab Laurel back as she had so long ago at the police station, receiving and holding her to convey that she would never again let go. But Laurel simply got in the car, pulled the door closed, and composed herself in the corner.

"Vera?" Elinor began, her anger, bewilderment, and fear all merging in the single word.

"It's nothing, El. Don't worry," said Vera from the back seat. "Drive. Don't worry."

Alcohol! Was it? A hint of it, an *idea* of the smell, came to Elly from Vera. Amazement dissolved Elinor's anger, confusion absorbed her fear. What was happening here? Elly twisted around to stare at her mother, her mouth literally gaping with astonishment.

"It's nothing, Elinor," said Vera. "There was courage involved here, that's all. Drive, dear. We'll talk at home." She broke from her daughter's speechless stare, brooking no more conversation. Laurel remained silent, but there was a suggestion of self-consciousness in the way she brushed her hair back off her forehead and gazed studiously, silently ahead.

\* \* \*

"Yes, I did it on purpose. After great thought," said Vera.

"Ma, what the hell are you talking about? What are you dragging her to, Mother? What *thought*? She's frail. You saw her at the Buddhist place out there. You don't know what you're doing, you don't know what she's been through."

"No, darling. Exactly. No one knows. Only Laurel knows, and she's a baby. What she knows is a terrible burden to her. She's got to get it out, Elinor. *Any* way we can do it—*any* way, I'm telling you. We've got to help her get it out. My darling, I'm telling you. I know this."

"So you take her to see blood and sex and killing on the screen to jar it loose?" Elly stopped pacing and let herself yell at her mother. "You put her at risk of a complete panic without me?"

"I took that risk, yes," Vera answered quietly.

"You took the risk and about how many drinks to boost your courage, by the way?"

"Sometimes I take a drink. For confidence."

Elly resumed her angry pacing while Vera smoked, composed. The old woman's silent claim to expert knowledge infuriated Elly further, and she stopped and wheeled.

"What gives you the right?" she hollered, her body bent toward Vera and stiff with rage. "What gives you the right to come in here and take Laurel over? What have *I* been doing for her for two years, working with Lovejoy, Ma, for God's sake?" Fury, and the old fear for her daughter, choked her.

"Listen. Elinor, sit." Vera patted the couch, moved over from the exact middle, extended an invitation.

Elly slowly dropped her hands, which were held wide in agitation.

"Come. Sit. Let me tell you," Vera said quietly. "Let me."

Elinor sat down. She crossed her legs and folded her arms, silently daring Vera to find a way in.

"Elinor, she's dying with guilt."

"Oh, I've been through that guilt bit with Lovejoy. Come on, I know that."

"But it's guilt in front of *you*, Elinor, that's what you have to understand. These things that were done to her, the hell she endured—she's ashamed. She's holding them back from *you*. In front of you, she's ashamed of what she knows."

"So you take her to the movies and scare the complete shit out of her?"

"It was a risk, yes. But a risk of what? Getting scared by a movie? I decided that if being scared got her *moving*, and out of this box she's in, it was worth it."

"But you still felt you had to take a little nip in the morning to see you through, is that it?"

"Yes. That's right. I did."

Vera smoked, and looked at her daughter unwaveringly. After a moment, Elinor sighed deeply and relaxed, defeated by Vera's calm logic.

"So what happened?" she asked, the anger gone from her voice.

"She grabbed for me and hung on like bloody murder. I asked her many times if she wanted to leave. She said no. After the movie we just sat there holding onto each other until the theater emptied out."

"Did she cry?"

"Not really. But her hanging on was something to me. She let me hold her, comfort her. That was something, coming from her."

Elinor sat still and dropped her hands.

"I'm dying of jealousy, Mama."

"I know, darling. But on that score I think you're just going to have to sit it out."

A moment passed, and Elinor's high feeling drained out of her. "How'd you get so goddamned smart, anyway?"

"It's my work, Elly. It's what I've always done."

"So, don't you ever take time off?"

"Elinor, will you trust me on this? I know I'm right. She needs to change or she'll be stuck forever, holding on to you for dear life, barely eating—"

"She never does anything but those fish—"

"Oh, those fish. Thank god for those fish. She *lives* in there with those fish."

"Yes," said Elinor with pride.

"So, do you trust me on this?"

"Who wouldn't trust you, Vera? Haven't I always trusted you?"

With this question, the image of Sandor rose up between them. Had he himself risen from the dead, walked over, and seated himself on the couch, turned his back to Vera, and mussed his daughter's hair in the joking way he had, he would have ended the conversation no more effectively than his shared memory had done. Suddenly, purposefully, Elinor stood, feeling the need to check on Laurel in her room.

Vera considered and rejected the possibility of having another drink. She'd had enough courage for one day, she decided. And she was exhausted. What she needed now, what every old lady needed and deserved in the late afternoon, was a nap.

\* \* \*

Elinor leaned wide on her arm, gazing abstractly across the table toward Jack, who was similarly relaxed and sipping honeyed tea. The lights were off in the dining room. A single dim lamp in the living room cast its light indirectly.

Elly laughed soundlessly, mirthlessly, and then shook her head on her hand.

"What?" asked Jack, on cue.

"I'm knocked completely off center. I'm not kidding. I don't know what to bloody think."

"What did Lovejoy say?"

"She said it's just a movie and Laurel knows it's just a movie, and that it probably had a good effect in suggesting that Laurel wasn't the only one in the world that something like that could happen to."

"Sounds reasonable," he remarked. He sipped his tea audibly.

"Yeah. I know it sounds reasonable, Jack, but is it true? Do I have no situation at all or am I going to have two raving lunatics on my hands for the rest of my life?" She looked up at him from under knit brows. "And one with a drinking problem yet. An old lady with a drinking problem."

"One drink, Elinor. And to ease a difficult situation. This is not a drinking problem, dear. It's what it is: one drink to ease a difficult situation."

"A drink at eleven o'clock in the morning taken by a seventy-eight-year-old lady with blackouts? That, my *dear*," she said, leaning on the word, "is my idea of a drinking problem. In fact, I can't decide what has me more flabbergasted. That

Vera would actually go to a liquor store, buy a bottle of bourbon, and take a drink in the middle of the day, or that she would conceive a program of therapy on her own—to take her sexually assaulted, emotionally miserable, probably anorexic granddaughter to the most abusive, violent, rancid, decadent movie of the century"—she affected an ingenuous voice—" 'to get things moving, to help her get the poisons out.' In fact, even *Vera's* seeing that movie makes me uncomfortable. I'm even worried about *her* seeing that crap."

"I'd say that Vera could absorb anything seen or heard. She's been hearing the real-life version of that stuff for years. What else did Lovejoy say?"

"She asked me how Laurel was. I said quiet, doing her fish. You know, she did an entire new tank today after the movie? I'm completely confused. After the Buddhist fiasco I expected the utter worst, and she went in there and made the most beautiful environment in one of those tanks she has stacked up in her closet."

She stretched out her arm, indicating his mug of tea. He handed it across the table, and she blew at it and took a series of quick sips.

Handing it back, she continued. "About seven she came out and said she needed to call Lovejoy."

"She called her?"

"I told you this."

"I didn't realize she called."

"Well, yes, I *told* you."

"Keep your shirt on, El. I'm just trying to get it straight."

"What's to get straight, Jack? She called up Lovejoy at about seven and huddled over the phone like she was talking to her best friend. I thought I told you this when you got here."

"Well, maybe you did, boss, maybe you did."

"Your memory's getting pitiful. Smoke more dope, why don't you?"

Slowly, elaborately, he reached into his shirt pocket, extracted a joint, lit it with a long, stagey pull, and leaned across the table handing it over to her.

Elinor rubbed at her face vigorously, let the irritation wash out of her, and after a long moment during which Jack held the pose, reached over and took the joint.

She took smoke into her lungs, held it, coughed, and drew her feet up on her chair, pulling her knees to her chest.

They passed the tea back and forth in silence once more.

After a long, meditative sip, Jack said, "What you all need around here is room to breathe. To stretch out and breathe." He sipped again and then put the cup down. "It would do everybody concerned a world of good to get out of the city."

"Oh, no. You're not going to bring that up now?" she asked, incredulous.

"Chiefly me," he went on, unperturbed by her tone. "I have to say I'm feeling cramped. Daily I ask myself, Why am I commuting to my office if I'm in business for myself?"

"I don't believe this. It's blackmail at this point. What are you doing, Jack?"

"It's not blackmail, it's a solution. It's a solution I'm posing to an increasingly impossible situation. We buy a house in the country."

Elinor half laughed in exasperation. "And where am I going to get money to buy a house in the country? What are Laurel and I supposed to be, your wards?"

"Haven't you heard? That's what families are all about. You declare yourself a family and then you're all in it together."

"That is, we use your money."

"I'm talking family, not business. Besides, Vera could sell the place in L.A. She wants to do it."

"How do you know that?"

"We've talked. She told me. But it doesn't take much to see it. She could sell that house and check into a rest home or sell the house and ensure all of you some comfort and security. And she hands on to you and Laurel something from your father in the process. What's she going to do, Elinor?

She knows that going in with me on a place we'd have no problem."

"So what's stopping you two from just packing us off to the country right now?"

"She doesn't want to push you."

"Oh, boy." Elinor closed her eyes.

The subject of moving out of the city was coming up more and more often, each time imbued with less humor. And each time it arose it threw her into confusion. She knew Jack was right, that more space could only do them all good. And yet something in her resisted mightily. Was money really the problem? Was it fear of upsetting Laurel? Was it her own independence she was reluctant to give up? Or was it simply a failure of courage in making a real life with Jack? The last consideration always set up a counterpoint in her mind. How could she live without him? Wasn't she asking too much? Why did she think she could have it both ways—with and without him, at her convenience?

"Jack, what's making you bring this up now of all times? I can't go into this now."

"Listen, Elinor," he said, "hasn't it ever occurred to you that the drama of Vera and Laurel is the kind of thing you lay on a husband, not a boyfriend?"

She stared at him frankly. He was not going to let up on this.

"Yes," she said finally. "Yes, it has."

"Don't you think we all owe it to ourselves to make things as comfortable as possible? For me that means getting out of the place in the city, quitting this deal of camping out here, and having some kind of real family setup. Someplace where I can bring Mike for summers, vacations. Right now I feel like I've got all the mishegoss of a family and none of the creature comforts. I've got a weekend mother-in-law, a weekend teenager, both with their problems. And a weekend ladyfriend."

"Be fair. It's more than weekends."

"Yeah, but it's patchy. I'm too old to be sleeping over, Elinor. I want to soak my feet."

She drew her hand over her face and covered her mouth with it, leaning on her elbow.

"There's one more thing," he said.

"Christ," she muttered through her fingers.

"It's a good time to make a move. With Laurel ending junior high."

She let time pass. "I know," she said finally.

"She'd be changing schools anyway."

"I know." Her hand still covered her mouth.

"What do you say?"

"I don't want to talk about it."

Under the table he poked at her knee with his foot.

"Think about it."

"I don't want to talk about it."

With her drawn-up foot, she nudged his intruding one off her chair. Then she reached out for the empty mug. She turned away and tipped back the mug, shutting him out completely and letting the sluggish honey drip into her open mouth.

# Twenty-two

Laurel sat on a low stump between the two chaise lounges, sanding the barnacles off a shell. On one lounge sat Vera, eyes closed and legs out straight. Elinor perched at the end near her feet. Goldy, a book face down on her chest, occupied the other. To Laurel, their conversation rose and fell within the sound of the leaves stirring on the backyard elms.

"Goddammit. I just can't believe you're really leaving," said Elly. With her hands on her knees, she leaned toward Goldy, intent on her friend's face.

"I know. I can't believe it myself. It's the same old force of habit that's been keeping me here miserable all this time. I should have left long ago." She paused. "But I just didn't know where to go."

Vera made a sound of comprehension in her throat.

"And now you're sure?" asked Elinor, an undertone of doubt apparent in her voice.

"Yes, I'm sure. Before I just wanted to break and run—tie up the old life and drop it in the bay. Now it's different. I can't bury this. I can't drown this. I have to go where I can look at what's happened to me and really study it. Study myself. See how it happened that I wrapped my whole life around a man I never even knew, never understood. For fourteen years!"

"Oh, damn it," Elly said again, lifting her face to the small triangle of clear sky visible above the elms.

"Why are you so mad, El? What's bothering you?"

"She's losing a fine friend, for one thing," said Vera, her eyes still closed. "A good neighbor."

"Not losing," said Goldy. "It's only across the bridge, an hour away."

"Yes, and here you're a minute away, thirty seconds away," said Vera. She turned her head and looked at Goldy. "She'll miss you. We'll all miss you."

"It's not only that," said Elinor. "Maybe I just have bad associations with the place because of the shrimp here."

"Oh, Laurie," Goldy said. She rested a hand on Laurel's bare knee. "Honey, that was bad luck that day. Maybe it wasn't such a good idea to go to the lecture. But Laur, it's not scary there, really. It's mostly just a farm. I wish it hadn't happened, but that was more Laurie than the place, don't you think, Laur?"

The girl smiled down at her shell.

"So what are you going to do for money?" asked Elinor.

"I've got money. Paul will give me some. I don't need much money, and maybe I can eventually get a residency at the farm."

"But what are you going to *do* there?" Laurel asked suddenly.

"Study," answered Goldy. "Try to understand myself so I can leave this old life behind. And then I'll have a new kind of life near people who are interested in the same stuff I like to think about."

"Not like us, right?" asked Elly, giving her twisted smile.

"*You* said that," said Goldy. "But I'm not leaving you. I'm just taking care of some old business and starting up some new."

"Shit, Gold, you sound just like you know what you're doing."

Goldy smiled. "I'm going."

The women fell silent and a warm breeze set the leaves to spinning and clattering softly. Laurel continued to rub on her shell. In the center of the triangle defined first by the trees and then by the three women, she worked as if in a safe, three-sided room. The wall that was Elinor was blank and white, Vera's wall held a still-locked door, and in Goldy's wall was a window with a view of a narrow path.

# Twenty-three

When Elinor started to object to Lovejoy's closing of the blinds, a warning went through the room, clear and shrill as an alarm. Elly recognized Laurel's silent warnings well enough and held her peace.

The slats fell to, and what little natural light in the room had reflected off the dark wood paneling and the battered fake leather chairs now disappeared. Fluorescence whitened all their faces, and the air itself seemed suddenly neutralized.

No one pretended not to be nervous. Lovejoy presided, looking austere and beautiful. Elly glanced around the room. Laurel hugged her chest and held her elbows tightly. Even Vera, usually upright, was sunk in upon herself, aligning and realigning her cigarettes and lighter on the wooden arm of her chair. Lovejoy alone sat composed.

"You need to start now, Laurel," said Lovejoy, her firm tone permitting no choice. "But don't worry about the time," Lovejoy went on softly. "Time is no problem today. Okay?"

"Okay, Janet," Laurel said, breathing down at her tightly clasped hands. She was visibly scared to death. Elly could see her stomach working back and forth like that of a watchful animal about to flee.

"Okay," she said again, and looked directly at Elinor. "We've been talking, Mom. Did you know? About the men? About that time?"

Elly nodded, the fear spreading to her. These mild references, couched in gentle interrogations, were the most explicit either of them had ever been with each other about the kidnapping. The police investigations had been focused on facts—on the van, the house, physical descriptions of the men and the clothes they wore. Mercifully, Metzger had gone easy on the details of what had happened, mostly eliciting painful nods from Laurel with his sordid yes-or-no questions.

"I need to talk to you about it some," Laurel went on hurriedly. It didn't escape Elinor's notice that she looked first at Vera, then at Lovejoy, for confirmation. Vera nodded. Lovejoy sat motionless, her customary affirmation.

"What do *you* think?" asked Elinor, aware that she was utterly at a loss for what to say. A great revulsion seized her for what was taking place, and she was suddenly sickened by the oppressive institutional feeling of the room. The solid wood paneling, the ugly chairs, the streaked black linoleum, all reminded her that she was deep inside the police station, a place she had been in too many times, always actively hating it.

"I don't want to. I've never wanted to," Laurel answered, the whites of her eyes suddenly going red in the instant way she had of beginning to cry. "Because I never wanted you to know what it was like, or what they did. . . ."

"What the men who held her did to her, Mrs. Landau." Janet Lovejoy picked up the thread, which had come from Laurel in a labored whisper. Though Lovejoy and Elinor had been through the fundamentals many times, and particularly lately on the phone to arrange for this meeting, Lovejoy seemed to be colluding with Laurel's need for a formal explanation, one more time, of why they were all putting themselves through this grueling group entrapment.

Lovejoy continued. "It seems probable that Laurel's great

need to protect you personally from the details of what happened is a way of protecting herself. Worrying about you and about whether you will still love her once you know what she was made to do could be a way Laurel has of worrying about what she herself thinks about Laurel now."

Laurel gagged dryly and held her body more tightly still. She bent over her arms, eyes closed, and sat motionless while all three women leaned toward her, their identical impulses to hold her head arrested by her stillness.

"This is not an uncommon reaction, I might add," continued Lovejoy. "The lasting damage that sexual violence leaves can be a terrible self-loathing. Our job is to cure Laurel of self-blame. Our work now is to help Laurel get back the self-respect those two men stole from her."

"Oh, the pigs, the filth," breathed Elly, allowed to say it now, and testing.

"Amen," intoned Vera. "Amen."

"How do I start?" Laurel asked Lovejoy, still holding tightly to herself.

"You tell the story. You start with leaving school that day and just keep telling."

Laurel breathed in and settled more deeply into her posture of self-protectiveness. She was doing her best to hold off Elinor's presence, as Elly was fully aware. The silence settled and bound them together like a feeling of doom.

\* \* \*

She began in a whisper, speaking down to her hands, now clasped tightly in her lap.

"Well, you know . . ."

"Louder, just a bit," said Lovejoy evenly.

"They just pulled me into their car. Van. It was a van, like I told the police. They pulled over to the side of the street near a corner—just below Telegraph on Channing. They just slid the side door open, and one of them grabbed me in. And drove away. The van drove off and I was inside. And for the longest time nobody said anything at all. I didn't know what was happening. And I was so scared. I must have been crying or something because after a while the one in the back said, 'Shut up,' and the other one driving said, 'Shut up, you'll scare her.' So the first guy said, 'Scare her? Hey, man, *scare* her?' and he started laughing so hard he let go of me, and I tried to get out. But I didn't know how to open the door of the van. I remember I couldn't even see a handle or anything to turn. But the guy laughing, he was still laughing, and he just pulled me back on the seat real hard, and the driver yelled back, 'Don't hit her,' and he yelled back, 'Yeah, sure, man,' and then yanked at me like he was going to. That's the way it always was. The one guy not wanting the other one to hurt me."

When she stopped talking, it was as if their eyes had been released. Elly's gaze, Vera's gaze, flew off the young girl, seeking something, anything, in the room to rest on. Laurel looked spent already.

"So where did they take you?" prompted Lovejoy.

After a long beat, Laurel took the cue. "Oh," she said, "to a house. After a long, long time of driving, a house somewhere, I don't know. I never did know. Somewhere where it was hot, somewhere."

Someone's watch ticked. Someone's chair scraped the linoleum. Outside, car doors slammed, engines started, a fan belt screamed.

"Then they just kept me there."

Elinor had the wild temptation to bolt. She glanced at her mother, who looked sharply back at her, as if divining that she needed a clear admonishment. Vera's mouth was drawn in tight. It was torture for her too.

Now Laurel went relentlessly on. "They had this room for us downstairs." Her voice was gaining strength now, as well as neutrality. "I guess it was a basement or a storage room or something. It was very dark usually. Just a funny kind of narrow window way up toward the ceiling. We stayed in there the whole time mostly.

"They brought other kids there sometimes. Mostly one other girl, Martha, the one whose picture I recognized. And a boy they called Chick. His name was really Chuck—Charles—but they called him Chick. They always told us never to ask each other's names, or they'd kill us or something. They were always saying or you'll die or we'll kill you or something like that. We knew they would. I saw one of them kill a dog just with his bare hands when he got mad at it once. There were other kids. I don't know, maybe they killed them too, who knows?"

"Oh god, nobody. Nobody knows," thought Elly. These children, from various parts of the Northwest, were still missing. Long investigation had turned up nothing. In a terrible way, Elinor felt grateful to the two hideous men for permitting her daughter to survive. Perhaps a similar kind of insane gratitude accounted for the neutrality—the utter lack of hatred, fear, or anger when she spoke of them—that now characterized Laurel's voice. Elly thought of the movie technique where a character becomes invisible as the flashback begins and the images on the screen take over. Laurel became a disembodied voice for the women in the room as their mental pictures of what she described forced their way to consciousness. The van, the men, a hairy arm, a flannel shirt, a sliding door. And then a desert house, perhaps, a half-buried makeshift room, a child on a mattress, a threatening snarl. These pictures came and went, clamoring for attention, pushing each other aside, as the soft neutral child's voice talked on and on.

"The kids were great. We helped each other. They were as scared as I was, all the time. We slept together—there were beds in the room, nothing else. We slept a lot, and we all slept together sometimes." All the women, in their minds, saw young animals sleeping in a tight heap.

"So, Mom," said Laurel in a sharper tone, "I . . . I'm supposed to tell you what they did to us, but I don't know. . . ."

She grabbed hold of herself again and gulped down air. Lovejoy took over.

"We've talked a lot about language, Mrs. Landau. About words to use. In our talks we use slang. We say fucking, and sucking off, and going down, eating out. They work a lot better than, uh, making love."

Laurel laughed nervously at that, and Elly, freed for a moment from the horrible images Laurel had been conjuring, leaned toward her child and embraced her.

"Use any words you want, Laur. I've heard them all. Honey, I've *used* them all. You've *heard* me. Since when am I a wilting violet when it comes to language?"

"But *I* am," answered Laurel. "I'm embarrassed about saying this stuff to you."

"I see the problem," said Elly.

"Well, fuck it," Vera exclaimed.

"Ma!"

"Grandma!"

"Well, why not? I've worked with people living on the street for years. You think I don't know the language? Fuck, shit, blow, suck! So. Why not?"

This sent Laurel into a new spasm of nervous laughter.

"Shall we take a break?" said Lovejoy as she regained control.

"No, no," Laurel returned, composing herself.

"No, let's get it over with," agreed Elly, feeling free to speak her mind for the first time since the session began.

Silence settled. The women crossed their legs, sat back in their chairs, and bent to business.

"Well," said Laurel, when she felt the full weight of their attention. "All right." She turned to her mother now, still holding her own body tightly but no longer resisting what had to be done.

"So they came in and did it to us all the time, whenever

they felt like it. In front of the other kids." She clamped her teeth together and breathed in sharply, as one does in sudden disgust at finding the meat rotten. "And they watched each other. They talked to each other a lot—you know, encouraging each other, laughing at us. We all had to watch. Sometimes they made us watch."

She looked straight at Elinor now, and Elly stared back at her, unconsciously returning her clamp-jawed expression of repulsion and slowly moving her head back and forth in a gesture of pure negation. "Oh," she breathed at her daughter, barely speaking it.

"Oh, and they were terrible. They had terrible teeth, both of them. Smelly, awful teeth. And dirty, greasy hair. And my hair got that dirty too. There was only a sink. I washed my hair with a bar of soap sometimes but it never really worked, only seemed to make it worse, all separated and greasy. One time Martha and I told them together we had to have some shampoo. They made us work for it."

"Work?" said Elinor.

"You know, do more stuff to them. Together."

"Oh, the pigs, Laurel. The disgusting pigs."

"Mom, they were. They were shit." She pronounced them shit with utter seriousness and a cold hatred befitting the two she had described. At the sound of the feeling infusing Laurel's voice, Vera, in her atheism, praised the lord.

"I was always scared—*always*. Because, you know, they used to say they knew where I lived and—" She stopped cold.

"And," Lovejoy repeated, not urging but requiring her to go on.

"And they said if I didn't, you know, do what they wanted, they'd get you, Mom. They'd come and—"

"And," demanded Lovejoy again, monitoring the momentum, keeping it going.

"And they'd do it to you."

Silence, during which Elinor's fundamental understanding

of those five months of hell changed completely, as if a new light of a different color suddenly illuminated that time.

After a long while, Elinor spoke. "So you did a lot of it for me. Not only did they make you do these things, but they made you do them for your mother, for me." She said this to Laurel, staring at her, eyebrows raised in new understanding, in a voice tinged with a new realization of the obvious.

"Yes, in a way," said Laurel, suddenly skittish, looking everywhere in the room but at her mother.

*This* was the revelation that Laurel had to make; this was the point of the meeting. Not simply a recounting of the girl's degradation, not an unburdening of the gory details, but a telling of Laurel's courage on behalf of her mother. The two filthy men had laid on Laurel's frail, growing shoulders the burden of protecting her mother from physical harm. They could not have hit upon a more unnatural task. It was, Elly realized, a total reversal of the order of things: the young fawn, her thin body barely casting a shadow of any real breadth, barring the way by every unthinkable means to her substantial, able-bodied mother. An outrage! It was a hellish outrage!

Elinor saw now that in the two years since Laurel's return there had never been a way that Laurel could have conveyed this information to her—or her triumph, for they had both survived! Perhaps the girl had not even known she had this to tell. Perhaps she too believed that it was only the details of her humiliation—the hair, the teeth, the claustrophobic basement room—that kept her from moving on. Elinor grew wooden as she realized the enormity of what she had heard.

Into her memory flooded the feeling of embracing Laurel that first moment somewhere in this building. She had felt Laurel's lack of substance then, and the continual quaking coming from within her. So thin she was, so young. But a firmness of purpose had brought her intact through the ordeal.

"Ah, Laur," she said, guided by pure instinct. "Laur, you strong girl."

Momentarily, pride transformed Laurel, and a new staunchness seemed to lift her taller in her chair, though tears slid down her cheeks. Elly felt a new respect for the girl. A threatening feeling of sickness, and horror at what could have been, she forcibly ignored, giving Laurel her due.

In a ritual gesture that ended the session, Lovejoy looked at her watch. Completing the tableau, Vera, like an old and untamed white owl, remained still in her chair, erect and alert to all that might yet happen.

# PART FOUR

# Twenty-four

Laurel walked Vera slowly to the passenger side of Elinor's old car and eased her into the seat. She let her small canvas pack fall onto the yellow lawn of mowed weeds and, in a careful manner, fastened the old woman's seatbelt as if strapping in a child. Then she walked around the car, slid in behind the wheel, and drove slowly down the long gravel driveway to the road.

In the low morning light, the house and outbuildings looked as if they had been scattered over the top of the hill by a careless giant. Below, the small town of Cascade, population seven thousand, was hidden by a quirk of the topography, and the result was a fifteen-mile view nearly clear of buildings all the way to the bay. The pure rural vista belied the city-dependent nature of the place. Cascade was forty miles north of San Francisco on the outer edge of the suburban sprawl, backed up against a curve in the coastal range that stood between it and the ocean.

When Elinor and Jack had decided on the place more than two years before, it had been designated Hilltop by a wooden sign dangling crookedly from the mailbox. Behind the house at the row of giant eucalyptus that marked the edge of the property began a true wilderness of increasingly rugged hills. It was seeing Laurel venture past that line of trees, breathing in the air, peering into the oak woods beyond, that led Elinor to agree to buy the place—that and the barn out back that was to become her studio. As soon as she saw the old peeling structure that first time, she couldn't keep her plans from forming.

Down the hill in town, Laurel pulled to the curb at the town's one major intersection and left the engine running to walk Vera slowly across the street to Ben's. Then she nosed the car through the city-bound traffic to the Cascade High School parking lot. She switched off the ignition, pulled a drawing tablet from her canvas pack, and engrossed herself in a half-finished pencil drawing—a deer nearly hidden in the bush, which she had seen behind the house the day before. She worked on the texture of the coat in minute pencil strokes with the tablet propped up against the steering wheel.

She ignored the students streaming by the car but kept glancing at her watch, a nurse's watch that Vera had worn for decades. With some difficulty, the old lady had unstrapped it one day and handed it over to Laurel. "I can barely make it out any more," she had said. "Besides, at eighty the last thing you need is a watch strapped to your arm. You take it."

At a quarter to eight, Laurel closed the tablet and slipped it back into the pack. The pencil went into an aluminum cigar tube she kept in the pocket of her shirt. The first period bell rang at seven-fifty; it was no good being late. She was never early, never late. She never allowed herself to stand out alone, but kept to the outer edges of the crowd. She leaned over to the glove compartment and pulled some money from her secret cache between the folds of a Marin County map. Laurel kept money everywhere. Her room at Hilltop was filled with hidden money—twenties in books, tightly rolled fives and tens in the back corners of dresser drawers. She was always needing money for paper and pencils and the animal books she bought to practice from.

The girl who emerged from Elinor's old car looked different from the other girls headed for class. The clothes they wore reflected the small town's proximity to the big city, calling out for attention with their bright bold colors and high-fashion lines. Mixed with the girls were boys in jeans and morning-fresh shirts. Laurel slipped in among them like a shadow. She wore two jerseys, the sleeves hastily pushed up to midforearm, and over them a loose, open, dark green shirt of Elinor's. She had bought her black baggy pants at a surplus store. These she had rolled up at the cuffs to reveal thick socks and soft, foreign-looking shoes, folkdancing slippers she had found somewhere for herself. One who looked closely could see pockets bulging with money, the cigar tube, an apple grabbed from home. Her thin body was hidden and camouflaged. And though her wild, puffy, wheat-colored hair was hastily drawn back at the neck and pulled together into two or three twists of a single braid, long wisps in the front dropped over her face except when she pushed at it in a swift gesture of impatience.

Laurel looked like a young runaway, ready to bolt and hide. Still, she had an emerging beauty. She took no interest in it at all, but the other students had been drawn to her since she first arrived at Cascade. The girls at the school courted Laurel, the boys looked after her down the hall. She never spoke to anyone. She just did her work and was gone.

\* \* \*

At lunch, she carried her tray out to a side lawn and leaned up against the scratchy yellow stucco of the gym. She made herself eat half the brown mess they called meat loaf and then reached for her tablet and opened it on her knees.

"Hey, Laurel. What you got there?" The voice was friendly. She recognized it as belonging to Jess, from her English class, who looked at her sometimes.

She snapped the tablet closed and squinted up at the couple on the path, shading her eyes with her hand.

Jess's arm encircled his girlfriend, Susan. The two stood

above Laurel on the path, and the boy's thumb, visible to Laurel from below, moved rhythmically up and down along the side of Susan's breast. Now and then the girl brushed at it as if at a pesky fly.

Jess looked down at Laurel, frankly making an overture.

"Your place up there about finished?"

Laurel nodded.

He spoke to Susan. "Laurel lives up there at the top of Blue Hill. Bet that place took a hell of a lot of work to get it into shape."

She nodded again, snapping her eyes away from the rhythmic thumb. She wasn't sure he knew she could see it working there like a nervous tic.

"Great old place, though. My dad and I used to go hiking up behind there. Must have taken a hell of a lot of work though. That place was a wreck."

"It was okay," Laurel muttered.

"Are you helping to fix it up?" asked Susan in a bright voice.

"Not really," Laurel whispered, looking sharply off down the path.

"You like fishing?" asked Jess. Susan gripped him more tightly round the waist, hearing possibilities buried in his voice. The thumb relaxed, though imperceptibly the breast became more available to it. "There's some nice fishing back there in the lakes behind your house. Do you hike up there sometimes?"

He was playing with her with his all-American voice, using it to poke and prod her in a preliminary way. But Laurel was used to deflecting these overtures, especially when they were fueled by sexual curiosity. She used silence like a wall and waited for the sightseers to go away.

Susan was punching Jess impatiently in the back now. "Let's go," she whispered. "Come *on.*" Laurel squinted off down the path.

"Yeah," said Jess in the tone that routinely ended these

encounters when the sightseers were boys. His arm tightened around Susan's waist, and his large man's hand, the stocky fingers outspread, drew her away with him toward the crowded lunch area.

"Nice talking to you, Laurel," he called back in a voice acrid with sarcasm.

Laurel waited until they were out of sight before opening the tablet on her knees.

\* \* \*

Study hall, the last period of the day. As she entered the work area of the library, Laurel saw Mr. Harvey going through a stack of papers at the teacher's desk and felt a surge of pleasure. Great. Mr. Harvey. She had brought a drawing to show him in case he was here today. He still liked to see what she was working on and encouraged her to bring her work by the art room. She rarely did that, but often laid a drawing silently on his desk, face down, when he was presiding in study hall.

She wasn't ready to show the deer but had a finished pencil drawing of a pair of quail. She laid it face down on an empty corner of the desk and he nodded. He would get to it.

Laurel felt let out of school—she always did when Mr. Harvey was at the desk in study hall. Now she could find a place off by herself and just draw.

She sat down near the back window at a table that held atlases and a globe. Carefully she arranged the oversized books so that no one would be tempted to share the table. She propped the largest atlas on her purse to serve as a makeshift drawing board, opened her tablet, and sank into the rhythm she had been practicing at intervals all day—short, rapid strokes of her mechanical pencil to compose the animal's shadowed coat.

In front of her in the hall, waves of restlessness rolled among the other students in the form of creaks, coughs, slammed books, and sharp whispers. Occasionally Mr. Harvey looked up from his work, and his cool eyes momentarily suppressed all sound. But the students knew him to be a benign authority, and it wasn't fear or careful attention he inspired; only the simple reflexes of children conditioned to react to their teachers' eyes.

One part of Laurel waited for him as she worked. Mr. Harvey was her mentor at the school. Almost as silent as she, though economical with words rather than shy or withdrawn, he had unknowingly led her to abandon her fish for the drawing of animals and birds. In his art course, which she had taken in her first year at Cascade, he had the class page through a stack of the old naturalist notebooks and bird portfolios that were his passion. She had been moved to copy an old lithograph of a pair of Audubon birds. "Hmm. Fine, fine," he had said over her shoulder of that first tentative drawing. "Yes," as if he could see that she had struck a major vein.

She spent that first semester of his class and all her time at the house drawing birds and animals from books. These were highly detailed, increasingly perfect pencil copies of *National Geographic* photographs, Audubon plates, pictures of African animals from heavy coffee-table books.

Soon after they moved to Cascade, Laurel began to walk out behind the wild yard, through the band of eucalyptus, and off across the hills, carrying a sketchbook. She would find a place and wait motionless for animals to appear. She learned to draw fast, taking what she could of the wild creatures before they moved on.

These preliminary sketches were tiny, minute, for her movements had to be nearly nonexistent in order for her to conceal herself. Perhaps she drew only a few lines, barely moving anything except her fingers, making records and reminders for later. She would finish the drawings, surrounded by books for reference, when she got back to her room.

She drew birds—jays, meadowlarks, hawks, owls, and the ugly, omnipresent turkey vultures—many rodents and deer, raccoons and skunks in the evening near home, and one glorious bobcat, astoundingly alert yet missing her for long moments while she stared motionless, memorizing. She never drew a line of the bobcat, but let every hair, curve, whisker on the proud, lifted muzzle burn itself into her brain in the slanted afternoon light.

She stored her pictures, along with her pads and pencils, in the bottom of an old cedar chest in her room, showing them to no one but Mr. Harvey.

He never said much more than "yes" or "fine," but she stood on these words as if they were wide flat rocks forming her path. When she'd had a particularly good sighting, she often pictured the moment when she would lay the finished drawing down on Mr. Harvey's desk, and the anticipation added to the excitement of the moment.

Now Mr. Harvey languidly pushed back his chair at the front of the hall. Watching him stand up was like seeing a stork lift itself off its nest. He had long, seemingly hinged legs, and a thin body, stooped and ruminative-looking at the shoulders. One slender, veined arm generally crossed his waist, the hand cupping his other elbow. With the second arm thus propped, his hand inevitably lay against a thin, solemn cheek, as if his head, which was quite handsome and saved him from appearing comical, was in continual need of support. So he glided up and down the aisles, occasionally pausing over a seated student like a large, thoughtful bird.

Now, returning down the aisle between the tables, he picked up the drawing Laurel had left on his desk. Laurel sensed rather than saw this gesture, and her breathing speeded up slightly as she drew. Slowly he advanced to the back of the room, his gait characteristically slow and gliding. So loosely strung did he seem that Laurel amused herself with the thought that she could hear his bones knock together. You always knew without looking when he was coming down the aisle from the clear sound of the change in his pants pocket. He was so thin it clanked against his thigh.

"Nice. Nice," he said to her from above, carefully laying the quail picture on top of the atlases. His comments were always short and spare. "Yes, absolutely" could set her to soaring for a day. "Mmm. Check the proportions" would make her wonder why she tried to draw at all. But it was his fingers, immensely long and knobby, that carried the real message. With swift signs above the image, he managed to convey all he had to say about balance and composition, the use of line and light.

His fingers spoke eloquently to Laurel. They urged her on from her first pleasure at the feel of pencil on paper into an enduring obsession. At his suggestion she had even taken two biology courses to study vertebrate anatomy.

Instead of ending with "nice" this time, Mr. Harvey folded himself down onto the chair next to her. He arranged himself so that his back was to the rows of students, and he leaned his elbow on the table, propping his head close to hers. He made a rather elaborate effort to whisper as he spoke.

"I have heard of a school you might look into."

She frowned down at her drawing. Several times he had asked about her plans after graduation, half a year away. And quietly he had urged her to apply to one of the art schools around the bay area. She never answered him.

"This is a new school in the Sierras. There is a naturalist painter there—Tom Shelton. Very famous. You've seen prints of his work in some of my books."

"I can't leave," she whispered.

He raised his eyebrows questioningly.

"My grandmother's too old. I can't leave now."

Any courage Laurel needed to roam the empty hills behind the house she would have traced back to Vera. In some unspecific way, for she did not tend to think back or consider the past at all, she had the idea that Vera's coming to live with them had saved her life. Now, in the house above Cascade, Laurel protected Vera and anticipated her needs. Laurel's place in the house was next to Vera. She helped the old woman to rise, sit, cut her food, as old age steadily robbed her grandmother's strength. Across Laurel's bond with her mother, across the new filament tentatively growing between herself and Jack, stretched a loyalty for Vera as tough and unyielding as steel.

At Laurel's reply, Mr. Harvey opened his mouth, and there was an infinitesimal pause before any sound emerged. It was a soft, accepting "ah." Then, "At any event, I'll keep the catalogue for you. This will be a place you'll want to know about."

He pushed himself up. "Yes. The quail are fine," he said. Then, about the deer picture, he said, "Find a sharper contrast between foliage"—his fingers waved above the unfinished drawing propped against the book—"and the animal." His other hand spoke another line. He glided away, his feet dragging lightly as if through water, his pensive face causing the students to lean closer to their work.

# Twenty-five

Vera tried to discern the features of the man across the table. If he would only hold still, she thought irritably, for he was blocking the glare of bright sunlight that shone into the dark bar through the door. Every time he bent forward to take a sip of beer or leaned sideways to shout greetings to one of his cronies, the light hit Vera like a bolt, and the man became a dark silhouette. Worse luck, she thought, as she nursed her soda water. She was having enough trouble remembering who he was without having to struggle to see. That the mind could slip and *know* it was slipping was a variation on the wearisome theme of aging she had never anticipated.

"She's a cow, though, she is," the man was saying. "Glad to see me out of the house so she can get on with talking to herself." He had a Cockney accent, barely muted by fifty years in California. He and his wife had come to San Francisco as newlyweds, Vera remembered him telling her. He was nothing at all like Sandor—and yet she kept thinking momentarily that he *was* Sandor. How could she make the same mistake over and over again?

"Tells the walls what a scoundrel I am, works herself up over it. By noon, she's shrieking her lungs out and glad for no contradiction from me."

"Oh, come now. She's old," responded Vera, finding her

way back to the present. "She needs care, companionship. She can't love your coming down here to get tight morning to night. Who takes you home?"

"Who takes me home, did ya say? Who *takes* me home? Nobody takes Eugene Duffy home, my girl. Eugene Duffy takes to the air whenever he damn well pleases."

"Why, Eugene, I've seen you myself leaning up against the side of the building, many's the night. Ben calls a cab for you and picks up the tab half the time. It's a regular charity show, the way that man looks after his old-timers, and everybody too proud to admit it. You ought to show some gratitude instead of ignoring the favor."

"I walk home every night of my life on my own two feet, you old crow."

"I've *seen* you standing there, ready to hit the sidewalk and break a hip."

"And who takes *you* home, then, old lady?" he returned. "I've seen *you* holding up a wall or two of your own."

"You're dreaming, dear. *That* you've *never* seen. My granddaughter takes me every day."

"*That* luscious sight, it's your granddaughter, is it?"

Her last remnant of control left her. "Shut your foul mouth, old man," she ranted, furious. "A wreck like you leaving your wife locked up in the house all day, and talking about young girls like that." Disgust silenced her.

A blast of light hit her eyes, and even the silhouette disappeared as Eugene scraped his chair back and left, offended. They had often had this argument, and it always ended in the same ugly way, with both of them too furious to speak. She snickered at him wickedly each time he joined her at her table on the day after one of these angry exchanges, for she knew he had forgotten the whole conversation. But lately, in the chair he'd left, she somehow perceived the presence of Sandor, and sometimes, unknowingly, she went on talking after Eugene had stomped away, pulling as much righteous indignation as he could manage into his stiff, arthritic gait. When it was Sandor, now dead thirty years, she saw sitting across from her, she gave him hell. Where he came from she had no time to consider. Whether she spoke out loud or merely thought herself into ascending spirals of anger she never bothered to find out.

She would pull herself out of it for minutes at a time, thinking clearly about Eugene. He's probably right, she would growl down at her drink. His wife probably waits for him to leave. What does she want with him shuffling around the house, scratching at himself and leaving wet towels and food around? And then she would glide across a memory bridge: Ah, Sandor was never like that, she would think. Meticulous, that was his word. "Why, that man is so meticulous," her mother had clucked in wonder. "Not a hair out of place, clothes sharp as a tack. Look how he dresses for you, Vera. Will you straighten up, now?" And she would reach over without being able to help herself, tugging something here, righting something there, unfastening and then refastening a button, though Vera was by then a grown woman, a virtual spinster at thirty-two. Her mother couldn't keep herself from making Vera presentable for this dapper small-time businessman with his faint European accent and his impeccable courtesy.

After they were married, he would sometimes scrub down their place on a Saturday, especially after Elinor was born and they were living in the Hollywood bungalow. Vera would wake up to the sound of a rug being snapped on the kitchen porch, or the smooth, taunting slide of the broom. Not that she had ever left the place dirty or unkempt. She always straightened up mornings and then again at night before bed.

It was living with him that opened her eyes. While they were courting, she had somehow never noticed the tight pull around his mouth at the sight of the Sunday newspaper piled carelessly on the floor next to her father's chair, or the near panic at a coffee spill. In the grand flush of romance she'd just never seen his streak of prissy fastidiousness. Those sex-shot days were too strained by the tension of love. It was so high between them that the touch of his hand made her close her eyes while the warmth spread down her thighs. They would go out driving—it was too dangerous for them to stay indoors together—both dressed to the shining teeth.

Later, when he began his philandering, or simply ended all efforts to hide it, how, *why* did she endure the ritual: the brushing of the suit, the shower down to the last drop of hot water, the shaving that was like a loving examination of each square inch of skin, every pore? Then came the laying on of garments and the myriad adjustments, much like her mother's pullings and tuggings, refastenings, rebuttonings—but with his eyes, like a lover's, never leaving his own image, even if she walked in to ask him a question, even if Elly walked in.

Ach, it was a disgusting show of vanity, Vera recalled, shaking her head at the empty place across the table. It was an intolerable display. How ashamed she was that she had stayed on through it all, and all in the name of love. Love had nearly threatened to eat up the best of her, the part she brought out at the clinics where she worked, the part she relied on still. What was that feeling, irrationally aroused, oh, nearly half a century ago now? Simply a lurch toward a man in a boater, with the collar of his shirt showing off his brown cheeks, that and the sight of his hands on a steering wheel, masterfully controlling the car. She could still see the very hairs growing on his fingers. And all summer of that first year, courting, when they went out to his uncle's farm and drove the country lanes, she would watch his hands on the steering wheel and feel the need to draw her knees together and push back more deeply in the seat.

They went out on those ritual drives for years, all during their marriage, until he turned sick. They took rides to the country, and in Los Angeles that meant seeing the wildness, the harsh red rock and desert vegetation that made up the true landscape there, even under the light surface of the city. It often scared her to go out into the rocky, blazing emptiness, especially when Elly was small. But by then Vera was used to keeping her thoughts to herself. So they would wind slowly up the dusty red mountains, the buzzing air scorching their breath, and spread a tablecloth at the side of the road, at the rim of the sheer wicked cliffs.

It wasn't until she went back to work that the pain of loving a selfish man began to subside. When Elly started going to school, Vera fought a vicious battle with Sandor to win the right to have her daughter looked after, and then she took a job with the county as a social worker. She brought in the indigents and placed them where she could. She talked all day in her direct, practical way, listening to herself explaining, reassuring, dispensing information. But her mind was filled with suspicions and gross imaginings, and the busy workday was framed by silence.

She came home every day to make plain meals, clear up the dishes, and then read for long hours in the chair with the ottoman. Sandor read to Elly, or the two talked, always in the next room. Their time together was filled with talk, chatter, soft musings—all coming through the walls to Vera as plays of sound, not words.

Elinor never understood. She always believed that Vera chose to remain apart while she and her father forged the family feeling. To this day, the image of Sandor stood between them: his face, animated in conversation, to his daughter; his back, broad and blank, to his wife.

Disgust made Vera hiss at her glass on the table at Ben's place. She remembered Sandor, a traitor, as constantly on the phone when he wasn't with Elinor. And Vera herself eternally staring at a page in a book that had gone suddenly jumbled at the sound of his voice, low and intimate, through the wall. She could see herself under the lamp with the yellow pleated shade—oh, *how* could she remember that shade while she could barely recall coming to Ben's that morning? How *galling* was this slow dissolution and decay!

Enduring the silence Sandor imposed on her was Vera's worst sin. Standing for being shut out! It made her sick, with the noise and sour smells of the bar and the sticky floor welling up around her now, to think that she had stayed there with Sandor long, long after her lust had burned out, stayed grim and determined, ignoring her humiliation, until he finally died.

She realized the irony: she would never have been able to stand it now. She could no longer abide silence—it made her think of death. Now in Cascade, hearing Laurel getting ready for school in the morning, she forced her limbs to move against the stiffness, dressed as quickly as she could, and left her room to ride into town with the girl before Elinor could object. It was like escaping from jail to leave the house.

Boredom was the jailer. Vera fled with an acute sense of relief each time she managed the getaway. Even sitting in Ben's all day, watching the regulars slowly pickling themselves to death, even walking slowly around Cascade, settling here and there in the sun for an hour when the weather allowed it, seeing herself as the children saw her, skinny and witchlike and vastly old—even these slight occupations were freedom when compared to the terrible silent nothingness in the house on the hill during the long, long day.

For a long time after they moved to Cascade, Elinor tried to convince Vera to go off to a center in the next town where old people met and ate together. It had stirred Vera's social service instincts, and finally she agreed, with the idea of carving out a job for herself. But by now the workings of time had completely obliterated the expression that had served as her professional face, and she was simply past mustering the authority it took to separate herself from the clients in the place.

The day Laurel drove her over, Vera was herded with the

rest into a school auditorium that still smelled of sweat. The far end was filled with long tables covered with paper tablecloths and plastic place settings. A hundred old people found places, viewing their neighbors, their settings, the steaming tureens, with caution if not outright suspicion. Vera's reactions to the intolerably noisy scene were simply those of one more elderly lady irritated beyond endurance by the metallic scraping of chairs.

At one point she reached out to catch the attention of one of the women serving food—a young matron in fine clothes volunteering her time—and received a vapid smile so poorly disguising disgust, and perhaps fear, that her inclination to offer her services died in her chest. Such bustling! Such noise! And the servers, the young, rich do-gooders who had left their children with au pairs for an hour or so to do their good deed "for the com-*mun*-ity," did all they could to deny the existence of the hundred old people they served with gluey potatoes and gravy. The result was a two-tiered circus—the busy keepers on their feet, smiling and nodding at each other, the old tired animals seated in rows, sullen and hopelessly bored.

Vera found herself wedged tightly between two silent diners, barely able to move. The gooey food on her plate looked like three congealed puddles—white, greenish, and brown. Could they have mashed lima beans for the green ones? she wondered, revolted by the mess and its smell. With a supreme effort and a terrible screech of metal that was lost in the general din, she pushed her folding chair back as far as she could and squeezed out of her place at the long table. More folding chairs lined the sides of the hall, and she headed to one, reaching for the cigarettes and lighter in her jacket pocket. Settling on a chair and lighting a cigarette, she knew she had been in danger of blacking out at the table. She exhaled in relief at having avoided causing a scene.

A hand grasped hers—two hands. The cigarette was removed from her fingers and ground out underfoot. The pack and lighter were removed from the chair beside her.

"No smoking here, dear," said the smiling face.

Vera was speechless with rage. This large young woman had simply lifted her hand and taken the cigarette from her as if removing something filthy from a child.

The woman was clothed in silk and leather. The foot that ground the cigarette out was shod in a tall, highly polished brown boot. Excess weight gave her a spoiled, overfed look, the look of a sensual sadist. The woman's perfume reached Vera, mingled with the smell of grease and beans.

"My cigarettes," Vera managed to say, holding out her hand.

"That's all right, dear," the woman said, turning on the heel of her boot. "Don't worry about it now." She tossed this inanity over her shoulder as she walked away.

"My lighter," Vera shouted, to no effect.

Nearly in pain from fury, Vera went after the woman and grabbed her arm. There was fear in the woman's eyes as she turned. Touched! By one of them. The Old.

"Give me my cigarettes and lighter," Vera demanded in a voice pitched low, like a growl.

"But there's no—"

"Give me the goddam cigarettes and lighter," Vera hissed, tightening her grip on the woman's arm and visibly increasing her alarm.

The woman held out the objects.

Vera held onto the pliant thick skin and pressed her advantage by staring straight into the woman's painted eyes.

"And don't you *ever* so much as touch one of us again, do you understand me? Or take anything away from anybody without asking permission. You ought to be ashamed of yourself, you thoughtless thing. Now go away from me and think about what you've done."

With the intense satisfaction of seeing the woman's eyes

fill with tears, Vera left the hall and found a pay phone in the church across an inner courtyard. "Come get me here," she demanded when Elinor answered the phone. On one more folding chair she waited the long half hour, in grief for her working years.

Eugene Duffy moved with dignity past her table, keeping himself supremely unaware of her presence. Still in Ben's place, she realized the bar, as dark as a cave, made a far better refuge than that sweltering auditorium. Old eyes could relax here and water unchecked. The place served as a kind of living room to the sagging residential hotel across the street, but few watched the TV hung in the corner above the bar; it would have had to be turned up to a roar to be heard by most of the patrons. The smell of spilt beer was terrible; sawdust congealed underfoot. Occasionally slow shouted arguments erupted from one of the tables lining the walls. Or a thin, high-pitched insult would be hurled down the bar in anger. But mostly it was quiet at Ben's save for the country music coming from the radio. That and Ben's laugh, which sounded out like a bark whenever one of the old-timers leaned over and, sometimes laboriously, sometimes slyly, sometimes with great solemnity, told him an ancient joke.

Vera didn't talk much and rarely had a drink, but after two and a half years she knew all the regulars and the sometimes hair-raising details of their current lives. She partook of the hospitality for hours at a time, well aware that Ben was keeping an eye on her as he did the rest, making sure she didn't expire at her table—he'd had the young paramedics in a time or two—and had a safe way home. She knew Ben walked out and looked down the street after some of the old people who left on their own. If he saw somebody leaning against a building, he called a cab.

Laurel always came for Vera on her way home from school, driving Elinor's car. She never came in, but stood at the darkened door and called, "Grandma." Vera could take the house and the silence once Laurel was inside. She usually went straight to her bed for a nap, knowing the girl was down the hall in her room doing her work for school and then working in silence on her animals.

# Twenty-six

Jack and Elinor headed south on the Golden Gate Bridge under a heavy sky. Jack drove easily, thinking about his son Mike. As usual, he saw the boy's face in isolation, a small shining medallion in his mind. No mother, no stepfather, no Mexican architecture to measure the distance between them—just Mike, starting to show a strong resemblance to his father, especially when his hair was allowed to grow long enough to curl some. Six years old. Funny how recent Mike's birth, yet how long ago Jack's marriage to Lee seemed—a geological era, a part of the distant past. Moving to Cascade and working on Hilltop seemed to sever any connections he had ever had with that time. Perhaps it was the eternal construction that had been necessary to pull the ramshackle place back on its feet. He could barely remember when he wasn't working on one of the buildings up there, learning the trade as he went.

Elinor gazed out over the rails of the bridge, orange like the muted sun drifting down through heavy fog and burning the horizon. They were making the hour and a half drive to the airport to meet Lee and Mike, who had a short stopover on their flight from Mexico City to Washington, D.C. Lee's father had had a massive heart attack, and the two were probably heading toward his death bed. Elly knew Mike—

he'd visited twice at Jack's city place. But what a time to meet the ex-wife. With some forced sympathy, Elly imagined herself just one more minor ordeal for Lee to contend with on a terrible trip.

"Is she close to him?" Elly asked. "Lee, I mean. With her dad."

"God," Jack answered with a groan.

"What does *that* mean?"

"If you call it close to be locked in combat, yeah, I guess you could say they were close. In fact, yes. I would say fiercely close, as in it's surprising they haven't killed each other by now." After a pause he went on. "Though, come to think of it, Lee has that kind of relationship with everyone she's close to. She just loves you literally to death, won't let you get away with a goddam thing. That's why I worry about Mike down there. The kid could be suffocating."

"You seem to have gotten out alive," she said, wondering at the flash of female loyalty she felt to this woman about to be bereaved. A fierce closeness with her dying father. What was it that she herself would be left to dismantle when Vera died? She almost envied Lee's fiery attachment to her father. Between Vera and Elinor there was only a standoffishness, and for Elly a continual awareness of her mother, now eighty, blanching and fading away.

"Didn't you?" she said, inviting him to spar.

"Oh, barely," he said absently, and she watched the heavy sky go from pink to gray as the traffic to the city bunched up and slowed to a crawl.

In the darkness the airport radiated excitement. Elly never failed to feel it when pulling up to the airport at night. They stood in the plush carpeted waiting lounge watching the passengers from the Mexico City flight until Jack made a subtle movement of his chin—while his body remained unnaturally stiff, at rigid attention—and Elly knew that the competition, foregone as the conclusion might be, was on.

In all that bustle, Lee stood out, tall and cool. She moved straight through the crowd like a spear, with Mike trailing behind, a small decorative feather. As Elly appraised her, recognizing her from pictures she'd seen, she felt the thrill and tension of the challenge. Had she been alone, she would have pinched her cheeks for color, would certainly have run her fingers through her hair to give it height and a look of disregard. Amused, knowing that this beautiful woman posed no serious threat, Elly watched Lee approach, then come one step too close, and almost thought she could hear her sniff, like an animal approaching a potential enemy.

"Lee, you look great, great." Elly detected a false heartiness in Jack's voice and laid over that the faintest tinge of irony. Seeing the two together, she could suddenly imagine the upward scaling force of an angry onslaught of words from Jack. She could feel the potential confusion right away. Why, they were practically squinting at each other right now, assessing each other, straining to keep the focus.

Of course, there was the boy. Jack had him in his arms, with Mike's legs encircling his waist, and was pounding him repeatedly on the back. Elly guessed he was pounding in an awkward imitation of a light-hearted welcome, and to diffuse the urge to squeeze, to caress, to embrace his son to death—to encase him in his fatherly love and flee through the crowd to the car. How many hundreds of times had she opened her arms or her hand or her mind to let Laurel go, suppressing the intensifying urge to crush the girl and keep her pressed up against her, with love?

"Great? Hmm," Lee answered Jack's careful opener in a flat, expressionless voice. "It was the world's worst flight with the world's stupidest stewardesses. If the second half's that bad, the little brat here ain't gonna be much fun for his grandma."

She had beautiful planes to her face—strong bones, exquisitely visible arches to the eyes, a broad mouth of great sensual potential. And yet her eyes, though well shaped and heavily lashed, had a dullness to them, a simple practical quality that lacked beauty or interest. Elly noted that Lee hadn't smiled once since she arrived.

"All right, let's find a place to settle and get this guy some hot chocolate," said Jack. "What happened? Did he throw up?"

"Of course he threw up. He always throws up on takeoff. The stewardess took personal offense."

Elly felt a catty satisfaction, which caused her to smile.

"You look amazingly unrumpled for having just come off a difficult flight," she said. She took pleasure in rising above the obvious fact that she had been neither introduced by Jack nor acknowledged by Lee, though Mike had unclenched one of his arms from around his father's neck to take her offered hand in greeting. She and Mike liked each other—they had hit it off well from the start. Everyone liked Mike when he visited, even Laurel in her silent way. Now the little boy smiled at her with his face laid sideways on Jack's shoulder.

At Elly's remark, Lee turned her full attention to Elinor, intensifying the squint and scrutinizing her openly, as if she were trying to understand the precise meaning of what she saw. After a long moment, she replied, "Thanks. I'm surprised," and turned to search the corridor for a restaurant. Elinor felt she had just been lumped with the unfortunate stewardess and the rest of the bumbling flight crew.

In the crowded café, Jack played game after game of tic-tac-toe with Mike while Elly wondered whether she dared impose onto the delicate situation the small present she had brought him. She decided not to try.

"How's your dad?" Jack had asked as they slid into the booth, and Lee had answered, "Like shit. Like absolute shit. If he's still alive. I've got to call." Jack began to pull back out to let her go, but she made no move to leave the table. Elly marveled at Lee's total indifference to the conventions of conversation among strangers. She made no attempt whatever to soften the effect of her words, and sat glaring at them both across the table, pulling at the side of her lip with perfect white teeth.

"Is he in a coma? Does he know what's going on?"

"What the hell's the difference, Jack?" she snapped back instantly. "What possible difference could it make? He's just about finished, whether he knows it or not."

Elinor was chilled by Lee's retort. Here was a woman utterly without empathy, she concluded with interest. Or perhaps Lee was choosing to feel no empathy in order to prepare for what she had to face.

"My grandpa might die," said Mike, looking up at Jack.

"Yeah, I know, babe," Jack answered.

"It's really sad. I haven't got to see him much."

"I know, honey. It's sad," said Jack smiling wryly down at his son. After a pause, in which at least two of the adults involuntarily estimated the number of weeks Jack and Mike had spent together since the boy's birth, Jack said, "This summer's going to be great, Mike. You're going to love our new house, honey."

"Your dad's getting your room ready, Mike," Elly said. "With a bed you climb up high to, on a ladder."

Mike smiled up at them, his face showing none of the cold observer in his mother.

Elly thought of the old man dying, conscious or unaware, and saw Vera. She thought of Mike being led away in another few minutes by this disconcerting woman, and saw Laurel. She looked at Jack, winning a tic-tac-toe game with a flourish and holding back his arm from his little boy, and she felt a terrible impotence in the face of the inevitability of people disappearing forever.

\* \* \*

Jack let his shoulders relax as he steered the car out of the airport maze and onto the freeway. "Jesus goddam bloody fucking Christ," he breathed.

Elinor lifted her eyebrows, looking straight ahead. "Woo," she said. "Whadda woman, right?"

"Okay, so say what you have to say." His tone had changed. Defended, he was ready to take on her ridicule for having Lee as part of his past. "But with a prize like Allen behind you, I'd hesitate about getting into this, El."

Annoyed, she turned to his surly profile, barely visible in the dark. "*That's* nerve, Jack. This woman is a complete original. I've never seen anything like it. Are you telling me you're not going to talk to me about her after subjecting me to an hour of that kind of downright nastiness?"

He let a moment go by.

"Incredible, isn't she? A goddam barracuda. I actually forget from one time to the next."

"Ten years of marriage and you forget? That's some job of glazing over. Especially when the lady in question seems so truly unforgettable. Hey, she is a case."

"Yeah, well—" He gave it up and simply drove.

Elinor sat back to gaze through the windshield. It had rained since they'd been out, and the freeway was slick. Back at the airport a monstrous jet lifted into the black sky and wrapped the car in thunder as it passed overhead. She was appalled, without wanting to admit it, that Jack had been involved with Lee at all for any amount of time. He had always seemed to her so certain of what was right for him, impatient to rid himself of anything or anyone not fitting his idea of how he should be spending his time. He'd slam shut a book after a single page, he'd walk out of a movie he didn't like, he'd leave parties that didn't suit him. She was used to his signaling to her silently—let's get out of here, this isn't right. Elinor, less certain and needing more time to assess, enjoyed his decisiveness in shaping his life to fit his desires.

Their own love affair had seemed rooted in this same quick certainty. Here's where I'm stopping, he seemed to say, once the initial sexual fever had abated and he and Elinor stood back to assess the possibilities. He never seemed to waver in his choice of her; he never seemed to ask himself, as she'd had to then, Is this the time? Is it worth risking the autonomy I'm finally learning to use? Can one *make* a life decision in the midst of a crisis?

He was ready, he had told her. He was sure of wanting her. As for changing his life to be with her, to him, the penthouse across the bay was an empty box. "Lonely at forty-two," he had said once. "There's no precedent for it, no meaning in it. You can go crazy from loneliness in a day and a night." It had seemed that simple for him.

But Lee, now, this cruel, beautiful woman, put a different gloss on Elinor's understanding of Jack. Maybe Jack hadn't always had the genius for self-determination she admired in him so much. Where exactly was the soft spot in Jack that Lee had found and entered? Or had she bored it through herself?

"Was she always so, I don't know—so horribly direct? I know this must be an awful time for her, but—"

"She never held anything back. She came off feisty at first, when she was young. That's what I liked about her. Most women I knew then seemed insubstantial, but Lee was a speeding bullet. Smart, knew what she wanted. She was spectacular, really. She fit right into the ad crowd. Because she was so good-looking, they got to thinking of her as that American woman who haunted them, the one they had to think about and write for all day. But of course she had them thinking what she wanted them to think about her, and she'd lay them to waste, one at a time." He paused. "That is, she'd lay them and then lay them to waste, until they all hated her guts."

Elly knew Lee had slept with the ad boys, but Jack had glossed over the particulars in earlier accounts of that time. Gently, she probed, "Did you know it all along?"

"Oh, somehow I knew it. Nobody said anything—come on, I was the boss. But one day I realized I was married to goddam Eva Braun. Everybody hated Lee's guts—everybody but my partner, who was a cool fish himself—and all of a sudden, very very clearly, I could see what they saw. She was exciting and wild and beautiful, but she was mean as a goddam snake."

The San Francisco skyline was stacked up against the black sky like a beautiful electric toy. She thought of the thousands, the hundreds of thousands, of invisible souls, as she always did passing this way. All those people thinking, working, loving, dying behind the lighted facades.

"So you came to your senses and walked."

"Not quite. There was Mike. We never did work it out until she told me she was marrying Marco and moving to Mexico. And so there she is and here we are, and there's Mike, the human Ping-Pong ball."

Off the freeway now, they crested a hill and the bay was before them. "Look, El, let's set up the wedding," he said in a new tone.

Here it was again: they always came around to marriage on the way home from places. Many, many conversations in the car had hit this rock and foundered.

He went on. "I just feel like I have to find a way to take care of Mike. I want to arrange things so I can take him for long stretches, maybe get him up here to go to school. I think it might be smart to get married so they can't get ugly on the subject. It's something I wouldn't put past Lee for a minute."

"No, I think you're right about that."

Elinor rested her head on the back of the seat and watched the road through half-closed eyes. What was she holding out for, anyway? She loved this man. At Hilltop they were building a home together. He had endured Laurel's troubles and Vera's presence with patience and humor. Why couldn't she do this thing, perform this technicality, for Jack?

Laurel would be leaving soon—she gave her two years at

most. And Vera was slowly disappearing right before her eyes. Was Elinor ready to take on more family as the one she already had slowly dissolved? She saw little Mike holding onto Jack's neck for dear life, having to be pried off at the departure gate. Mike, so young, with years of care and feeding still ahead. Miserable Mike throwing up on the plane, self-conscious and embarrassed at six years old.

In the darkness, the Golden Gate Bridge swung imperceptibly across the mouth of the bay. As they crossed, Elinor watched the lighthouse beam sweep the dark water from Alcatraz, the crumbling abandoned prison on its rocky island. Specters of men like those who had taken Laurel flashed across her mind as they always did when she saw the island and, farther up the freeway, the huge complex of San Quentin. To close them out she concentrated on the old ruin. It was an empty, hollow, useless old place haunted by the strange and lonely. Being out there in the middle of the bay must have driven those trapped creatures crazy: the sound of waves lapping, the water breaking against concrete buttresses. Loneliness can drive you crazy in a day and a night, he had said. Those outcasts, trapped together, must have all been mad with loneliness and the constant awareness of waste.

They ought to burn the place down or raze it, Elinor thought. Somebody wanted to make it a park. Oh, do it, do it. Take down the ruins and plant something soon.

She reached out to grip Jack's solid shoulder. "Okay. All right. Let's do it. We'll make it official. You set the date."

# Twenty-seven

"At school I'm the outcast. Don't you know that? You know how there's always one?"

Lovejoy remains motionless. "Did you ever see those movies. There are two I always get mixed up. In one a girl's mother is so strange that everyone is afraid of her and of her daughter too. And in the other one, a horror movie, a girl lives alone with her mother, and this girl is an alien. Did you see it?"

Lovejoy somehow conveys no though she barely moves.

"I get them confused because both girls live with their mothers in old dark houses, no one visits, and their clothes are weird. Both movies make a big deal about how the girls have funny clothes." She pauses, comparing point by point. "It's all supposed to be because they live alone with their mothers. No fathers on the scene, you know, going to work and back, keeping things regular."

Pause. "One blows up a dance finally with her weird eyes. She's supposed to be an outcast just wandering through, and so angry and hurt she can somehow . . ."

One beat. "What?"

"Murder them all. Wipe them all out."

One beat.

Laurel looks up, and without warning delivers a wide sunny smile, more of a grin because it contains a trace of irony. "Oh, no, that's not me. That wasn't what I meant, Janet."

"What? About being alien, wandering through?"

"Oh, yes, I do that. I slip around. They're all so noisy. I stay quiet." She bites at her lip.

"And I do see the other kids thinking I'm strange. Maybe they do see me as some crazy girl who's going to blow them all up at a dance."

"Who? Who thinks you're strange?"

"Everybody thinks I'm strange. The kids think I'm strange. The teachers." She looks up sharply to the ceiling, raises her eyebrows, pulls at her top shirt, one of three, two open over an old jersey. "My *mother* thinks I'm strange. My dad's scared to death of me."

"Really."

"Oh, maybe not really scared. But, you know—appalled."

"Why appalled?"

Another smile, this time pure irony, inviting complicity.

"Why? Because I'm appalling. Because they're right—I'm weird, I'm strange."

"What do you mean by that—strange?"

Annoyed, "Quit it. Stop quizzing me."

"No. I'm genuinely puzzled. What is at the root of the strangeness? Why do you say you're strange?"

Laurel thinks before she answers.

"Because I really am something outside them, unlike them. Something from nature. Sometimes."

Lovejoy lets the answer settle and take hold.

"Why sometimes? When?" She is conscientious; she doesn't ask why.

"Mostly."

"When not?"

Laurel draws her feet up onto her chair and grasps her knees. She wears loose gray sweat pants, striped socks, worn-out sandals. "When I'm drawing I'm not. When I'm alone I'm really not."

She presses her lips together and makes a concession. "I don't think Jack thinks I'm particularly strange. I'm just human with Jack."

Another set of spoken words settles in the silence and takes hold.

"And your grandmother. What are you when you're with her?"

Deep thought, careful. Laurel recognizes where they are: where words have more than ordinary weight. They handle the words as if they were objects, not the ephemera of ordinary language. These words remain. The memory takes them up permanently.

"I'm both with Vera. Vera sees both. I'm normal and strange both for Vera." In the silence, Laurel ponders her meaning. "We can talk, you know, but I can feel her too, very clearly."

"Meaning . . . ?"

"Come on, Janet. I know you know what I mean. I'm tuned in to her: I smell her. I hear her very well, not just her words but her body. Her mind sometimes. Her meanings." Eyes glazing slightly as she contemplates the memory. "But we can still talk. Not like my mom—when I smell her, hear her, she's like a nervous horse, and we can't talk. A weird, wild thing and a nervous horse—they can't talk to each other."

"What about me?"

"You? You mean, what am I here? With you?"

"Yes."

Laurel laughs outright. "Don't you know? You're the ultimate human. You're just about as human as it's possible to be." She smiles, a little mocking. "Didn't you know that about yourself, Janet? You're the pure stuff. All you do is hear me. It's like I'm only a voice when I'm here. I love it, just being a voice, dropping everything else. It's a rest. If I came in here the other way, we'd never be able to talk. Didn't you know that, you ultimate human, you?"

Lovejoy cocks her head slightly. This gesture, which Laurel has seen her make before, is the closest she ever comes to acknowledging a loss of clarity.

Laurel laughs again. "I practice on you, Janet. Didn't you know that? Someday I'll get so good from coming here that nobody will ever know I can smell their feelings and hear their thoughts. They'll think I'm only a human being, like you."

# Twenty-eight

Elinor stood against the doorway of Laurel's room. She had stepped in front of Allen as he was about to enter it. "Oh, no you don't," she warned him, barring his way. "Uh-uh, Allen. She doesn't like it."

"But how can you—?"

Elinor struck what she hoped was a casual pose in the doorway facing Allen in the hall. With a familiar rush of embarrassment, she searched his face, now tight with anger, for a clue as to why she had married him nearly twenty years ago. What was it she had ever loved in this nervous, fussy, angry little man?

"How can I what?" she delivered coldly. He faced her in the hall, already slightly defeated from the loss of momentum at the door.

He looked away, recalling the outing with Laurel. He and Debby had picked her up for a two-day stay at a campground up the coast. On their return to Hilltop ten minutes ago, Laurel had sprung out of the car and bolted up the hill and out of sight. On the driver's side, Allen smacked the wheel with sudden determination. "I'm going in to talk to Elinor," he resolved. For once, mercifully for Elinor, Debby waited in the car.

Inside Allen strode down the hall to inspect Laurel's room.

Now he demanded an explanation. At least, Elinor observed, his attacks of fatherly responsibility were becoming fewer and farther between—that was something to be thankful for— and less impulsive. Once he had herded Laurel into the kitchen, pressed her into a chair, and frantically piled fruit and bread in front of her, demanding in a high-pitched tone up close to her white, scared face that she eat, *eat*.

"How can you let her go around like that? She looks so goddam *grim*. What is she trying to *prove*? I don't think she combed her hair the whole time. She wouldn't even let Deb touch it."

"Hey, I wouldn't let Deb touch *my* hair with a rubber glove."

The fight rose in Allen's eyes. "She's a licensed beautician, Elinor, for one thing."

Elinor withheld comment, and Allen leapt into the breach. "Don't you start on Debby now. I'm talking about Laurel, and I'm saying she's a mess. She's a wreck. I don't think you're doing enough to get her into shape."

Elinor drew in her lips, rubbed her mouth. Counted to ten. Leaned a shoulder harder into the door frame. "Oh, no you don't," she said when he made another move.

"Look at this room. This is a dump, not a room." One small lamp on the floor next to the bed illuminated the pictures of children and animals Laurel had clipped from magazines and pinned up on the walls.

"This is Laurel's room, the way she wants it. It's a room, not a dump. She's fixed it up the way she wants it, and she doesn't like people walking into it uninvited. And just what did you have in mind, by the way?"

"I'm going to take a look at her clothes." He took a step to push past her, and she thumped him hard on the chest, her withheld fury shooting through her arm. "Nope. I'm telling you, Allen, she hates people going into her room. We don't go into each other's rooms around here unless we're asked, and neither will you."

"Hey, maybe somebody ought to throw their weight around a little and tell Laurel a thing or two about how to behave in the real world."

Again she took her time responding. "Maybe somebody ought to. But nobody's goddam going to." Her voice remained remarkably steady. In her stance she was unmoved.

He blew his lid, and the subsequent tirade brought Jack to the door of the room down the hall where he had been working on Mike's loft bed.

"Are you crazy?" Allen shouted, his voice escalating with each word. "You can't let her go around like this—she's completely out of it, Elinor. She doesn't talk, she doesn't eat. She looks like she's been pulled off the street somewhere."

"She *has* been pulled off the street, Allen. You forget."

"Look. I don't forget what she's been through, et cetera, et cetera—but that's *years* ago now. She's got to get on with her life. She can't go around like this. She's too big at sixteen. Don't you teach her anything at all about her appearance?"

Elinor knew that the clothes and hair were the crux for him. Allen loved clothes. Well-dressed women of a certain size had always triggered his lust. From down the hall, Jack dared to intrude. "Nifty jacket, Allen." It was—the latest in ski gear, covered with zippers and Velcro flaps.

"Shut up," Allen hurled at him, flustered and angry. He hadn't seen Jack come to the door.

Elinor prepared to begin placating. It was an old routine, soothing and rhythmic. She borrowed the tone from Vera: one removes oneself from the fury of the other and stands outside, a calm, reasoning presence. "You must understand. It goes deeper than clothes. We're doing what we think is right, Allen. We're waiting—"

But Allen surprised her. Apparently he had rehearsed this tantrum before he came in. "It goes deeper than clothes, all right. Elinor, did it ever occur to you that Laurel might be on drugs?"

Her self-control vanished. "*Occur* to me? What do you think—I'm not watching my daughter? Do you think I'm just drifting around without paying attention to what's going on with Laurel?" She folded her arms and looked off down the hall, widening her eyes at Jack, who retreated, smiling slightly at the floor.

"*Drugs? You* tell me drugs? You, who haven't been fully awake in fifteen years, who has to get stoned to go to the office, who is *dying* right now to light up the joint you always carry in your pocket? *You're* deciding that Laurel's on drugs, and I'm not doing anything about it? Get out of here," she shouted, pushing sharply at his breastbone with the heel of her hand. "I'm not kidding. Just get the goddam hell out of here, Allen."

"*Look,*" he yelled, digging in his heels. "I'm concerned about my daughter."

"Let me tell you something, boy," she returned, dropping her voice and narrowing her eyes. "You don't know what concern *is*. You're way out of your depth around here, so just you go back to your little ski bunny in your cute little car out there and trundle the fuck out of my life. Because where Laurel is concerned you simply have *no idea* what you're seeing or doing or talking about. And the truth is you've never cared. Where was your great concern when she was a baby?" Elinor counted on her fingers, "Where was it when she was a child? Where was it all during junior high? What's blindingly clear right now is that you have absolutely no idea what is going on. None."

Enunciating, he reiterated. "She is a mess. She's a *mess*. She needs straightening out. She's odd."

"You're right there, bub. She is odd. You have no idea. But she's okay. Hey, do you ever tell her how much you like her work? Do you *look* at her drawings? Have you ever even seen them?"

"I'm not talking about her drawings."

"So all you really want to talk about is her hairdo, is that it?" Her fury returned full force. "I'm mentioning to you that she's doing some really good work, and that she's completely taken up with it in a totally *positive, productive* way in spite of the dire predictions, the awful prognosis." She took a breath and let herself shriek. "And you're worried because she doesn't iron her blouse before she goes to school? Is that what you're telling me?"

Jack reappeared briefly, checking out the silence that followed this outburst, and then withdrew again.

Allen shook his head. "You're a witch, Elly. Do you know that? I'm showing some concern here, and all you can do is scream. You're a real witch, Elinor."

She sighed a deep sigh, momentarily cleansed.

"Yes, well, Allen, you might be right. So why don't you just get the hell out of here before I beat you to death with my broom?"

He walked down the hall and let himself out of the house. Elly could imagine him reaching for the joint in his pocket as he walked down the path to his car. She ardently hoped he was washing his hands of the whole situation, having done all he could and acquitted his conscience. She pictured him driving across the bridge with growing relief, Debby's tiny manicured hand at rest on his bony knee.

## *Twenty-nine*

Goldy lived near the Jade Mountain farm now, in a tiny studio cottage behind someone's house. Slowly over a two-year period she had transformed herself from a busy, stylish working woman into a humble student in the ancient, classical mold. She worked in the library at the center and meditated for long stretches of time with the other farm residents and students who came to learn and practice. She kept mainly to herself, finding it hard to meet the puzzled, sometimes even demanding, expressions of people from her old life. Oddly, she wrote letters to Elinor to stay in touch, though after the move to Hilltop she lived less than ten miles away. And on a warm February day, after breaking two engagements by mail, she visited there to have lunch with her old friend. She showed up with her head shaved clean.

"Ay, Goldy—" Elinor cried, swamped with confusion at the sight of her friend's bald dome. In another moment she had to suppress a fierce urge to laugh.

"So what do you think?" Goldy asked at the doorstep, forcing herself to meet Elinor's eyes.

"Think? Give me a minute, will you?" said Elly. They faced each other across the threshold, motionless for long seconds. Elly unconsciously blocked the doorway, unwilling to admit this new development.

"You're going to let me in, at least, aren't you? Come on. It's only my head."

Visibly fending off self-consciousness, Goldy stood on the carpet before the open fireplace, her back to the small crackling fire.

Elinor gazed at Goldy from the old couch, the couch on which they'd spent so many hours talking. She had to work to recognize her city-wise friend in this stark, strange being before her. Goldy wore loose black pants, a black jersey, and black cloth slippers. Elly thought briefly of the expensive leather shoes Goldy had favored when she worked at the university. Were they such a serious indulgence in Goldy's mind that they had to be banished and replaced by these modest, noiseless, somehow self-deprecating slippers? And now the thick, dark red hair had been discarded as well. Goldy's unadorned face was starkly revealed and, Elinor perceived with some gratefulness, icily beautiful—an effect quite the opposite, she was sure, of that intended. The hair had softened Goldy's beauty and lent it a casual quality. Now the lovely lines of her face defied the humility Goldy had imposed, and the eyes seemed bold and judging—not diminished in their power, as was the point, Elinor assumed—below the taut, smooth dome of the head.

"So. A wedding—," Goldy opened.

"Hey, I can't talk to you about getting married until you tell me what's going on. What are you doing? Why did you do this to yourself?"

"My hair?"

"Of *course*, your hair. I can't believe you've done this. Why did you do it?"

"Oh, boy," Goldy sighed. Finally she said, "To get clean."

"*What?*"

Goldy sat down in front of the fireplace, apparently comfortable enough now to give Elly a full view of her head, top to back.

"To get free. It's a symbol. It's a way of reminding myself that I'm trying to disentangle myself from what I brought to the center."

"To me it looks like you're trashing yourself," said Elinor.

"I can only tell you you're wrong," returned Goldy, a shadow of irritation crossing her face, which was remarkably revealing now of every inner shift. "Look, you don't want to go into this again, Elinor. You never get it when we talk about it. I don't really think you want to understand. It always makes you mad, you know," she ended, smiling.

"You're right, it does. I keep wanting to shake you back into life, the deeper into it you get. I can't figure out what you're doing."

"It *is* life, El. It's just learning a different way to think."

"Getting *clean*? This is a way to think? The premise is that you're dirty somehow. I don't hear respect in that for what you are."

"Oh, that's the trouble with words," Goldy answered, exasperated. "Saying that about getting clean was just a way of trying to make it simple." After a pause she raised her face and grimaced toward the ceiling. "My mind really is full of garbage. It's rancor, pure and simple. Tirades at Paul. And I haven't even *seen* the guy in a year and a half. I *have* to get rid of the racket and get on with it." She bowed her head. "Whatever *it* is. I've lost track."

"Well," said Elinor coyly, giving her cocked smile, "you might feel like the newest acolyte, but you look just like Yul Brynner."

"Ha, ha!" Goldy shouted, and they let the subject go.

Mild February sunshine entered the room through the high windows, bringing up the yellow tones in the wood-paneled walls, calling out the blue and violet of one of Elinor's woven panels hanging over the fireplace. "Hey, do you want to *really* get clean?" Elinor asked with sudden inspiration.

Goldy lifted her eyebrows in question, and from her seat

on the couch, Elly saw, with fascination, the whole scalp shift.

"I mean *clean*," she said again, "right down to the soul of your soul, or whatever you guys call it over there. Laurel found a fantastic place—the original cascade, a true cascade, and after the rains we've had it must be running powerfully. Jack and I walked out there once. You've got to see it. Do you want to go, maybe take our lunch out there?"

"Sure, anything."

"No, you have to really want to go. It takes a hike. But, Goldy, it's a wonderful place."

"Sure. Let's go."

\* \* \*

Spring was present, just barely, as a smell in the air, a quality of the light. They took a muddy red fire trail down the side of the rounded hill. The road curved back westward into the wilderness and eventually joined a system of dirt roads and trails traversing the mountains to the sea.

Crocus and other new shoots pushed up at the puddled edges of the road, and here and there were clumps of wild iris, ivory and purple, just out for their scant week on the hillside. Elinor and Goldy walked with their jackets swinging open, enjoying this first chance to do so since the start of the winter rains.

At the bottom of the hill, Elinor led the way onto a narrower trail, heading back through the woods and then gently up another grade along the bed of a swollen, fast-running creek. In the open air, with an awareness of the infinite sky, Elinor felt released from the press of daily life. The surrounding trees breaking up the light, the faint smell and spray of the fast-running water, the mild sweet air itself gave her a child's lightness of spirit.

"Funny how you and I are now absolutely opposite in the

way we live," she said to Goldy, consciously taking her turn to talk. "You're alone, living in a one-room cabin. You seem sure of what you're doing, I think."

"You're not?"

"Oh, I'm sure of my work. But living here I'm not just in a house but in a kind of compound with more family than I expected, and more on its way, with Mike coming up for the summer. You're looking to yourself only. I'm worried all the time about Vera dying, Laurel getting crazy."

"And you'll be married now, again."

The idea that the marriage might be an additional encumbrance, another sort of entanglement, floated off into the trees.

"Why now particularly?" asked Goldy.

"Why get married? Oh—" Elinor asked herself if she wanted to burden Goldy with the fundamental happiness that lay below her shifting concerns.

"Oh, we figured things have progressed pretty far beyond the boyfriend-girlfriend stage," she answered, choosing her own shorthand to spare her friend her new certainty. "Besides," she added, recalling one of Jack's more pointed jibes, "would *you* lay Vera and Laurel on your best beau?"

\* \* \*

The trail climbed gradually to twenty or so feet above the running creek. At the high point it narrowed, and they followed it between a damp, rootbound hillside and a pile of giant boulders to emerge above a small deep pool. Across from where they were standing and from the top of the high rock wall fell a smooth cascade of water, breaking in a lacy fringe at the edge of the pool and slipping over the boulders in shining rounded sheets.

"Oh," Goldy said simply, in surprised pleasure.

The place had the perfection of scale that landscapers strive for. It seemed linked by unbroken wilderness to the mountains, hours to the east, while it housed two human figures as if in a room. It was exactly the size to make a person feel enveloped and secure, safe to relax for an afternoon.

The rocks caught and held the warmth of the sun, and, tired from their walk, the women allowed themselves to relax. Elinor settled on a bed of smooth pebbles at the edge of the pool farthest from the cascade. She lay back and looked straight up into the clear sky, feeling a sailing freedom from the clinging concerns of life.

Around Goldy's monkish presence the pool took on the look of a classical Japanese scroll painting. She climbed onto a boulder and, lining herself up with the sun, leaned against another.

Within the rock bowl, they were encased in the waterfall's steady roar. Early dragonflies skimmed and hovered over the pool. Water spiders lay on the surface. The two friends, practiced in spending time together silently, may even have slept in the sun.

* * *

Elinor opened her eyes and sat up. Here, somehow, Goldy's shiny head didn't look so odd. Perhaps Elly was getting used to it. Needed sun, though, she observed. The scalp was white in the daylight.

Elly was warmed through. She took off her jacket to stuff it under her head, and on impulse shucked off all her clothes and hurriedly made a pallet of them on the stones, which had begun to bite into her skin. Upright, she caught the chilled mist drifting off the cascade. She lay back down to take the sun's warmth again, wriggling out slowly to make contours in the clothes and stones with her body.

Oh, glory be, oh glory. Hip bones, ribs, strong clavicles. Her breasts lay out heavily to the sides, nipples drawn up hard in the open air. The very surface of her skin tightened slightly in the fragile heat. Fully stretched out as she was, her deep breaths seemed to originate nearly at her pubis. A swift branching flow of pleasure traversed her body at the thought.

A scream broke through. In an instant Elinor was up and alert. Goldy stood against the rock wall opposite, naked and hunched against the falling water breaking over her. In another second, her willfulness apparent, she pushed her back up straight, and there she was at full height, naked and shining from scalp to toe, the frigid water encasing her like a liquid chrysalis. With another perceptible surge of will, she stretched her arms out wide into the curtain of water and lifted her face. Eyes closed, mouth wide and laughing, Goldy screamed again.

Without daring to hesitate, Elinor accepted the challenge and stepped across the pool, chilled by the spray breaking from all around Goldy's body, and entered the cascade herself. Cold flashed through her like electricity, and involuntarily Elinor added her voice to the din. As the frigid water pounded their heads, seizing and reseizing their naked bodies, the friends sent yells and hoots and screams pouring over the boulders and down the canyon to join with the roar of the rushing stream.

Was it clean Goldy wanted to be? As the shadows darkened the pool, they would leave it with the feeling of being scrubbed, inside and out. And throughout the night, as they lay in their separate places, their long friendship sealed anew, their bodies would twitch with brief somatic memories of the thrilling, bladelike cold.

# *Thirty*

Eighty, nearly eighty-one. The numbers are preposterous, laughable. Yet they are present in Vera's life like ancient ruins—there forever, only now come upon.

Her body is impossible—arthritic, stiff, and bent. She wavers every time she stands up; to sit takes major concentration, often interrupted by a rush of irritation as someone—other than Laurel, who knows her bones—rushes to her assistance and breaks her momentum. Most mornings, it makes going to Ben's out of the question, though Vera often forgets the built-in impediments, wakes with the intention of catching a ride downtown, and then lies furious under the sluggish weight of her body, supremely frustrated at its refusal to move.

She stays in bed for hours now, or sits in a deep chair that Laurel has built up with pillows so she can push herself out when she wants to. She knows the others think she's asleep at these times, but she rarely sleeps—this is something else: a foreknowledge of nothingness that she fights off. When the blankness rises up in her, Vera garners the shreds of memory and sensation that float loose before it. She hangs onto anything—the pain in her swollen knuckles, a bilious stomach, fatigue in the eyes. Or she smokes, going through the motions of feeling for her cigarettes and lighter, of setting up an ashtray, of lighting a cigarette—inspiring alarmed watchfulness in anyone at home—of clearing her throat as she has all her life directly after inhaling. In this way she interrupts the heavy descent of oblivion, so unlike sleep in its lack of promise. In fact, she wishes for sleep at these times, to end this need to draw on her will.

She watches television now, and often sees herself there, and Laurel, Jack, and Elinor. Sandor never appears on the impenetrable glass screen, but others do—doctors she knew, other social workers, patients, and friends long dead. She knows it is simply a trick of the brain to see familiar figures on television. She has known old people who saw their dead relatives trapped behind mirrors or who heard them talking upstairs in a room in a remote, unreachable corner of the house. Vera understands these things. Unsurprised, she lights a cigarette and, with the sound of the set an inaudible whisper, watches the tiny familiar figures interact with strangers in a senseless minuet.

The toilet plagues her, the need to eat plagues her. Being in a bath having her sparse hair brushed by the ever attentive Laurel outrages her modesty and makes her wooden with embarrassment. It has probably been years since she has looked at herself directly, but having to expose her bending, nearly hairless body to Laurel brings fury up to choke her. This is too much. Why must it be that Laurel learn how the skin softens, puckers, and drops its hair from *her*, on whose upright body and continual presence the girl has relied now for years?

Yet how the warm water soothes Vera, seeming to melt the residue collected in the crevices of her joints. How subtle is the discomfort of hair not quite clean and smoothed against the head and face, how satisfying and simple the solution: the young grandchild, one hand on Vera's shoulder, steadying, one rhythmically brushing her short, newly washed hair. Vera's flannel nightdress and robe catch and hold the warmth of the bath as she sits on the edge of her bed, a small lamp casting a glow onto the roughly paneled walls of her room, her knobbed feet flat, relaxed, and at rest in warm slippers on the rug. Laurel first rubs her hair with a towel before starting to brush it. Wryly Vera sees herself as a huge baby being bathed and put to bed. Yet with the girl attending her silently, she slowly lets go of the watchfulness and yields to the delicious, now rare, and simple temptation of sleep.

\* \* \*

Laurel lays down light pencil strokes, building the outstretched wing of a hawk. Her mind is silent; she is hypnotized by the repetitive motion of the sharp lead point. She is beautiful and tall, long on the floor of her small room. She is surrounded by pictures of animals and children pinned up on the walls. Among them is a snapshot of Mike, Jack's small son, expected for the summer: a room is being prepared.

Wrapped in her layers of clothes, her long wild mass of crinkly hair all but hides her face as she works over the large tablet. Sure that Vera is with her for one more night at least, all Laurel's loving attention goes into shaping the wing.

\* \* \*

In Mike's room, Jack builds his pride of place one nail at a time. With each blow of the hammer on the ladder he is making for Mike's loft bed he feels the house coming closer to the picture he has in his mind. Only years to go—*years*—before the house is finished and the two studios are really completed. Elinor's workspace is a single quadrant of an old barn out in back. True, it's a fine piece of work—clean, spacious, good light. But the wind still rattles through the other three quarters, and birds get into the rafters. Elinor takes a space heater out there on cold days, unplugging it from their bedroom, where in truth the fittings around the sliding glass door might not be perfectly tight.

His own office, in another weathered, unpainted structure, is plasterboarded, and that's about it. A huge work table, a phone, an extension lamp on the wall, a file cabinet, and a bookcase make up the physical portion of his agency. But the lack of paint on the walls doesn't inhibit Jack's style. The business side of the operation is a restaurant kind of thing. He meets clients for lunch in the city.

Mike has a place now, at any rate. His room will be as finished as any in the house—tight and clean. Jack uses his pleasure in the room to block his concern for how the summer will go. He wants to give the boy a great summer—the greatest! And yet Vera will not last long. What kind of visit will Mike have with a slow dying taking place in the house?

He hates to think it. Vera has Jack's concern and affection. She has always made it plain that she likes him; she has taken pains to respect his privacy. And he frankly believes she has saved Laurel from serious illness. He is glad to have had Vera in his life. If that's love, then he loves her. He hates seeing her deteriorating health as an inconvenience to his plans. And yet there is so much at stake.

He lays down the hammer, picks up the sandpaper, and begins to smooth a step. Mike will spend a lot of time in this room over the years. Jack will see to that.

\* \* \*

In her studio, at a desk by the window, Elinor plans their wedding trip. They have abandoned the idea of a party— Vera is too weak. Instead Elinor and Jack will fly to Mexico, to a resort village on the tip of the Baja Peninsula. On the way back they'll stop in Mexico City at Lee's to take Mike home with them for the summer. Elinor is surrounded now by brochures and flight schedules. Goldy has agreed to stay at the house with Vera and Laurel.

Elinor wonders what Vera will wear to stand beside her at

her wedding. One of the pantsuits she had for work, no doubt. Perhaps they could buy her a new blouse or some shoes. Vera never wears any of the clothes Elinor has made for her—too showy, she always says, not efficient enough. After trying to scale down the flowing lines that she favors, and that show off her fabrics to best advantage, Elly finally stopped giving Vera gifts she had made.

It is the details of clothing and food, the imperatives of daily life, that are saving her now from the constant knowledge of Vera's steady weakening. That and her work, the intricate beauty of the fabric laid out and growing on her loom. Sometimes she works the loom for hours with barely a conscious thought except for the nearly imperceptible widening of the fabric. The rhythm, the sounds, the familiar efficiency of her hands, take her past her worries and past the sharp disappointment she loathes in herself when she sees her daughter slip down the hall and into Vera's room. Now she is caught by the familiar anxiety about the wisdom of leaving Vera even for five days, and she crosses to the loom as another might cross to a bar for a drink—as Vera sometimes reaches for her cigarettes, and as Laurel, reflecting her own mother's steady, habitual practice, opens her pad and begins to draw. Once into the rhythm of weaving, her hands moving lightly, her feet steadily, Elinor merges with the loom. And all four—Vera sleeping, Laurel drawing, Jack sanding, Elinor weaving—move forward in time together, unaware of their peaceful synchrony.

# *Thirty-one*

After a weekend of boredom spent nodding in a chair, Vera woke up on a Monday with some of her energy restored. She knew before she opened her eyes that her body had been granted a reprieve. She would be able to move freely through the day: there was warmth in her joints; she could stretch out her arms and feel the fingers respond instantly. She resolved on an outing.

"Wait," she said to Elinor after Jack and Laurel had left for the day. "Wait. Where are you going?" The tone was imperious. Behind it lay Vera's determination to escape the tedium of rocking in front of the television, fighting boredom with endless cups of coffee.

Elinor heard the old vigor in her mother's tone. "To work in the studio. And when Laurel comes home I was going into the city to show some work. Why?"

"You wait for Laurel to babysit me, don't you? Before you go out."

Elinor noted the warning signs. She proceeded cautiously onto ground they rarely trod.

"I'm afraid you'll fall down, Ma."

"You're afraid I'll burn the house down."

"I'm afraid you'll burn the house down *and* fall down."

"And how can I fall down when I can't even get up?"

Laughter cut through Elly's exasperation. "Vera, I just hate to leave you alone, that's all. Mom, don't get mad at me. I'm feeling my way."

"Ach, I'm like a child, don't I know it. You have to take care of me and here you are starting a new life with Jack."

"Ma, I've been practically living with the guy for four years. *You've* been living with him for two. What are you worried about suddenly? It's working out."

"Take me downtown today," Vera commanded suddenly.

"Oh, not Ben's, Vera—"

"*Take* me, Elinor, or I'll call a cab as soon as you leave." An empty threat. She had only enough cash for soda water at Ben's.

Elinor resigned herself. All day she would be vaguely uncomfortable knowing she had allowed her elderly mother to spend the day in a dark, smelly bar. But she couldn't play the mother with Vera, nor was she willing to sentence her to the dreary company of the television set.

"Okay, get your purse. I'll take you, I'll take you. I'll leave word at the school for Laurel to pick you up."

\* \* \*

The sun was shining, so Vera was settled on what they called Ben's annex, a city bench unaccountably placed on the very edge of the small town's street. In sitting on it one rested one's feet directly on the curb. Always on warm days two or three of Ben's patrons sat there, like old crows on a fence in their dark, thick clothes, solemnly observing the traffic.

Vera watched Eugene nudge his wife across the street. He looked frail but audacious, a tall, sickly Ichabod Crane holding a drink in one hand and cupping it like a flame with the other. It was his elbow he used to guide the old woman. Cars lined up behind the crosswalk waiting for the elderly pair to cross, but Eugene paid them no attention, and Nettie Duffy, the old woman, seemed permanently oblivious.

"They'll get you for bringing that drink out here," Vera called out to Eugene.

"They don't give a damn what us old farts do," he huffed at her, and with his free hand he heaved the old woman up the curb. He pushed her around in a slow spin until she came to rest on the bench. With the other hand he held his drink close to his chest, protecting it. "Just as long as we don't fall over dead on the streets, what do they care?"

He let himself down slowly. "About any chance she gets, Vera here lets me know how she thinks I ought to be carrying on," whined Eugene sociably.

"Nice to see you, Mrs. Duffy," said Vera, lighting a cigarette.

Eugene's wife said nothing. Her face was a sullen mask.

"Yep. Thought the old girl needed an airing," said Eugene. He settled back to watch the traffic, in slow motion crossing his long branchlike legs, folding his sticklike arms.

Bad luck for them both that they've survived together, thought Vera. She recognized in Nettie Duffy the near paralysis of years and years—decades—of holding back words. Vera knew Eugene, had listened disgustedly to his wicked boasts. But here on the bench was reality for Eugene: he was a dog dancing on a long leash, tied to this silent rock of a woman. Long ago, Vera thought cynically, blowing smoke out to the street, he could have gnawed his way free. But here he was wrapping the poor mad thing in her old coat and moving her out for her monthly constitutional. Served him right, but she pitied the woman, and imagined her distaste at his touch.

"Married fifty-seven years, and hated every minute of it," Eugene had crowed one day.

"That's nothing to be proud of," Vera had snapped back at the obnoxious old man. "You should have given your wife her freedom long ago."

"Hah!" he'd exclaimed. "She wouldn't have lasted two weeks without me. Would have died of hunger and exposure both."

"Oh, *you* think, you arrogant bastard." Revulsion had blinded Vera then, and she had seen Sandor, long buried, leaving her table for the bar.

Now, in the sunshine with the traffic glinting by, she searched for a way to reach the silent woman beside her.

"Do you smoke, Mrs. Duffy?" Nettie raised her hand two inches above her lap in a barely discernible negative gesture.

"Well, it's nice to see you out, though." The woman nodded almost imperceptibly.

The old lady's silence spoke messages to Vera: waste, regret, blind fury. Exhaustion, crazed loneliness, confusion. It spoke a misery beyond the hope of relief, an unrelenting depression that softened and absorbed life, blows and all. The woman's silence set Vera's mind churning, and she felt the urge to speak.

"The sunshine's a blessing on these old bones. Nice to loosen your coat and get out in it. Not like staring at the television, is it? With nothing of the slightest interest one hour to the next? You've never seen so many empty-headed young women crying love, love over the hours. They all need something to do, some honest work, a *book* to read."

Vera warned herself. This was dangerous territory. Most old women loved television. They loved those fluttering young women all dressed up and staring wide-eyed at their wooden, high-voiced men.

"Need fucking," Eugene offered to the traffic.

Mrs. Duffy turned her head an inch to the left, toward Vera, in protest at her husband's remark.

"They need taking off the television, Eugene," returned Vera. "They're making everybody stupid. Read *books*, that's what I say."

So she would do, those endless nights of her own dead marriage. Funny she didn't now. She no longer had the knack of entering a book. Back then in the bungalow in Hollywood, though—the life that was returning to her these days unbidden—she had kept library books stacked by her side of the bed and by her chair.

"Need to occupy themselves," she muttered, but she was seeing it so clearly now. That small bungalow with its thin, cheaply constructed walls. She'd put Elinor to bed, or he would—the girl's laughter at his bedtime games coming at her through the walls like handfuls of tacks, puncturing her studied calm. And Vera would read.

He would let Elinor watch him get dressed those nights. The little girl would sit there on the bed Vera shared with him—where he was to die in so short a time—and he would push out his chin like a boxer dog while he expertly tied his tie. Then he'd straighten his suspenders, he'd comb his hair, he'd fuss with his tie once more. He had such great concern for his precious looks. There's nothing so ugly as a vain man preening.

She pictured Elinor watching with brimming love. From the bed, the little girl talked to her father's back and watched his face in the mirror.

Didn't you once wonder where your precious dad was going, dressing up on those nights, with a wife and daughter at home?

It was a point of pride for Vera that she had protected Elinor from the truth all her life and had permitted her to love her dead father. She had determined from the moment he died never to tell her daughter the truth. Why, that was the point in those days, was it not? To protect the children. We women stayed on to protect the children from the truth. Why else stay? Why else? Mentally she addressed the stolid woman beside her.

Would I tear from a ten-year-old girl the memory of a loving father?

She had kept the secret from Elinor for thirty years, exchanging the loving bond they might have had for protecting, loving deceit. But these days the urge to reveal her secret pressed at her with new vigor. With Laurel enlivening her memory and Elinor aloof, she tantalized herself with imaginary revelations.

Elinor, Sandor was never what you thought he was. You of all people should know what I mean. He had a terrible eye for the ladies. Oh, my dear! Your father was a ghastly man.

The traffic was miles off now. Filling Vera's vision was the face of her daughter, shocked, astonished, at Vera's secret.

I know you never saw it. You really were too young when he died even to imagine. You had no idea then, at the age of ten, what people can do to each other. But, all those nights! You would watch him get dressed. You thought he was going out selling.

Ah, his professional pursuits. Lucky for him his wife worked, for all it ate at his terrible pride. His selling was really a kind of sporadic thing. It was women that were his steady occupation.

Vera could imagine it: the walls would come down. Elinor would cry, then sympathize. And Vera would feel her diaphragm relax, giving up the truth it had held in for all those years.

But why? Elinor would want to know. Why didn't you tell me before? Why?

Oh, you always loved him so. And of course, he treasured you too. With you he *was* that dapper, playful, trustworthy man. And of course you were just a little girl. And then of course he died. I was so relieved, Elinor, you can't possibly imagine how relieved I was when he died. I laid him to rest, refused to see his hysterical sister—how she wanted to come and sit with me, talk with me about her sainted brother—and then, you know, that was it. I forgot about him. I forgot about that fool for thirty years.

But why did you stand for it? she would want to know. Why did you stay?

Anyone would be bound to ask.

Why, indeed?

Things were different then, I could always say. Would I mark my daughter as one from a broken home? There was stigma then. One more humiliation laid over the original mistake.

But truly, was it for Elinor she had stayed? Or was it simply from paralysis in the face of finding out more than she could stand to know?

She ground out her cigarette under her foot on the curb and tapped out a fresh one on the bench. But Elinor's face persisted stubbornly.

Why, Ma? Why?

Once Vera had heard something through the wall. In a split second life in the bungalow changed permanently.

What, Ma? Explain. What happened?

A deeper relief promised. There was a darker secret. She had almost forgotten.

Ma!

Vera lit the cigarette and pulled her coat collar tight.

He got a phone call once. You probably don't remember how the phone was out there in the hall on a little table. Oh, I can see it—no dial, just a flat plate with the number on it. And he hated for me to answer it. But I heard him whispering into the phone, trying to hold his voice down like it was something very urgent. He was already sick by then, already getting weak. Just something he said, something about "her," about how he was sorry, something about *"right now,"* and there was some tone of voice that made me know suddenly there was a child involved, a baby perhaps.

There was a child involved. There were other calls after that that made me sure. But that first time I suspected it I could hear something was wrong. And I couldn't get it out of my mind. It wasn't just one of the women any more. Maybe that had stopped a long time ago. No, there was a child:

there was another family somewhere. No less than our own little family in the bungalow—mother father child, mother father child.

But he couldn't be in two places at once, could he? And by then he was sick, spending all day in bed, only getting out of the house after he put you to bed some nights.

And you know I can still remember—I felt sorry for the man. For the first and last time, I think, I felt sorry for him for the desperate mess he had made of his life, and he was a man who hated a mess more than he hated anything else.

I never let on that I knew. And soon after that he stopped getting up altogether. Getting showered, shaved, dressed— oh, those days came to an end in a hurry. He traded those in for a basin and a load of pills.

And he was happy enough for me to handle him then, I can tell you. I was used to the suffering of the sick by then. I had handled suffering by the truckload by then. People on the street, people in the hotels down there where they have the old people live—those folks down there suffer just as much as anybody lying in a sickbed being tended by his wife in a Hollywood bungalow. So I knew what *that* was all about. I knew what had to be done for him at night after I picked you up and got home from work. Every so often I'd be washing him or turning the bed sheets under him and the phone would ring. I'd see his eyes shift right to the side while he tried so hard to hold them steady. But he was way too sick. He didn't have the strength. Sometimes I'd answer it or you'd answer it, and the party would click off. Then I got so I didn't answer it at all, and it would ring and ring while I was working over him, even holding the basin for him or helping him sit up. We'd never mention it and finally it would stop in midring, and that would be the end of it.

She took a final drag of the cigarette and squashed it out on the bench, using the butt to smooth a circle in the gray ash.

So that's how he left her, or them, or whoever it was. Just let the phone ring and ring with no answer. That was it. I wondered as the time got near whether he'd have fixed something up in a will—I knew he had a couple of policies from when he was selling insurance himself. But it was all left alone. There was never a mention. That was the money I handed over to you when you found Hilltop, before the bungalow got sold. So that's how he left them, whoever they were. After a while, he just never answered the phone.

Eugene's derisive voice brought Vera back. "Books! Books is too good for 'em. If Nettie here tried to read a book, the effort would kill her. Right, old gel?"

"Have respect, Eugene," hissed Vera. "Keep your foul mouth shut, old man."

"Suppose you just mind your own business," retorted Eugene, his voice rising into its familiar whine. Elaborately Eugene pushed up with both hands to raise himself from the bench. He stooped for his drink and drew his bent shoulders as high out of the stoop as they would go. Then, holding off the traffic with an outstretched hand, he advanced imperiously toward Ben's.

"Good riddance to woman-hating scum," breathed Vera.

In empathic agreement, Mrs. Duffy turned her head a half inch more toward Vera. The traffic passed by the old women, who dreamed on in the sun.

# PART FIVE

# Thirty-two

In Mexico, making love was like swimming—and swimming in the warm, gentle swells of the Sea of Cortez kept the body primed for love. One early morning before the heat hit them, Elinor and Jack shook off the trappings of the hotel as if shaking street debris from their feet and walked three miles down the coast to a stark, deserted beach.

Getting married had made a difference, despite the casual, half-humorous attitude they had adopted toward it. Or perhaps it was the trip. As soon as the plane took off from San Francisco, and all through the long day of connecting flights it took to get them to the town just inside the tip of the Baja Peninsula, Elinor had been aware of having done the right thing. Their relationship had withstood the extremes of family life to a reassuring degree, and between them there was an easy friendship sharpened just now by relief at leaving their household behind. On this trip, they were poised, just briefly, on the brink of a new level of domestic responsibility, and they savored the hiatus. In four days they would pick up Mike to take him back home for the summer. Elinor saw the time between their San Francisco departure and their arrival at Lee's front door as a glorious island of sun and heat.

That early morning they tramped up the beach as the sun rose, their heels digging into the cold wet sand. The sky to the east streaked pink and orange; the water took the color but broke it up with gray. As the sun rose there was a moment, only the length of a stride or two, in which Elinor saw the gulf as if motionless on her loom—a panel taking up the sand colors, the narrow shadows in blue and the sea a bed of pink and reds.

Jack carried a big canvas bag containing an old quilt to spread, towels, and a change of clothes. Elinor wore a backpack that held their box lunches, their books, some water, and money. But they felt unencumbered, and they walked in amicable silence for nearly an hour after the sun had risen and wrapped them in its blanket of heat. Blue sky, an eye of sun, clean white sand, gentle lapping water—absolutely simple to the gaze and to the mind.

Some empty thatch shelters came into view far down the beach, perhaps one of the clusters of *cerveza* bars that sprang up like mushrooms together. Maybe they were approaching a town or resort. By silent mutual consent, they stopped and spread their quilt within the curve of some dunes. Then side by side, with an amused mutual awareness of lying there tiny on the long empty beach, they rested on their backs in the sun.

Elinor murmured, "Great. Hand me the thermos."

He didn't move, didn't open his eyes.

"You get it. You're the wife."

Elinor rolled on her side to look at him.

"You're not sorry about going public?"

"Not so far."

"No. I want to know."

He strained his neck to hold his head up and look at her, shading his eyes against the wicked sun.

"You were the one with the reservations," he said, his mouth stretched down by the tilt of his head.

"I know. But they're gone now. I feel great."

He let his head fall back on the quilt.

"Walking up here I was thinking," he said to the sky, "the chances of meeting somebody in your life you can walk three miles up a beach with comfortably without saying a word—and she doesn't even *look* half bad. You know, there's still some spring left to the skin—"

She rolled onto him and lay on his body, ignoring the sweat and grit. She breathed on his skin, almost blowing, with the growing intention, expressed in the urge to lick and bite, to take him in.

The regular lapping of the water on the sand accompanied her lazy work. Behind the jagged patterns the light made through her closed lids, an image started to form of a pebble on the sand. Small waves broke over it regularly. It was awash and deep black, then exposed and shining. Waves breaking over a smooth dark stone. She lay on him as upon a small island. Waves breaking over a smooth dark stone, waves breaking over a smooth dark stone. Together they waited for the sea change. When it came, for a moment all motion stopped. And into the silence, with their bodies pressed together like weighty beasts of the deep, a power flooded up: It was love, basic as blood, beating through.

\* \* \*

Elinor peered through her eyelashes at the silhouettes of sandpipers picking over the shore. Perhaps a hundred of them tapped daintily along the wet sand, first toward the land, then seaward, stopping, listening, eyeing the sand in a gentle dance.

It was hardly eight o'clock, but the morning sun was fierce, and Elly sat up suddenly and reached for the backpack to find the sun oil. Jack stretched and groaned beside her in a way she'd heard him do a thousand times. Old Monstro was stirring; little fish beware.

They swathed oil on themselves and ate oranges and bread and then walked naked into the Sea of Cortez. Casually the birds opened a path for them. Thigh-deep in the gentle swells, they tested the water.

"Ah, ah-h-h," Jack offered to the horizon in a full-bellied sound of satisfaction. To match the sound he slapped his ample midsection with outspread hands. Full and solid, it showed the frank suggestion of a swell above the hips. At forty-five he carried the bulk easily, with authority. His chest and groin were matted; his sex nested above the glittering water, the balls in retreat against the touch of the waves.

"This is something," said Elinor. "It's really something, being here." She felt her own weight—the circle of water that held her around the hips was larger than in the days when she swam in the ocean near Santa Monica, slipping in then like a knife after standing like this to test the water. Now each thigh felt substantial, each breast, its skin pulled tight from exposure to the sun, of significant weight.

They plunged in and swam slowly, separately, not too far out. The water buoyed them up, and they turned frequently on their backs, eyes closed, faces lifted, to float and be carried for a time. Elinor concentrated on the water line as she floated, lazily focusing on the difference between submergence and exposure. Past the low breakers, the motion of the water was only just wavelike, the crests of the waves only sometimes showing white, and once meeting shore, their energy spread silently in thick overlapping curves. The water held her buttocks; it nudged her breasts.

"Oh, shit," Jack shouted. "What the hell—?"

As she rolled to see him she felt something too—a quick, sharp crack of pain on her thigh. Two more, crisscrossing streaks of pain on her calf. A stripe on her shoulder, a flick on her hand.

Jack was flailing. And she was beset—surrounded by small ghostly presences, hounded by a commotion of small assaults.

"It's jellyfish!" shouted Jack, slapping out at the water. Elly yelled too. The pain sank in after a moment, and that under the skin was different from the surface contact. Soon her body was throbbing, superalive, in the quiet unchanging water.

They clambered toward shore, windmilling and trailing small semitransparent creatures of an unearthly nature, gelatinous, insubstantial, decorated in blues and purples of varying degrees of distinctness. Orange and pink subtleties flashed; tentacles unfurled in the water like a mass of party streamers. On the beach, free of the onslaught, Jack and Elly stood hunched over, assessing, as exposure to the air added a new dimension to the strange, just bearable pain. Looking at each other, their brows crumpled in distress, they found they were striped—long, thin welts covered their bodies. They had drifted into a floating colony of medusae, and for a time had been engulfed.

"Goddammit, goddammit," muttered Jack, dancing lightly on the sand in his discomfort. They were pathetic in their nakedness now, holding and rocking themselves, the statuesque quality they had achieved in the water ridiculed away.

Elinor felt herself begin to tremble. Could they be poisoned, she wondered?

Out of nowhere came a voice. "*Cerveza, señor.*"

A young man in bathing trunks and a buttoned-up white shirt stood upon a dune behind their quilt holding out a bottle of beer. "Oh, hell," muttered Jack. Behind the man stood a round-eyed little boy and an old, old woman in an oversized housedress. Both were loaded down with bottles of beer. So much for their romantic idyll, Elinor thought, vainly attempting to hide her nakedness with her arms. So much for hovering between two lives, et cetera.

"*Señor, la cerveza,*" repeated the young man, stretching out his arm to urge the beer upon Jack. But Jack snatched the quilt and ran to wrap up Elinor in her misery.

"*Mira, señor. Agarre la cerveza,*" the man insisted, "*y echarla así.*" He poured beer onto his arm. "*Para quitar el dolor. Debe que hacerlo.*" He ran down the dune to Jack now and took Jack's arm, pouring the beer up and down the length of it. *"Debe que hacerlo,"* he repeated, and then his meaning sank in. Jack took the bottle and poured beer onto his shoulder as the young man ran back up the dune to grab as many bottles as he could carry from the boy and the old woman. *"Más, más, más,"* he cried to them, and the two hurried each other along, back toward the thatched huts down the beach.

*"Más, más,"* he cried to Jack, and Jack shouted, "Here" to Elly, placing himself as best he could in his own huddled pain between her and the man. The beer took the sting away—perhaps the alcohol anesthesized the skin slightly. They made a strange display for the sandpipers as the young man poured bottle after bottle of beer over Jack, and Jack, adjusting the quilt in an ineffectual gesture of modesty, poured beer over a hunched and miserable Elinor. For a moment the relentless throbbing, the surface stinging, the violent sunshine, and the suffocating blanket combined to become truly unbearable. Elinor felt shrieking hysteria threaten, and the ghosts of violent men seemed to rise up in her mind. But the beer splashing down her body did take some of the clamoring away. Impatient for relief, she pushed off the quilt and grabbed an open bottle from Jack. She poured beer on her breasts and her belly and thought perhaps that if magic could transport them somehow to their hotel, as it had apparently arranged for a barman and his family to rescue them from their odd accident, she might decide to live through the day.

\* \* \*

Late that night, they tended each other with anesthetic ointment prescribed over the phone by the town clinic's doctor. They snapped and hissed, letting their extreme discomfort steam off in short bursts of irritability, and then they fell into a fitful sleep. Midway through the night Elinor woke.

Jack snored and turned. Elinor laid a hand on his shoulder,

and he flinched and growled like a bear. Simple, superficial, this noise nearly made her laugh aloud. Rolling onto her belly, experimenting with a new position for her arms, she passed through an instant of joy everlasting and back into pain-drugged sleep.

# Thirty-three

It had rained all night. In their sleep they had heard the water splatter heavily onto the patio outside their Mexico City hotel room. Now, under a clear sky, Elinor and Jack climbed stiffly out of a cab, avoiding the raging gutter in front of the house where Lee and Mike lived with Marco, Lee's builder husband. The house, a modestly artful assembly of interconnected stucco boxes cut off from its neighbors by a blue, shard-topped fence, now steamed in the sun as if it had just been lifted from a pot and placed there to cool.

The lawn was immaculately trimmed. The picture window that formed the front of the left-hand box caught the morning sun directly. A uniformed maid answered their ring. Inside the door, the hall floor was mosaic-tiled in bright blues and yellows, and fresh orange flowers spilled out of a bowl and onto the sideboard. A massive thigh-high pitcher, its unglazed surface covered with brightly colored matte-painted figures, stood near the doorway to a cool white living room.

"Hmm," said Elinor in shorthand.

"Oh, yes, very nice," Jack responded abstractly. He had never been to Lee's house before. Nor had he met Lee's husband, Marco, the faceless reason for his separation from his son. Jack hadn't spoken since breakfast. Now, readying himself for the meeting during which Mike would literally be handed over for the summer, his shoulders were unnaturally squared and his eyes stared straight ahead, on the alert for Lee.

The maid led them out a door, under a bower of newly blooming wisteria, and into the large yard formed by the boxes. There were a small swimming pool, a garden, a green lawn. In the background was a small, fenced play area containing a sandbox, a bicycle, and other shiny toys.

Lee and Marco, both handsome and brown in cotton shirts and shorts, sat at the white wrought-iron table on the lawn, colorful ceramic coffee cups before them.

Elinor began to swelter, and her welts, though nearly gone, throbbed slightly in the loosely woven top she wore over her pants. It was her favorite of the clothing she had designed, and she cursed her vanity for choosing to wear it today. She had composed her appearance that morning with unusual care, remembering Lee's riveting beauty, so casually displayed. She'd roast until they got on the plane.

Appearing from nowhere, Mike darted across the pool deck and threw his arms around Jack's hips, burrowing his face into his father's stomach. Jack grabbed him up and spun him around. The small brown legs flew out behind, the delighted scream pierced the apprehension that had clouded Jack and Elly's approach.

"Nooo," said Lee. She shook her head at the coffee she poured, drawing her perfect lips into a pout of disapproval. Jack set the boy down to say hello.

"Come, come, come," cried Marco in welcome. He stood at his place and opened his arms in a gracious invitation to the table. He was a small wiry man with a deeply creased face. Dark brows, luxuriant wavy black hair, and a brown complexion contrasted sharply with heavily lashed light blue eyes. These eyes seemed a strange fluke of inheritance in the classic Latin face, as if physiologically a European claim had been made on the man. Marco's manner and his welcome were cheerful but carved into his face was a permanent sadness, somehow linked more to Mexico than to the experience at hand.

Marco welcomed them, shook their hands, seated them, bustled slightly. Lee, however, would concede nothing to the social nature of the occasion. They might sip coffee in the sunshine, they might eat the lavish breakfast the maid was pushing out slowly on a white cart, they might exchange pleasantries and some light gossip, but Lee commenced at once to transact business and articulate terms. Her son would be let go for so many weeks. So many suitcases would accompany him; so many medicines would be handed along. His arrival back in Mexico City would be expected at such a time on such a day twelve weeks hence. He would review these books for one hour every day in preparation for the second grade at the American school. "He absolutely must go over this work daily," she said. "He is slipping already. I don't have to tell you—" she glanced at Elly, mother to mother, her lovely gaze rising to perhaps the level of Elinor's chin—"what a child can lose over the summer in terms of the progress made during the year."

"Ah, but he's only seven." Marco with his fingers spread wide dared to interrupt the flow of instructions and cautions.

"A prime learning year, Marco." Lee clipped his objection with a practiced efficiency. Undoubtedly, she cut new blooms in her garden in precisely the same way.

Jack had resolved to show no resistance whatsoever, but simply to collect his son. He sat hunched over his plate, apparently attempting to deflect the stream of Lee's words with the top of his head. It was Elinor who saw Marco deflate Lee's perfunctory answer to his remark and withdraw back into his chair with a slight philosophical lift to his brows.

"Also," said Lee, changing direction—and Elly sensed a slight hesitation here, a garnering of resolve in the face of certain resistance—"there are the vitamins. I have myself been under the care of quite a remarkable nutritionist—more, really. She is a healer with extraordinary powers of diagnosis."

Jack rubbed his nose vigorously and exhaled loudly. "Ah, Lee," he said, as if he had suddenly recognized her. The match was set. He stepped into the ring, and she greeted him there with a luminous, transforming smile.

"*And* she has seen in Michael," she went on serenely now, "some tendencies toward anemia, an iron deficiency that can have serious ramifications educationally. These children"—she made a sweeping gesture with her hand, indicating, as was somehow apparent, every native child in Mexico—"all have it to one degree or another. That, coupled with their abysmal system of education . . ."

Jack turned abruptly to Elly, and after a long pause during which he seemed to be cleaning his teeth with his tongue, said with a steadiness she admired, "You'll find that Lee's social analyses—and her political views as well—generally contain a strong nutritional theme."

Elly refused the invitation. She wasn't going to step between these two with even so much as a polite smile.

"So what insidious regimen has your remarkably psychic, highly intuitive nutritionist devised for our small boy Mike here?" The boy now played with two boats on the steps at the shallow end of the pool, muttering a sound track to himself.

Lee delivered another smile, and Elinor, increasingly uncomfortable as the sun pummeled her shoulders and sweat slid down her hurt sides, appreciated the rare beauty of the weapon as presented. Simultaneously she grew deeply, impatiently annoyed. This woman remained supremely confident that her loveliness, an arbitrary gift utterly unmatched by any inner charm, would carry her opinions into the world and give them merit. Even with Jack? They would see.

Lee went on, a lilt in her voice revealing her increasing confidence. "But this is no theory. She has conducted tests.

She uses a clinical approach, blood tests and so on. He really is quite deficient. We feel lucky to have caught it so soon, before his schoolwork and his learning have been affected to any great degree."

"As with the entire population of Mexico under twelve?" Jack suggested with a sidelong glance. "*All* learning disabled, *all* pitiful cases. No wonder the government . . . eh, Lee? No wonder inflation . . . ?"

Marco ducked his head over his coffee.

Lee chose not to react to Jack's sarcasm. "You may well laugh," she said, dismissing him lightly, "but Mike is on a high-iron diet and is required to take supplements. And then he has various natural compounds to aid his absorption and digestion. Iron can affect the digestion, you know." She turned to Elinor now, still smiling. "The program must be followed to the letter," she said, as an efficient nurse would. "Mike's education, his general well-being, depend on it. His health, his colds, his tendency to pick up anything and everything have improved remarkably since we began. You'll see to it?"

"We'll see to it, of course," said Elinor, choosing her words carefully, "that Mike is taken care of in every way."

"Yes, but the iron program in particular?" Lee returned like a determined dog tightening her grip on Elinor's ankle. "I'm most concerned—"

"Stop badgering, Lee," Jack snapped. "Elinor and I will take care of the boy. Period."

Lee smiled once more at Elinor, ignoring Jack's obvious fury. "I'm really quite concerned about this. I've written out the program."

"Please, don't worry, Lee," said Elinor. She began to wonder whether this brusque pharmaceutical manner wasn't the closest Lee could come to expressing concern about being separated from her child for three months. "We're going to have a great summer together. It's going to be wonderful for all of us having Mike there. My daughter, my mother—we're all looking forward to it."

"Ah, yes." Lee breathed, withdrawing the smile. "Your daughter." She stared at Elly in silence. Here was a woman who had never experienced the least self-consciousness, the least social uncertainty, in her life.

After the interminable silence, which effectively brought Elinor's trustworthiness as a mother and an adult under scrutiny, Lee continued. "I have absolutely no doubt that you will show Michael a good time. I am simply asking you for reassurance regarding the dietary program."

"You have my reassurance," Jack hurled at her. "You have *my* reassurance."

"Oh," she returned, smiling once more. "*Your* reassurances," implying long experience with *them*.

Marco, who had been tapping his lips, brought the standoff to an end. "Miguel," he called, with affection. "Run in now to have Carmel fix you for the airplane. Run now."

Elinor longed to follow the boy into the cool recesses of the house. Lee's towering egocentrism and her silly, shameless wielding of her own beauty reflected too poorly on Jack. How *could* he have lived with this grotesque, selfish woman? she wondered with distaste. Surely he had assumed a different style from the tired, wilted man, his kindness wasted and kicked aside, who endlessly stirred his coffee across the table. Combat! That's what Jack had called the marriage. He must have resigned all the trappings when he and Lee divorced, for Elinor had rarely glimpsed in Jack the inclination to do battle. Certainly he enjoyed being right, and certainly Elinor's own strong opinions met his in eruptions of temper. But the fights for survival Elinor could imagine between these two were quite outside her experience of Jack.

In the bright sunshine now, Elinor allowed herself a moment of intense satisfaction. She was the prevailing lioness as, with studied courtesy, she talked about gardening with Lee. That the four had arrived at this benign subject without a major blowup she took as a personal triumph. Poor Lee, left with only her beauty and her tired, kindly husband, in her garden clipping blossoms day after day, while Elinor, Jack, Laurel, Vera, and now Mike, tumbled on in a tangle through life.

Days later Elinor would remember her complacency of the moment with a wry, sorrowful shake of the head. Life, she thought, seemed to be the continual re-proving of the most hackneyed clichés. This time the remembered moment would ring with "little did she know."

# Thirty-four

It was raining at Hilltop. The sky was a gray sheet just above the house. Wind blew hard through the eucalyptus trees. The giant stems bent and threatened, their towering height newly apparent, their weight inestimable and dangerous. Everywhere around the house the rain made different sounds—drips, runnels, and thuds; steady streams from the gutters; a solid sheet off a section of the studio roof. The blowing wind swallowed the more subtle syncopations: of water working down through the scrub bush; of taps on the hard, curved oak leaves; of drops chattering on the driveway. Sudden splatters of rain against the window barely intruded upon Vera's tangled thoughts.

Elinor and Jack, along with Mike, were expected in early afternoon. Goldy, after glancing in at the sleeping Vera and eating breakfast with Laurel, had left to return to Jade Mountain as planned, to start an intensive practice session. Laurel watched Goldy drive away through the storm, and then quietly entered her grandmother's room. Vera's profile was razor-sharp against the pillows. When Laurel came in, Vera opened her eyes.

"I've sat by the bedsides of many old ladies," Vera said, or thought she said. "It's been part of my work to do that." She let her head roll on the pillow so she was looking in Laurel's direction, but not at her. "Don't you let anyone keep you from doing your work."

On the small table near her bed stood two whiskey bottles and a glass.

"Grandma—" Laurel went to her in alarm.

"I'm all right, Laurel. I'm not sick."

In reality she had not drunk much. At the most, four or five full ounces. She had kept whiskey for herself ever since Sandor's illness, as a totem against the hardest nights. Perhaps she had poured herself a total of six drinks a year until now.

During the course of the long, long night, she had had the eerie feeling, increasing over the hours, that she was pouring the liquid into nothing, so ephemeral had her body become. It was simply a net now, loosely holding the various nodes of discomfort and trouble together. Once past her mouth, the whiskey was a warm steam that slowly drifted downwards, magically relieving her of her flesh and bones. Not only the whiskey but also her body—except for her head lolling now on two pillows—was vaporous, compressed and trapped by the bedclothes.

"Pull out the blankets," she said, but it was a feat of great concentration to compose the sentence. And apparently she had not managed it. Laurel did not hear her over the rain and wind batting at the house.

"The blankets—pull them," she managed. The girl sprang to the bed and pulled the edges of the bedding from between the mattress and springs.

Only a thought, that notion of her body disappearing was only a thought—and yet Vera felt the vapors that had been her arms and legs, her foolishly thickened trunk, her organs, her hag's breasts, her shoulders, unaccountably still smooth, all drift slowly down toward the floor from under the blankets.

Why hadn't she known how easy it would be? She had watched the process so many times at the bedsides of others. One simply found a way to dissolve the body. So old and used were the bodies she had cared for that it rarely took much to release matter from mind. All that remained now of herself, she felt, was the thinking, remembering head—a heavy, substantial, unmeltable thing. How to get rid of that?

"Come here," she demanded of her handmaiden. Obediently, Laurel stepped in close.

"Are you all right, Gram? What's wrong with you?"

"I'm not sick, Laurel." Her voice was so thin it lodged in her throat, nearly a whisper.

The girl reached across Vera for the hairbrush on the table. By picking up the brush, Laurel knowingly entered a drama of high meaning in which her grandmother had already been engaged—for how many hours now, alone in her bed?

As Laurel brushed the old woman's thin hair, Vera felt close to laughing. Terrible to think about hair, its meaninglessness. She could imagine nothing farther from the solemnity of the moment, and yet she had seen many dying old women think only of their hair—muttering, worrying, suffering over the state of their hair as their last words fluttered past their lips, terrifying their children gathered around the bedside. One old one, so long ago now, had suddenly demanded that Vera brush her hair, and Vera remembered it as if it had happened just a moment ago. At the woman's frantic command, Vera had gently unpinned the thick gray braid that the nurse had worked on that morning. She had squeezed herself halfway between the bed and the wall to unfan the hair into a wide skirt of many shades of gray, and as her arm grew tired with brushing, the old woman died.

Vera's hair had been like Laurel's in her girlhood—unruly, always threatening to break free of the elaborate arrangements of pins, and sometimes ribbons, that her mother favored for her. It had been thick and curly, sometimes frizzy, a huge cloud around her head if she let it free after washing. Early in her marriage it had seemed a symbol of her surging sexuality—Sandor was mad for her hair free and billowing; he pushed his hands into it until the hair itself trapped them on either side of her head. Like Laurel's now. Often, lately, Vera had given up the struggle to sort them out, and let Laurel be either Vera or Laurel herself, just as her mind first willed it at the time.

There was nothing left of that wild bush now. Laurel brushed at Vera's hair in quick short strokes, more petting her grandmother than grooming her hair.

"Give me that glass," said Vera. Laurel's hesitation was imperceptible. An inch and a half of brown liquid remained.

"Help me with it. Lift me," Vera commanded. The old woman barely felt her body being hefted slightly to lean, back-to-front, against the girl, who sat on the bed near the pillows. Laurel held up the glass, and Vera drank.

"Put me down now," said Vera. The girl slipped one of the pillows off and lay the old woman down. Then she lay down herself and stretched out, gently placing her arm across Vera's chest and lightly clasping her shoulder.

"No, no, I'm not sick," Vera crooned. Yet the words were barely audible, as if someone were speaking quietly in the next room.

She could think Laurel into obedience—she was used to doing that. And now she wanted the girl near her on the bed. It was unlike Vera to imagine herself being embraced, but it came to her that the pressure of the young flesh up against the old bones that lay spilled beneath the bedclothes—there after all! not vaporized yet!—would satisfy her final appetite. She thought it out now, willing the girl step by step: Wait, Laurel. Get up first. Pick up the glass again. It still holds an inch. Turn the bottle upside down over the glass again and achieve an eighth-inch more. Now lift me from the back. Vera saw herself from above, a long, severe-looking mannequin, but somehow also a floppy baby that, left to fall too far forward, would slowly roll off the bed.

This doll-like figure is held now by a very young Vera, just starting her service, wondering with respect and some fear at the ravages of age to the skin, the hair, the *teeth*. So many of the old ones she had lifted and fed in the end had no teeth, no thought for the false teeth in a drawer somewhere, forgotten. And the grown children inevitably made a fuss about the teeth—"Ma, wear your teeth. We spent good money for the teeth. You look old, Ma, you look old without your teeth." As if the plastic teeth slowed the earth's revolutions around the sun or made the slightest difference to the perfect regularity of time.

As a visiting caseworker to the state hospital, Vera was never supposed to feed the old patients or help them drink. She was never to move them from their beds or bathe them or help them with the toilet. And yet some cried, some demanded; she soon saw she had no right to withdraw her able body from them merely to obey the rules.

She learned to love the old people early in her work and to respect their proximity to death. Many talked with her openly about it; some trusted her to witness their preparations. She became over the years, in a multitude of hospitals, clinics, and private nursing homes, a special kind of midwife to the dying. In fifty years, and as the observer of hundreds of passages, she learned the shape of the labor, the stages involved, the quality of the pain, and the point at which it gave way. Pain, she knew, was life. Where it withdrew and remained forgotten—as with clothing and jewels, and later with children and grandchildren—the crossover was virtually accomplished. All that remained were details of no moment: the closing down of the house.

Vera recognized herself now to be still too much alive. She had resolved to finish it, to speed it along with the hidden whiskey, yet she still had power enough to impose her will on Laurel, for there the girl was, the glass put back, lying down beside her once more. Vera's body was all but gone, a vaporous waste drifting now about the room, but the power of her mind, memory, and will, though softened by the whiskey and the long sleepless night, was still vital, nearly undiminished, safely encased.

With the bodily power gone irretrievably, how did one extinguish oneself? Several times over the years the old ones in their beds had begged Vera's aid in taking them past the last barrier. They would beg an overdose, divulge some secret cache of pills, or propose quite simply a pillow to the face. A pillow to the face—a pillow simply placed upon the face, and a strong substantial body laid across.

Composing the idea itself seemed to bring it close. The whiskey helped that. Vera concentrated on what was happening now. Laurel lay beside her, stretched out long on the bed. Her head lay near her own head. This prescient and wary girl had done what Vera herself had never once imagined of herself in all her bedside vigils—had climbed up beside Vera on the bed, stretched out and laid her head down on the pillow, bringing her eyes, liquid and unafraid, up close.

Could Vera send the message across? Help me. Help me. Could she find the way to send the message across? Their skulls were secure, two rooms closed tightly against each other. She found she could not speak. So that was gone. She was very close to gone now. Could she send the message across?

Only the eyes were left. The eyes of her child's child not five inches from her own. She could see their layer of water. There was a small speck on one lachrymal duct. She watched the regular blinking, so close and explicit she could even recognize, peripherally, the cleansing function performed by the closing of the enormous lids.

It was the eyes then. They were all she had left. Help me, she said with them. There is a simple way to let me out. Help me, she called through her eyes.

\* \* \*

Laurel had gotten up once to wrap up in a blanket. She lay curled now against the old woman's slack form. One arm lay across Vera's chest, one hand held the quilt against her grandmother's shoulder. Slowly darkness swallowed the corners of the room, the bottles and glass on the table, still perhaps showing the imprint of Laurel's fingers over those of Vera's own. Darkness absorbed the bed itself, and finally Laurel, wrapped in the blanket, pushed herself up carefully, needlessly quiet, and left the room. She closed the door and crossed the hall to her own room. In the darkness there she felt for the small squat candle and the matches she kept in her bedside drawer. She struck a match, and the faces on the wall jumped into view.

Wrapped up and alone, her wild hair merging with the darkness, the children and animals keeping watch on the walls, Laurel curled up and slept like a creature in a cave, bending round the knowledge of Vera's death as if it were a heavy package as yet unopened.

\* \* \*

Darkness fueled the storm, it seemed, and a chaos of wind currents bent the eucalyptus trees behind the house. The moans of the trunks abrading each other were lost in the violent sea sounds made by the lashing of thousands of leaves. But one forceful gust shook a white owl from its protected place deep within the branches, and suddenly the creature glided down—so huge, for a bird, a white reaching thing expert and silent in its curving descent. With a tip to its body, the owl lay down on the wind and, like a slice of silver, rode close to the contour of the grass-whipped hill, over the crest, and away.

# Thirty-five

It was eerie riding back from the airport in the plush limousine bus. North of the bridge, power was out in the county, owing to the rough springtime storm. Darkness had converted the orderly suburbs into the deepest countryside, unmarked by the slightest guidepost. Occasionally the black would be brushed by the long, tubular lights of cars. The freeway cut through the darkness like a pilgrim's road, and Elinor, Jack, and Mike rode it in silence, tired from the long trip home. The storm had closed the airport and kept their flight delayed on the stopover to Los Angeles for hours.

They called a cab in downtown Cascade. Mike slept against Jack, who, carrying the boy, had lowered himself carefully to the wooden bench in front of the bus station. Elinor paced the empty street waiting for the cab. The last scraps of clouds had blown away, the night was washed and warm, and with the hiss of tires in her ears, Elinor felt exhilaration at the sight of the stars in their hundreds.

Carefully, the cab crawled up the long winding driveway to Hilltop, picking its way through the branches and debris from battered eucalyptus and pine trees that were scattered everywhere. Elinor and Jack tapped up the front steps like a blind couple. The darkness was nearly total, and Jack still carried the child against his chest. The boy, a giant starfish, blessedly slept.

But before Elinor could slip her key into the lock, the door slitted open, and Laurel, candlelit, pulled her mother to her, nearly slamming the door in Jack's face. Holding the candle aloft, she burrowed into Elinor's body like a near-grown cub demanding milk. Elinor, confused by the welcome, so unlike Laurel in its unreined physicality, laughed.

But: "Grandma died. I think I might have killed her." Laurel hissed this into her mother's coat, burying the words in her breasts.

"What?" snapped Elinor, frightened.

Laurel's very breath conspired against her repeating the words. She had lain for hours with the message unspoken, growing against the inside of her throat.

Jack pushed in behind Elly.

"She says Vera died."

"Where?" Jack asked Laurel in a harsh whisper.

A slight movement of her head, the face still pushed against her mother's chest, indicated, "There."

"All right," said Jack. Reason and clarity had devolved onto him. Now he carried all three, not just Mike, as the meaning of Laurel's words rendered Elinor motionless and terrible gulps of fear and remorse racked Laurel. Bracing Mike's weight against his chest with one arm, he herded wide-eyed mother and frightened child to the living-room couch. Then he ran Mike back to his newly renovated room and laid him in the loft bed. Carefully he built up a pile of pillows against the child to guard against his falling out. Finally, he slipped out the front door to grab the luggage and pay the cab driver.

The driver leaned against the side of his taxi, smoking. He had unloaded the suitcases onto the porch. "Quite a storm," he said genially.

"Looks like it."

"Pretty rocky coming up?"

"Not bad, not bad. The storm was all over by then." Jack counted out the fare. He savored the moment, ignoring stray memories of his own parents' sudden death. As the taxi drove away, he stood still in the clear air, gathering his strength. Vera dead in the house, Laurel nearly crazed, Elinor in shock. He would count on Elinor to come through clean and strong, and he would keep his own mind clear to steer Mike through this strange welcome without being scared. Thank god the boy was asleep. With a start Jack ran up the porch steps and grabbed the suitcases. The sudden anxious thought that the boy might have wakened in an unfamiliar room, and in a house where death was present, propelled him down the hall to look in on his son.

* * *

The power was out at Hilltop. Leaving Laurel huddled under a quilt on the couch, Elinor and Jack, each overcoming a staggering inner resistance, carried candles into Vera's room to look at her body. Somehow the candles softened the view and brought out what beauty there could be there.

At the sight of Vera, Elinor's mind remained perfectly clear, but a never-opened door swung free, and unexpectedly she discovered a third plane of existence in addition to body and mind. From behind the door flowed sadness of a power and purity beyond words. As she stood, gripped by Jack from behind, grief spread through her body until she was simply a vessel filled with it. In a last lesson from Vera, Elinor learned the two-sided nature of grief: unfiltered comprehension of loss wrapped in a question: "Where are you?"

Yet Elinor's body, full as it was of feeling, remained steady, and she was even able to marvel at this mechanism she had not known existed within her, though she had sensed something like it before. This was the door that, during Laurel's disappearance, had remained shut tight, yet primed to swing open at fatal news.

She stared down at Vera and spoke to her silently. *How much we didn't say! Where are you?* The mystery of death asserted itself through the body's inconceivable stillness.

The phone was out, so Jack drove down to town to get Vera's doctor. As the light came up outside, the three of them settled the particulars. There were long silences among them as they agreed on the official story. There would be no mention of whiskey, no mention of Laurel's presence in the room. Perhaps Vera had decided to drink herself to death, perhaps Laurel had physically handed her the whiskey. But such facts, if they were facts, were incidental to the larger truth—half a pint of whiskey wouldn't have killed anyone who hadn't been ready to die.

\* \* \*

Convincing Laurel of her lack of complicity in Vera's death would be a new challenge. That night, once she had delivered herself of the message that had pinned her to her bed, Laurel became a study in adolescent defiance. Through the filling grief, which if anything sharpened her senses, Elinor felt the girl draw up into herself, stiffening her posture and moving farther away than ever from what comfort Elly could give. If Elly were to read those high shoulders, the rigid neck and back, the hips cocked, the chest lifted out like a shield, she would see emblazoned there: "I did what Vera asked me to do. I always did what Vera asked me to do." Laurel projected distance and pride, and only her still childlike face suggested doubt and the cousin to Elinor's grief. Soon enough, though, Laurel would buckle and plummet into a silent despair.

"She needs a shot," said the doctor, with an outsider's offhandedness, making them wince. The suggestion, overheard, sent Laurel flying out the door. They let her go, unconsciously trusting her more easily in the wild hills than in the house alone.

Jack drove the doctor down to the hospital to arrange for

an ambulance. With Laurel gone and Mike safely asleep, Elinor sat down beside the fire. No props had fallen from Elinor at the loss of her mother, but Vera's disappearance gave her a terrible restlessness of mind. With exhaustion from her trip making her quiver, and renewing grief, wave upon wave, filling her body, Elinor imagined Laurel hurt again, and moving far away. It had only been Vera holding Laurel home. Elinor knew now that the girl would go too.

Elinor remembered Vera plain as day as a woman of forty, Elly's own age, dressed up in a suit and hat. All sharp angles and long lines, the look of Vera bespoke competence, intelligence, and style. You pull up over loss, the picture said. You draw strength from misfortune and show it. Such was the example Vera set for Elinor from as early as she could remember. She recalled the feel of striding next to her mother, consciously raising her chin. Laurel had learned that from Vera too, perhaps even more precisely than she. By now Laurel had Vera's bold posture down pat. But although Elinor had raised her chin, she had found her strength more slowly, from the inside out.

Elinor turned to her own ways of mining strength from loss. She lay her head on the back of the old couch, closed her eyes, and set herself adrift among the memories, giving up her mother to the past.

# *Thirty-six*

High summer at Jade Mountain. A smell of the ocean hitting the beaches a quarter mile to the west mingled in wafts with aromas originating closer by: bay trees and dill weed, dry grasses and dust, something pungent—perhaps the Queen Anne's lace that rimmed the rough, unpaved parking lot where Elinor hesitated, suddenly scared. It had been three months since they'd brought Laurel here, full of trepidation, and a month since Elinor had actually seen her. She had come to decide once and for all whether it was working for Laurel to be living out here, with Goldy watching out for her at a distance.

That Laurel had even considered returning to the farm had filled Elinor with a sense of defeat. The girl was dying to get away from her, that was clear, even if it meant taking refuge at the site of her terrible panic. When Goldy had raised the possibility of Laurel's staying at Jade Mountain—"But away from the hall, Laurie. You'd never have to go close to the big hall"—Laurel had broken her silence to jump at the chance. "Oh, Mom, say yes. Please. *Please*. I'd be with Goldy." So it was Goldy to whom Laurel had turned in her grief and loneliness for Vera. It will never be me, thought Elly. There was never a chance of that.

At Goldy's request, the community had voted to allow

Laurel to come at a student's tuition fee though she would be under no obligation to study. She would simply live for a while, work at an assigned job. It was a charitable granting of succor to a troubled young girl. How much had Goldy had to tell them? Elinor had wondered, turning the strange proposition over and over in her mind.

Yes, Lovejoy had said. Let her go. She'll be safe there, and your friend can keep you informed. Let her. She seems to want to be away.

Elinor was galled by Lovejoy's composure and her apparent freedom from deep feeling. She seemed to glide through life unimpeded while Elly sank under its weight. In Mexico Elinor had gloried in the idea of her family as a vital love machine propelled forward by its own life. But since then she had suffered her mother's loss, watched her husband lean like one besotted toward his little boy, who was slipping away again, and seen her daughter shrink from what she could offer as if from certain contamination. Elinor had only her work to get her through this dreadful summer of mourning, but even the parts of her loom had conspired against her: repeatedly the motion of weaving failed to take her up. Even so, this morning, before driving to Jade Mountain, Elinor had sat before the loom for two full hours, resolving and resolving again to shed the emotion that was plaguing her. Wherever she went now, she felt, she trailed long filaments of grief for Vera, impotent empathy for Jack, and an anxiousness about Laurel that sent the girl flying away.

Elly started down the road to the farm, where the residences, offices, library, and prayer hall were grouped at the edge of the planted fields. Suddenly she remembered the feel of her hands on Vera and Laurel as she had embraced them on this road three years ago. They had walked here together, with Jack strolling casually behind. She could recall the very fabric of Vera's cotton blouse, the flesh over the old ribs thin but soft, lacking tension. By contrast, the skin of her daughter, tautly bridging the rib cage and hip under Elly's hand, was firm and resilient. Sharp grief for Vera came and went in its by-now familiar pattern—she could let it pass on through—and Elinor was left with a cameo memory of the four of them on the path.

Elinor had had hope then as now, but it was vague in those days. Then she longed in a romantic way for Laurel to let her love her into health. Now the hope was specific nearly to the point of pain. If Laurel's stay here in this strange, seemingly self-invented religious community wasn't working, if the girl still remained blanketed in the terrible grief that had sapped all her youth and kept her sleeping for hours, waking at night to eat furtively, speaking barely at all, then what was Elinor to do? She was farther from reaching Laurel than ever—the girl bent away from her, never met her gaze, and blocked off the flood of feeling that invariably flowed from Elinor at the sight of Laurel in pain. What was there left to do? Images of medical apparatus, sun rooms, pills, shots, low-voiced consultations intruded on Elinor's view of the dusty path.

But there, suddenly, was Laurel coming to meet her, the wild hair puffed out and free. The girl wore layers of shirts, but they were thin and light, Elly noted with fresh hope, not shroudlike, and her white pants looked gauzy and comfortable. There was a tentative suggestion about her that she was ready to unwrap and expose herself to the open air. Her step itself was light, her shoulders high. Even at a distance, Elinor could see that Laurel was free of the weight that had bent her down since the day of Vera's death. Relief close to jubilation burst up through Elinor's chest, followed by the start of resignation—the child would never come home.

"Laurel, you look wonderful."

Laurel smiled and they walked, untouching, down the shaded path to the cluster of buildings around the modest dining hall.

"It's lunchtime," Laurel said, nudging the air around her to direct Elinor's steps. Goldy waited for them at the door. A smooth, fresh fur covered her head. The friends embraced and Elly poured all her family affection into the gesture she had carefully withheld from Laurel.

"I like your do," she said. "It looks like red grass."

Laurel went off to fill a tray for them, and Goldy hurriedly reassured her. "She's better, El."

"Is she talking?" Elly asked.

"Not much," admitted Goldy.

"So what's better?"

"She eats. She seems to like going through the day. And she doesn't give off that awful sense of doom. Can't you see it? To me she really seems better, lighter."

"Yes, I can see it. I'm amazed, as a matter of fact. I was petrified that she was going to go around the bend at the sight of this place."

"She steers completely clear of the practice and the ritual. It's not the Buddhism at all that's drawing her," said Goldy. "But I think she likes the routine. It keeps everybody moving along. That's what it's for. I think it's that, and the animals."

"What do you mean, the animals?"

"Hasn't she told you?"

"She hasn't said a thing."

"She has a job now. She takes care of the animals. She's our animal girl."

After lunch Laurel took Elinor to her new room. She had moved from a little cubicle in the residential hall to a rough room in the barn above the stalls. Elinor's spirit lifted at the sight of it. New pictures covered the walls, fine animal drawings, highly detailed, in lead and colored pencil. The wild creatures and haunting children were gone. These pictures showed farm animals, fat and calm. Seeing the pictures on the wall, Elinor had the feeling Laurel was pulling the farm in around her like a comforter.

Two unscreened windows, their wooden shutters thrown wide, cross-ventilated the spare, whitewashed room, and a hot summer breeze stirred mildly. Cicadas buzzed, and steady incessant clicking sounds, seeming to ride the heat itself, emanated from the trees around the barn. The warm, sharp smell of horse mixed with the odor of hay.

Laurel sat on her bed and drew up her knees while Elinor looked at her pictures, working to contain the gladness they inspired. Two cows grazing side by side, nearly touching at the belly; a fat ewe with its lambs; a horse stretching its head over a fence post, inviting attention. These were solidly present animals, not caught in a flash, not about to flee as the ones at Hilltop had been. These were placid, enduring, staunch beings. Elinor saw in them Laurel's depiction of ways to be in the world.

"I like these a lot," said Elinor.

"Let's go see them," Laurel replied.

\* \* \*

The animals dozed in the noon heat. Two horses and a cow had taken to the barn, where Elinor followed Laurel now, entering the darkness gratefully. She luxuriated in the coolness that clung to the concrete floor and soothed her hot sandaled feet. Squinting against the glare, she saw chickens and geese in the gravel. From somewhere in the barnyard came the weak bleat of a goat, from somewhere in the barn the heavy thud of a hoof. Grain dust circled in a tubelike shaft of sunlight cutting down through the gloom from a high knothole. Elinor felt that the barn itself held Laurel like a mother, one who blessedly lacked the hungry eyes with which she herself scoured the girl, searching for signs of health.

Laurel unlatched a gate to one of the stalls and tapped her tongue softly against her teeth. "Hey, Sugar, hey, Sugar," she crooned to the brown mare standing there. Behind the horse,

Elinor could see the vague outline of a colt curled up in the hay. Lazily it pushed itself up, rump first, when Laurel entered, and stepped between the girl and the mare.

"I helped pull her out," said Laurel, her voice studiedly flat. "It was pretty amazing—uh, about a month ago, just after I saw you last."

"You helped deliver the foal?"

"Yeah, with Jim, who used to work here. I was lucky he was still here. But I guess he stayed around especially, waiting for Sugar to foal and showing me how to take care of the animals. When it came time, Sugar couldn't do it on her own. We had to help pull the baby out."

"You pulled?"

"Well, I pulled Jim and he pulled the foal. Sugar's labor just stopped. The nose and front hooves were out, so Jim wrapped a towel around what he could grab so it wouldn't slip and then he pulled. He had to brace his leg against the side of the stall, and I pulled him from behind. And Lolly here slipped right out." As she spoke she worked hard to sound casual, pressing all but a remnant of pride from her voice.

Elly shook her head, smiling. "Mike would sure like to see that little colt," she offered tentatively. She feared spooking Laurel in her rare loquacious mood with talk of Hilltop and the family going on there without Vera. But safe in the barn, with one arm flung over Sugar's solid back and the other resting lightly on the foal, Laurel seemed secure. "Oh, bring him. Sure."

"He's only got another three weeks with us. Then he goes back to Mexico."

"Oh, sure, bring him by. Bring him next week. Bring them both."

Elinor felt a final tightness in her chest give way. She was sure the fever had broken on Laurel's grief.

"Did you ever ride, Mom?" Laurel asked her.

"Oh, sure, as a girl," she said. Suddenly she remembered Sandor on a large pinto leading her own horse on a rope around a lakeside trail.

"Want to ride down to the ocean?"

A crowd of objections rushed into Elinor's mind to resist this radical idea. Her clothes were all wrong, and the heat outside the barn seemed to roar.

"We'll walk all the way," said Laurel. "We'll have to go slow, for Lolly."

\* \* \*

They went bareback down a narrow winding trail below the planted fields. Laurel rode Sugar, and the colt Lolly followed closely behind. Elly sat on an old solid workhorse named Jim. After her initial surprise at how high off the ground she was, Elinor relaxed into the easy swinging gait as the horses picked their way down the trail, their hooves dropping onto the path with heavy, solid sounds. The heat was magnificent: it baked her shoulders and head with a kind of pulse. The hillside below the farm was wild and steep and completely sapped of moisture by the sun. The horses' hooves raised dust from the trail and kicked free tiny landslides of rocks and dry clods. Lolly picked her way less steadily than the grown horses, not fully in control of her overlong legs.

Elinor watched the sway of Laurel's horse and learned from the girl's relaxed posture to round her back, unlock her hips, and sink into the motion of the ride. A grand indifference engulfed Elinor, and the heat along with the insects' buzz held mother and daughter apart. No tight bands of feeling bound Elinor to Laurel. With neutrality, Elly watched the girl's feet swing free against her horse's belly, and she realized her acute concern for her daughter was tempered—by the resilience she saw in the girl's back and by a certainty that Laurel had inherited Vera's strength. With calm acceptance of the world's certain dangers, she let her daughter slip free.

The trail dipped steeply down the mountain to the sea, but Elly, watching Laurel, found her center of gravity and rolled over it loosely. Birds called; two quail skittered across the path, scaring Lolly. A light sweat coated Elinor and Laurel. They melted in the heat; sleep dogged them.

But at a turn in the trail they felt the first sea breeze, and the ocean spread out before them boundless and serene. In its sight the brittle harshness of the afternoon softened, and the promise of relief—from the heat, from the season—flowed up from the horizon like the dawn.

# Thirty-seven

"I was scared without Vera, but now . . ."

Lovejoy waits. Then she intrudes carefully into Laurel's pensive silence. "Now?"

"You know, at first I thought Vera was trying to help me back in. Bring me back into the family circle. But now I don't think so. Now I think she was coming out to be with me on the outside."

Another pause.

"She didn't exactly hold a place in the inner circle anyway. She was kind of an outsider too."

"What do you mean by the inner circle?"

"Oh, you know," Laurel throws out impatiently. "The love birds. My mom and Jack." She leans over to fumble in the canvas bag beside the chair. She pulls out a single cigarette and a pack of matches and lights up. Lovejoy is impassive.

"So I returned the favor. When she wanted me to, I stayed with her, and when she asked me I took her all the way out." Fear has become bravado, guilt a sharp defiance. Will Lovejoy challenge her lightness of tone, the new flippancy she's just starting to practice? Laurel has only begun to discover that it keeps her free of pain. She draws smoke in, then exhales carefully away from Lovejoy.

Lovejoy merely crosses her legs and watches.

"And then I took myself out."

"Not exactly."

"Well, no. You're right. They found a way for me to leave."

"Are you saying that you think your mother sent you away so she could be alone with Jack?"

A degree of uncertainty enters the picture: Laurel tips her head slightly.

"A little. I guess that's some of what I'm saying."

"That your mother wanted you out?"

"Yes," she whispers down to her chest, carefully rubbing out the cigarette in the small glass ashtray she has taken from the table beside her.

"*No,*" she says sharply, snapping her head back up. "No, she didn't want me out, she wanted me in. She's always wanted me to crawl in with her and Jack, leaving Vera out. She's never liked it that I'm . . ."

The brash flow is over. Laurel is deflated and Lovejoy has to coax. "What?"

"What I am. An outsider."

"Yes?"

Laurel smiles at Lovejoy. "Yes. Of course, yes. *You* know."

"So?"

"So now my mother and Jack can do their family thing without a weird kid and a weak old lady always hanging around in the background."

After a moment, Lovejoy says, "Your mother misses you. *And* Vera."

"She misses what she wanted me to be." She reaches down toward the canvas bag again. "Besides, it's not the same. I'm not dead. She can come visit me whenever she wants." She pulls the pack of cigarettes from the bag and holds it lightly in her lap.

"True."

"And it's funny, you know, when she comes to the farm she seems more relaxed about who I am, not as worried as before. I think it's because in a funny way I fit in there. In a funny way, they're all outsiders there." She grins broadly at the thought. "Look at Goldy, out in the hall. With her furry head." She grins again, enjoying the contrast between Goldy, in her soft dark clothes and cloth slippers, and Lovejoy, composed for work in her suit and heels.

"I think you've found a comfortable place for yourself at the farm."

"Yes."

"What will you do about school?"

"Graduating's not a problem. I didn't miss that much school."

"And then?"

Laurel's face turns serious, alarmed. Have Lovejoy and Elinor been making plans?

"I want to stay at the farm. I don't want to go back."

"Will they let you stay on indefinitely?"

"I think they think I'm doing a good job with the animals."

"And your mother and Jack will keep paying for you to stay?"

Laurel is suspicious. Why is Lovejoy insisting that Laurel acknowledge her dependency? "Don't you think they will?"

"I haven't discussed it with them. I'm asking you."

"I think they will. I just want to draw for a while. Mr. Harvey thinks I should go to art school."

"Art school costs money too."

Lovejoy is insisting on reality. Laurel doesn't want to think about it now. Slowly, as if studying the operation, she draws a fresh cigarette from the pack. She pulls it through her fingers, then lays it on her knee. She places the pack and the ashtray on the arm of her chair, lines them up precisely, then picks up the cigarette and lights it, drawing deeply. To the little line of objects on the arm she carefully adds the matches. Then she draws her feet up onto the seat, wraps an arm around her knees, and leans back into the chair. For the rest of the hour she drifts in silence—she knows how to do it so well—and watches the burning cigarette make its beautiful ribbons of smoke.

# Thirty-eight

Elinor made a shirt for Jack from a soft fabric she wove in light sand colors. He wore it on Mike's last day. At Hilltop, the August heat of a blazing afternoon slowly gave way to the balm of early evening.

After dinner, Jack, Goldy, and Mike played Frisbee on the sloping yard in front of the house, while Elinor sat on the porch, watching and listening. With Mike going back to Lee and summer noticeably fading, Elly felt the complex mixture of emotions that she had associated with the last day of summer as a child—fear and excitement at school's beginning mixed with the urge to extract the last of summer's sweet freedom.

With Mike gone tomorrow, life at Hilltop would change again. The last remnant of family, which three months ago had been their motivation to marry, would be gone, and Elly and Jack would face the task of shaping a new daily life. There would be just the two of them then, not the five they had anticipated in Mexico, not the four they were after Vera's death, not the three since Laurel had moved away. More lessons to learn. Would they be enough? Elinor wondered. Would the natural balance Jack and she had together hold out in their new solitude?

"Are you admiring me or my shirt?" Jack called.

"Oh, the shirt," she answered. She had been loving the look of the shirt as she sat there. It was loose fitting, light-colored, and soft, and yet it held the shape she had worked into it—good collar, clean shoulder lines. He wore the sleeves rolled up twice, and she enjoyed the look of his arms against the fabric she had woven—beautiful!

"It's the shirt *on* you! I can't take my eyes off it. It definitely does something for you."

"Quit bragging," he called, turning to toss the Frisbee to Mike. "Daddy, too high," cried the boy, and he chased the plastic disk down the slope like a bounding calf. Jack watched him run with an expression of naked longing on his face, but he clamped on a look of concentration when the child returned and sent the Frisbee wobbling back. "Great throw," yelled Goldy. "Great!" Mike had charmed Goldy, too.

The sun was at its last daytime point as the earth rolled on toward evening, and it shone nearly horizontally from just above the western ridge. Everything took the illumination separately—stalks of tall grasses, loose gravel in the driveway, yellow flowers of the wild rabbitbrush bordering the yard. Backlit trees showed their branches through the foliage; some leaves became translucent. Even Goldy's hair, two inches long now, became a fuzzy halo, which Elly regarded with amusement. The myriad details of the world were called out sharply to Elinor in her place on the steps, and she completed the view with an imaginary picture of Vera standing near a tree with a sweater over her shoulders and a cigarette burning in her fingers. She could picture Vera's eyes gazing at the players. The old woman wore the calm, slightly inquisitive expression that had invited everyone's confidence but Elinor's own. The picture came to Elinor unattended by grief. Here was Vera restored—calm, self-contained, physically at ease—standing by a familiar tree.

A restlessness to use the glorious light seized Elinor suddenly. "Call me for dessert," she hollered, and headed for her studio. She thought the new fabric started there might be lighted through the huge windows of her studio in a way she hadn't seen before.

At the sight of the loom and the strands she'd dyed herself, she knew she would find the rhythm that had eluded her all summer long. She felt pleasurable anticipation in her hands. She even dared music, an old jazz suite she had listened to while weaving since the days when she first began. Unaware of her voice, she hummed lightly along with the music, found a way to start, and then worked on, easyhearted, as the clear country sky turned gray.

**Suzanne Lipsett** lives in Petaluma, California, and reviews books for several West Coast newspapers including the *San Francisco Chronicle* and the *San Francisco Review of Books*. *Out of Danger* is her second novel.

**DATE DUE**

f  D-313126
Lipsett
Out of danger

WEST GEORGIA REGIONAL LIBRARY SYSTEM

DOUGLAS COUNTY PUBLIC LIBRARY